almost then

Margot McCuaig

Published by Linen Press, London 2020
8 Maltings Lodge
Corney Reach Way
London W4 2TT
www.linen-press.com

A CIP catalogue record for this book is available from the British Library.

Cover art: Arcangel
Houses illustration: Penny Sharp
Typeset by Zebedee
Printed and bound by Lightning Source
ISBN 978-1-8380603-3-6

This book is dedicated to Art; thank you for providing me with love, support and encouragement, *always*.

About the Author

Margot McCuaig is a writer and award winning filmmaker. Her acclaimed debut, *The Birds That Never Flew*, was short-listed for the Dundee International Book Prize and longlisted for the Polari Prize. She was shortlisted in the 2018 *Words and Women* prose competition. Her non-fiction work has been published in books and anthologies. She won Royal Television Society Scotland awards for documentary films she directed, produced and scripted in 2015, 2016 and 2019. She lives in Glasgow, Scotland, and in the home she built at Maoil na nDreas, Rathlin Island, Ireland.

Find the author on her website:
https://margotmccuaig.com/

Reviews

'Age-old themes of betrayal and family violence are skilfully mined to bring new insights for the contemporary reader. A story of love and passion, hate and despair, jealousy and guilt, violence and tragedy, beautifully told, about the past's impact on the present and the future, and the unbearable burden of unbearable losses.'

— Hilary McCollum, author of *Golddigger*.

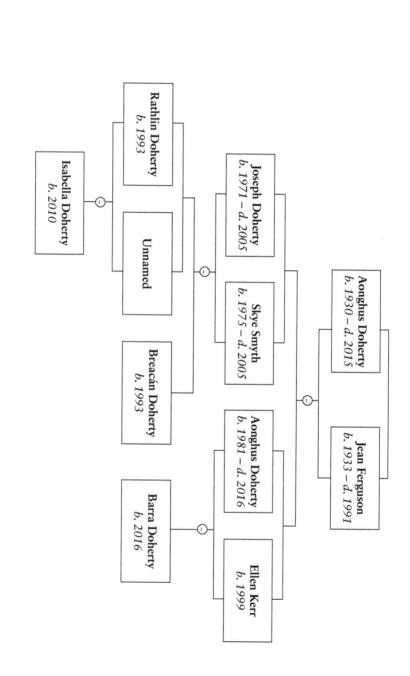

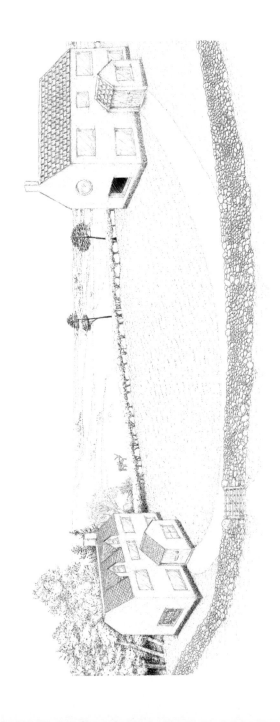

Rathlin

Home. Ballynoe, Kintyre peninsula

Rathlin was born in this house, in this bedroom, in Ballynoe. Memories of her mother live in every cavity of the walls, on each thread of carpet, in the lived lines of the creaking floorboards. But it is here on this bed that she feels her mother's presence. That first coming together is tattooed onto its mattress. She's smothering herself in it and the house is bending in, wrapping its arms around her, sheltering her from the fall. Because she will fall, she always, always falls.

Rathlin is pressing her fingers into coiled springs, their pulse a connection. She's remembering tasting her mother's blood on her teeth, the stench circling and settling on the back of her throat. She's trying to clear it but it is clinging to her tonsils, tiny metallic puffs releasing with each c c c of her forced coughs, spraying a reminder onto her lips. She's licking the reminiscence greedily, knowing it's all she has left.

Rathlin senses the forest beyond the window calling her and using her arms as a crane she's raising her neck, watching trees swallowing the hill that's pressing into the horizon. Its shadows are stealing her but she's a willing traveller all the same, following their inky path, letting her mind wander to the past.

She's walking through heather. She can feel its foliage tickle her ankles. She's wearing sandals, the T-bar pinching her foot. She's stopping to touch it, moving her thumb under the leather. She's looking at the imprint of the strap on her skin. It's summer. Her feet are brown, even under her shoes, so she knows she must have been walking barefoot, sucking in the sun's rays like a sponge. She's wondering why she isn't as free now so she moves to untie the buckle, stopping when she sees her bike lying on its side, the back wheel spinning. It's new. The white tyres are as pure as the lime-stone chalk on a cliff, the metal spokes glimmering in the sunlight. She's standing up, dusting bracken from her bare leg, turning to listen to laughter in the woods, its cry strong and deliberate.

She's running quickly towards it, her binoculars bouncing on her chest. She's grasping the lanyard, holding them in her outstretched hand so they don't ram the flesh that's beginning to fill the space in her bra. The laughing's harder now and she's recognising the sounds of her mother. She's imagining her throwing her red hair back into the sunlight, the overhanging pine leaves catching her chuckle, muting its soft sound, releasing it so it can stretch freely into the bluest sky. She's skipping beyond the wild flowers, heading for the silver lights, gentle rays of sunshine meandering in and out of tree roots, their long fingers passing her into the forest. Then she's stopping. Hard. She's curling her toes and pressing on to her heels, pulling from a forest floor edged with sharp claws that will tear her to shreds.

Rathlin never gets beyond this point. She knows it's when she falls.

Part One

Chapter One

Rathlin

Glasgow

Rathlin is done fighting. She's going to find the morning and with its arrival the ease it sometimes brings. She opens the front door and steps into shards of early dawn without fear of consequence. Her dog is more reluctant and she has to tease its frame over the threshold. Molly is not as ready to start the day. *Trying again*, or *putting the past behind you* are things that don't seem to matter in the same way to a dog. Lucky dog, thinks Rathlin.

She tries to close the door softly behind her but her sleeve snares in the letterbox and its metal lips chatter like a parliament of magpies. She mouths *fuck* silently into the changing light and the empty word slips into the dim street. Orange streetlights are still pushing down on oily pavements even though morning is closing in. Rathlin can feel its imminent arrival in the softening of her breath. Or maybe that's because she is awake and not being forced back to *Then*. Why do people always want to go back?

Molly seems to want to. She has slammed on her brakes and Rathlin lets the tightening lead drop to the ground. Both hands now free, she pulls her hood over her head, stretching the fabric as far as it will go. Blinkers to start the day. She holds on to it and stretches her neck skywards so she can fix on the setting moon. Which, she wonders, of the powdery grey lines on its surface lead to her crater.

Undecided she turns her attention back to the dog.

'Whit you worrying about, that wiz just the door clattering.' Rathlin tickles the dog's head encouragingly, pushing her chin so she's facing the letterbox. Molly responds with an indignant yawn and collapses her limbs so she's resting on the ground, her back legs folding first, her front legs stretching out long in front of her. She's looking directly at Rathlin, her jaw loose. Rathlin smiles in retort but it's only in the moment. A reaction. She's stressed. Up to high doh as they say. She really doesn't want to venture north today but she will because she has to. Her brother is in trouble. They both are. They need one another and for the first time in a long time they will do what they always did as children and fight for one another. Rathlin and Breacán will form the united front of Ballynoe.

Rathlin takes a breath, remembering a moment, perhaps when they were six or seven. They were holding hands, refusing to say who broke the window with the football. The twins know how to build a wall. Trouble is, Rathlin thinks, it used to be *their* wall, but now she keeps building giant blocks her brother can't penetrate. And he her. She knows he has his own walls too.

It's shit that it turned out like this but she's going to try to change it and she tells the dog that she and Breacán are going to get back on track. For definite. Well, she hopes so anyway.

She moves through the memory and encourages Molly to get moving. Time needs action, interaction. They walk into the day together and the dog pees in her usual spot, lifting her hind legs when the job's done. She pushes ahead of Rathlin, her nose knowing the route well enough to take the initiative.

Rathlin yawns and shrugs her shoulders. She's thinking about action again. Quite often action is futile. It certainly doesn't take the edge off her tiredness. Broken sleep is still taking control, almost always brooding in the pit of her stomach whilst the moon sets, pushing into her throat as it rises. Night-time brings with it a familiar pattern, a dream of nightmares that almost but never quite take her back there, back to *Then*.

Rathlin
The forest behind Ballynoe, 2005
She's wiping her palms on the grass, burrowing her head into her neck and stretching her arms away from her face. Her hair is smothering her and her hands are back with her, trying to untangle it from her neck, her fingers sliding through its wetness, soaking in the deep red of the blood.

. . .

The council scheme where Rathlin lives is finally quiet. The low drone of song pulsating from drunken mouths has been silenced by sleep. When the memories woke her she had stayed awake and listened to their constant rabble, piecing together a who's who of her neighbours as they stumbled over their doorsteps and into the shelter of home. She looks around her, searching for any evidence of the slice of night they left behind them. She watches her step on the pavement, her trainers leading the way. She stops to thread her lace behind the tongue of her shoe and notices how wrecked her trusted favourites are. She sighs, knowing there is no money to buy more. There's never any money to buy more, only enough to get by.

A fox stumbles upon Rathlin and Molly, for it is they that are cutting into its moment, walking in the shadow of its foraging hour. Rathlin gives a nod to its territory, encouraging Molly to sit by her heel. The fox strolls past nonchalantly and Rathlin is enchanted, tumbling into its gaping jaws of indifference. Finally, she pulls on Molly's lead, turning back. They navigate a path across the sun-scorched grass, darting over broken glass, a used needle, and around a supermarket trolley that is on its side, exhausted. Rathlin scans the scene, her hand on Molly's collar, wondering as she does every day if it's okay to let the dog run in the only green space near to them.

'Sorry, Molly, we cannae take the risk of you getting one of your wee paws hurt, a vet bill is no gonnae get paid anytime soon. C'mon, we'll head up early tae Breacán's and you can get a good run in the fields when we get there.' Rathlin is squatting and her nose is almost touching Molly's. 'What else are we going to do at this hour eh?' She climbs back on her feet and peels a treat from the tiny pocket in her jeans that has no real purpose. Molly accepts it greedily, pushing her wet nose into Rathlin's hip in the hope for more.

When they turn the corner into the familiar surroundings of their flat, they walk directly into a high-pitched squeal. Rathlin recognises it as a safe hello and smiles warmly.

'Frances, how y'doing? Looks like someone's had a good time.' Rathlin centres her weight, getting ready to embrace her neighbour, Frances. There's a police siren walloping her ears even though it's somewhere in the distance and for a moment it makes her dizzy. She can feel her breath quicken. Women are so vulnerable at night but she relaxes when she sees the red lights of a taxi disappearing into the corner at the end of the road. Its purring engine lingers, its music an accompaniment to their meeting.

'Hey, careful, you'll knock me out wae that bag of yours.' She ducks just in time to avoid Frances's swinging handbag. 'You're out late, are you no, where's Frank? It's the middle of the bloody night. You werenae on your own were you?'

Frances steadies herself but in the process her foot buckles and her ankle folds awkwardly into her wedged heel. Her body topples like a used Christmas tree into Rathlin's path.

'Rathlin Doherty you are worse than the weans, I've had more nights out than you've had hot dinners. Just cos I'm old, doesnae mean I'm stupid. I can get myself up the road at the end of the night.' She points her finger, trying and failing to be stern, pausing for a moment to take her hand back and gently rub her eye. 'I put some bloody mascara on the night and it's really annoying me. Don't know why I bother at ma age, mutton dressed as lamb, eh, hen.'

'Here, move your hand, let me see.' Rathlin leans in, examining Frances's eye. 'All I can see is an eyeball, is that whit you were looking for?'

'That's a relief, hen, thought I might have taken it out and left it at the side of my bed wae my teeth.'

'Still got the patter, even when you're pissed, I see. So where were you tae this time anyway?'

'I went back tae Donegal Mary's after the bingo. She's still no used tae being on her own after her Tam died.' She continues, the level of her voice increasing. 'Here. Did I tell you it turns out he had a few quid put by, and I mean a lot of dosh.' Frances is drunkenly using her arms, swinging them wide to illustrate that it was a lot of money. 'Mind you, as Mary says, she could have done wae him letting her have it when she was in her forties when she could make good use of it. It's no much use tae her in her eighties.'

'Whit, Donegal Mary's in her eighties?' Rathlin is raising her voice now. 'I wouldnae have thought that for a minute. She looks much younger.'

'Ach she's no quite in her eighties, she's seventy, but that's no a kick in the arse off eighty. The years all start tae roll into one after you hit the big six-o.'

Rathlin smiles. 'Jeez, don't be wishing your life away. So what were you two celebrating?'

'Well.' Frances draws breath, ready to continue her story. 'I had tae go out and get blotto, the doctor ordered me tae.'

Rathlin curls her lips. 'Hmm, sounds a bit suspect, Frances, no that I'm calling ye a liar.'

'I'm telling ye, she did. You may think I'm talking a lot of shite cos I'm pissed but she said tae me, "Frances, there's nothing better for you right now than a night on the tiles."'

She raises her eyebrows and stares at Rathlin. Rathlin is staring back, transfixed by the wrinkles that are furrowing on Frances's brow. What stories they must hold, Rathlin thinks. They begin to tell another one and fold and unfurl as Frances continues.

'I don't think it worked though as tae be honest I feel as crap as I did before I went out so don't listen tae the doctor, she doesnae know whit she's talking about.'

Frances stumbles and reaches out and grips Rathlin's shoulders. Rathlin bears Frances's weight while she pulls herself back to a standing position but she knows the anchor has slipped. The alcohol has got the better of her and she has fallen into the chaos of it. Her mumbled speech is slurred, her eyelids gently folding.

'Hen, will you come in? I want tae tell you something. I was gonnae give you a wee knock in the morning but it's in the stars that I was tae meet you. It's pure important.'

Frances tugs at the underwire of her bra, settling her breasts before smoothing the waistline of her black skirt. Rathlin can feel herself respond to the gentleness of her face and she devours more, even though she wants to be alone. She has enough drama to deal with already. She scans Frances's hairline next, taking in the whiteness of the short cut, following the severity of it as it sculpts the hollowness of her cheeks. Frances's dangling earrings are catching the light and Rathlin looks more closely, giggling when she realises they are *Yes* slogan earrings. Frances keeps the independence campaign going and her rage still regularly boils over when she pontificates about the 'three wise men' who 'knew bugger all'.

Rathlin knows she hasn't answered Frances's question yet so turns her head away. She is happy enough to lie to her, but she's not that keen to do it to her face. 'I'd love tae come in, Frances, but Molly's dying for a walk and then I'm gonnae try an' crash for a couple of hours.' She has to pause. She wishes she could steal the lies from her voice and crush them under the heel of her shoe. 'I'll call in later this evening though. We can catch up then.'

Too late. They are already entrenched. She can hear it in the way Frances's voice falters.

'Rathlin, that's bullshit.'

Shit. Caught.

'I know, and you know, that you're off tae your brother's the day so you've got nae intentions of coming in.' Rathlin presses forward, trying to narrow the filthy space between them but Frances has raised her arm and created a void. Or is it a wall? Probably. Everywhere there are walls and it is Rathlin who is building them. She can see it, but does nothing about it.

'And you can haud yer wheesht.' Frances is waving her finger in front of Rathlin's face so she tightens her lips, knowing it is heading for contact. 'I know you're stressed and the last thing you want tae be doing is listening to ma shite patter.' Frances curls her fingers around Rathlin's chin and their warmth embraces the coolness of her face. Rathlin drops her hand to her side. It hangs loose and free.

'Do me a favour though, hen, gies your arm an' walk me tae the house. Ma feet are bloody killing me. Whit was I thinking wearing these mad shoes.'

Chapter Two

Rathlin

Glasgow

Rathlin is back in the flat, folding clothes into her holdall. Her two jumpers are already in, softening the base of the bag. She squishes them down and throws in her other pair of jeans. She wraps her ankle boots in a poly bag and adds them along with her hoodie and three t-shirts, two of which she alternates for bed. She piles on pants and socks like a cairn. She wonders if it's overkill before deciding that you can never have too many of either.

She stretches into the wardrobe and pulls her one dress from its hanger. It's their birthday. In a few days. Birthdays are for celebrations and she and Breacán did that with vigour eleven times. Well, she thinks, eleven and a half. Three quarters even. It didn't get totally obliterated until towards the end of the day and it has remained utterly shit ever since. Still, she wants to wear her dress when it comes. Not for fun but because it's the day that she and Breacán are meeting Ellen, the lovely aunt who is selling Ballynoe, and her lawyer. Our house, *ours* Molly, it's nothing to do with her. The dog responds and barks encouragingly. She's grateful that someone is listening.

What a bitch. Rathlin is still talking to the dog but she's ignoring her now, preferring to lick her paws. She suddenly has a vision of Ellen and she's pissed off that she has come into her head. She's thinking about the first time she met her. It was in Kebble, her father's childhood home. He was born there but moved across to Ballynoe when he married Rathlin and Breacán's mother, Skye. She quickly puts her parents out of her mind and refocuses on the first meeting with Ellen. It was her granddad's funeral and her uncle Aonghus, her father's much younger brother, a 'change of life' baby, had found a teen bride for himself. He might have been her daddy's younger brother but he was still ancient compared to Ellen. Or 'the money grabber' as she became more familiarly known. Well, it couldn't have been love. Rathlin was pretty clear about this to Breacán. Aonghus was an alcoholic mess. Ellen, just sixteen at the time, definitely couldn't have been after him for his charm and intellect.

Rathlin rolls her dress up like a swimming towel and stuffs it into the side pocket of the bag. She's not quite finished. She takes a breath and picks up the framed picture of her mum and dad and places it on the bed. She stands over it, looking, her hands almost but not quite touching. Molly barks impatiently but for the moment Rathlin ignores her and pulls her phone from her pocket. She takes a small step forward and snaps an image of the photograph, deleting it seconds later, her lips curled in dissatisfaction. She moves the frame away from the light and tries again. She nods and smiles, tracing her finger along her phone and then the photograph before putting it back on the bedside cabinet.

Rathlin has still to pack the most important thing. It's there, under the bedclothes.

The teddy bear is white, but its once soft fur is coarser now, matted from the nightly grip of her hands. Rathlin teases it out and removes a tiny paw embedded in the pillowslip.

'Right, your turn, little one.' Her voice is soft and gentle. A tone a mother would use to her newborn child. She hugs the bear's sadness into her chest, her eyes shut tight. The fur is warm now, as it was when she found it in the bright lights of the Build-a-Bear shop. She had wandered in, looking for something to love. She shook her head when the assistant asked her if she wanted to record a voice message in its heart. It wasn't possible. Rathlin didn't have words.

'That's enough cuddles for one day, it's time to get on. You snuggle up in there for now.' Rathlin is fine about talking to the bear. It's a teddy bear, that's the whole point. She slips it in the bag and ties the top of her rucksack, drawing the lace tight.

'Hang on, we forgot something.' Rathlin takes a small yellow blanket from a chest of drawers beside her bed and inhales deeply. She wraps the bear in it and tucks it into the bag. Rathlin slots her arm through the strap before lifting it onto her right shoulder. She picks up the holdall with her other hand, exhaling sharply at its weight.

The space between Rathlin's bed and the window is narrow so she turns her body and walks sideways like a crab, her heels echoing on the thin carpet that was part of someone else's existence long before she moved in. When she gets to the living room she dumps her bags on the floor.

'Right, magic couch, this is where you do your stuff.' Rathlin pulls the cushions off the sofa. She's done this before. She works swiftly, forcing her hands down the tight edges, searching for loose change. She discards the fluff and crumbs into the bin and counts the haul that's left behind with her left index finger.

'Shit, one measly pound and fifty-one pence isn't going tae last us long, Molly.' The calendar is on the wall in front of her and Rathlin gives it time it doesn't deserve. There's no point to looking at it but she does anyway. It's still ages until payday. She bundles her tiny steal into her purse, her find clinking against the other coins. They shuffle together, the heavier metal clambering for a prime spot.

'Four pounds and one pence it is. There's nothing magic about that.' She flips open the back of the purse, her breath quickening. Her last tenner is still there. Rathlin has already decided to buy petrol in batches of under thirty pounds enroute so she can use contactless. The monthly saga of swallowing her pay bit by bit before it even arrives in her bank. It'll have to do because that's all she's ever able to do.

'And now it's you, little brother.' Rathlin clears her throat. It's still early so she closes her eyes and pictures Breacán asleep in Ballynoe, the house awake, waiting. She presses his name on her phone and his answerphone eventually kicks in. She's right. He's still asleep.

'Hey. It's me. I've changed my mind, I know I said I was going tae head up tonight but I'm heading up the now, well as soon I've finished throwing some stuff I don't need in ma bag.' A nervous giggle slips to the floor and she sits down on the cushion-less sofa. She hauls herself back up immediately, the dog following her movement. 'Look, this is shit, I know it is, but we'll sort it out, we always dae don't we? I should be there about lunchtime, okay?'

Rathlin hangs up, turning the handset towards her so she can check the time. It's 5.35am. She heads to the kitchen in search of breakfast, looking despite knowing there's little hope of finding sustenance. Her stomach is tightening and she grips it, wondering why the hunger pangs always kick in so viciously when you allow yourself to think about food. The trick is always to avoid, avoid, avoid.

'Yes, success.' Rathlin jumps triumphantly when the bread bin reveals an outsider inside the plain loaf packet. Her fast fingers tear it from the paper and she lets out a loud whoop when there's no evidence of mould. The grill clatters loudly when she draws it back and places the bread on the metal shelf underneath, its sound as sweet as the crunch of an apple. She lowers her knees so she can watch the bread toast, her hand turning the gas knob as she shimmies from side to side. But there's no point. The magic cooker isn't on form either. There's no money in her meter. She tries again anyway, hoping for a slither of light, something to spark her day into life. There's nothing. She eats the hard bread, a thin layer of margarine easing its passage.

Chapter Three

Ellen

Kebble. Kintyre peninsula

At the other end of Rathlin's phone call, Ellen and Breacán are in her bedroom at Kebble. She's turning her body, wriggling out of the spoon position. She has realised that the ringing isn't in her dream. She's a little dazed but alert enough to lean across Breacán and try to reach the phone from his side of the bed. It has fallen silent, its ring sinking into the pillow along with their parting sleep. She sits up sharply, her emotions heightened by the intrusion into their private space. She picks up her own phone and examines the time. *Jesus, thanks a million, sleep wrecker.* She throws it onto the side table in disgust and it clatters off the wood. She holds her breath until she's satisfied that it hasn't woken her daughter, Barra. She keeps her voice low but she drills her words to Breacán.

'Who the fuck is that phoning at this time, or do I even have tae ask?'

The dawn is slicing into the room like a carving knife. Breacán is groggy, but less on edge. Typical. Always on another flipping planet. Ellen can see that he's stretching his eyes, trying to focus. She also knows he will be retreating, hoping the moment will pass. He's not one for drama. He says he likes a quiet life. Ellen tells him that even after all these years together, he's still feart of a bit of healthy confrontation. He's always the one to pull back or not even rise in the first place. She swallows his silence and it jags her throat on the way down. She's waited far too long for him to catch up so she climbs over him and this time manages to grab his phone. His sister is the last caller.

'I might have known it would be her.' Ellen chucks Breacán's phone onto the bed, her action swift as if she's tossing a hot coal. It lands between them, lost in the heaviness of the duvet. She unfurls herself from the bedding and clambers to her feet, marching across the wooden floorboards until her heavy steps stop at the window. The room falls silent, briefly. She opens the curtains and raises the blind, turning back into herself. Breacán's attention isn't on her. *Not a good start to the morning, pal.*

He's still in bed, stretching his neck so he can see through the window. She knows that he's finding strength in what he sees, the shape of the fields and trees like breath to his lungs. She feels her shoulders tighten as he pulls himself up on the bed. Her body keeps reacting, her back muscles hardening as she looks at him looking at the house he lives in just across the field. She can feel him wishing he was at Ballynoe instead of here with her. Ellen is ready to say it, *just go why don't you*, but he gets in first. That's a first, a voice says to Ellen, from inside her head. The visit of the voice isn't unusual. There's always a din in there but Ellen has long stopped worrying about it, if she ever even did. Did she? She shrugs her shoulders in response to the question and then repositions herself, remembering that Breacán is the one having a moment.

'I better get out tae those fields. There's work to be done.' Ellen watches a shadow that's settling on his cheek. It moves when he does. He exhales a long, low sigh and moves again, swinging his legs to his side of the bed. The same bed they've shared for what, more than five years now? She's pretending to herself that she doesn't know the exact number of years, months, days, moments even that they've been together. If you can call it together. Is it a relationship when it's a secret? She looks at the bed again, and Breacán sitting on it. They share it, frequently, but he doesn't always sleep there. Sometimes he just pays it, and her, a visit and she's fine with that. Well, she was. Not anymore. She just wants to be together at night, every night. But that's too much to ask, apparently.

Breacán has settled his elbows on his thighs and moved his weight through his arms. His hands are cupping his face. Ellen is ignoring his question and she's choosing to focus on a different one. She has found it among the high-pitched voices that are in her head, drilling quick-fire words. She speaks in her own voice, a calmer tone than the one snared in her brain.

'What is her problem?'

Ellen flaps her arms dramatically. She knows she's doing it and knows it's making her look ridiculous but she's letting it happen anyway. The voices in her head are telling her that nothing about this moment is right. 'It's five thirty-five in the morning. Does Rathlin no want you tae have a life of your own?'

Breacán is calm and shrugs his shoulders, stretching his body over the bed to retrieve the discarded handset. Ellen watches him, feeling her temper rise as he rubs his fingers over the glass. *Why is he always so bloody oblivious to the argument we're having?*

'Earth tae Breacán. Whit does she want? Is she still in Glasgow?'

'I'm no a mind reader, I havenae listened tae the message yet.'

For fuck sake, what is he like? Ellen shakes her head, agreeing with the voice. 'Well how about listening tae it then? I need tae know whit she's up tae.'

'I will once I get a chance. Chill out, I'm still waking up.'

Ellen knows he's stalling. Avoidance technique is his forte. It's annoying but in the moment she's satisfied that she knows him better than anyone. Especially his sister. When his response comes, it is all about her. His precious Rathlin. Surprise, surprise.

'And here we go again. Rathlin is my twin sister. She's no up tae anything. It's hardly her fault that I'm lying tae her about us and neither is it her fault that all this shit is because of what we are doing behind her back. Why do this now, Ellen? It's the way you wanted it for years. It just doesnae make any sense. Things are alright as they are.'

He stands up slowly, his tall frame suddenly awkward and unyielding beneath the low ceiling. Ellen's anger is lost in the narrow space where he might hit his head. She guides him from the eaves, gently lowering his head as he moves forward.

'Thank you.' He looks up and the light snares his hair. His head is like an orange on a tree. 'How many times have I actually cracked my nut off that bloody roof? You'd think I'd have learned by now. Jesus.'

'You'd think, aye'.

'Can you no just think about it logically, Ellen. Why would Rathlin not want tae help me? Our parents' home is about to be ripped away from us.'

Ellen catches Breacán's eye just before he turns away. He's sad. He's ill. He's wincing in pain. His joints are burning, an ache that sets the tone of most days. She knows he's using more energy than he can afford so early in the morning.

'How would she not want tae help?' Ellen is mimicking Breacán, deliberately pitching high, emasculating him. 'Well, you know exactly whit you need tae dae tae take all of the stress out of this. It's no rocket science.' She stops for breath, lowering herself on to the mattress beside him. The difference in height centres her and she calms her tone. 'Can we no just tell Rathlin the truth, for god's sake, how hard does this need tae be? It's always about how she's gonnae feel, but whit about me? You never ever think about the damage this is daein tae me. And tae Barra. She's nearly four and a half, Breacán, she's no daft. You're here every day at some point or we're at yours. Is your sister knowing you're a lying prick more important than losing us?'

Breacán is pressing his forearm against the wall. He follows through with his body weight, pushing his forehead back and forward against his wrist in frustration. Ellen stands alongside him at the wall and tugs his arm. She wants to take his pain, transfer it to her. He concedes and it only takes a gentle nudge for his body to follow as she directs them both back to bed. She straddles his bare torso, settling her hips on his, curling her back to form a protective shell around him.

'Breacán, don't. Please stop. Don't.' She takes his arm and circles her fingers around his wrist. 'You'll waken Barra. Jesus, you know how much of a monster she can be if she wakes up too early.'

Breacán laughs softly and there they are, being them, smiling at one another. The way it should be, all the time, not just when no-one else is looking. Ellen can hear herself sigh as she kisses him softly on the forehead, moving her lips down to his, kissing him full. Her tenderness earns a response and they embrace for a moment, their breathing settling into each other's hair, circling familiarly.

'Please don't do this tae us, Breacán, I love you. And I know you love me.' Ellen entwines her fingers in his but she draws back sharply when he winces. 'Shit, sorry, ah didnae mean tae be rough. You feeling bad the day?'

'No more than usual. Time I changed the bloody record, eh? You must be sick of it. Might be no bad thing for you tae sell the house and put me down while you're at it. I'm fuck all use tae anybody.'

Ellen rolls her eyes skywards, a voice telling her that Breacán is looking for sympathy. 'Jesus, Breacán, don't be so dramatic, you're not a bloody dog and if you were I'd be caring for you, no killing you. And besides, it's no as if you're that bad, you're still working on that farm, there's tons of folk out there a lot more worse off. You're not in a wheelchair.'

Breacán shakes Ellen's weight from his body and she slips backwards as he climbs to his feet. 'You mean I'm okay? Who knew? I should've stopped wasting my time going tae the hospital years ago.'

'Ach don't be so childish. I'm rubbish at sympathy, you know I cannae do right for being wrong wae that stuff. You're always saying *I'm fine*, but now that I'm trying tae buck you up by playing your arthritis down, I'm the dick? This is ridiculous. Wise the fuck up and just tell Rathlin. It's that easy.'

Ellen moves aside, giving Breacán space to pull on his jeans. Their skeleton is still straddling the floor from when they climbed into bed, their tone hushed until they were confident that Barra's breathing had deepened into a snore. He pushes his arms through the sleeves of his jumper and Ellen watches his head appear through the neckline, his bad mood still apparent on his face. She waits for the right moment to intervene and thinks she has found it when she sees that he's struggling with his boots. She edges closer but holds back as he succeeds, exhaling loudly at the effort it took. In her mind, her arm is mirroring his as he raises it to wipe the sweat beads from his forehead. When he settles, she smooths his ruffled hair with the palm of her hand. For a hint of a breath she thinks his eyes are smiling, the fight forgotten as it almost always is. She picks up Breacán's phone and dials 1-2-1.

'We best have a listen and see what Miss-high-and-mighty is after then, bound to be something dramatic knowing your sister.'

It was the wrong move. She realises as soon as she hands the phone to him. He thrusts it dramatically to his ear, turning his back as he walks towards the door. Ellen throws a pillow at him which flies through the air in front of him, narrowly missing his head. He doesn't turn around. *Why the fuck is he not turning round?*

'Breacán, don't be such a wean. You cannae just storm off. Whit's she saying?'

Breacán stops but he keeps his back to Ellen. He's clutching the handle of the bedroom door with his right hand. 'If by *she* you mean Rathlin, she's on her way up to Ballynoe to try and stop you selling it. By the way, what you're doing is blackmail, Ellen, pure and simple. A bit ironic given you also keep telling me how much you love me.'

'Shut up, Breacán, you know I love you, that's why it's so simple. If ye love me tell her, if ye don't ye can both get tae fuck out of my house.' Ellen knows she'll win. She knows he loves her too much to lose her.

'My house, *my house*, that's all I hear fae you these days. Fine, do it. Ballynoe means the world tae me and my sister but I'd rather lose it, and you, than hurt my twin. Aye, she hates you, but maybe there's a fuckin good reason to, Ellen.'

Ellen is racking her brain for a move, but the shock has sent all her voices silent. But wait. Her heart thumps when she hears some tenderness push back into his voice.

'I'm sorry. You know I love ye but I'm no changing my mind. I need tae get on with my life. Sell it, Ellen. As you say, it's yours anyway.'

He opens the door. Ellen stays where she is, rooted to the spot. She can't open her mouth in case the *come back* words escape. She needs to hold firm. She can't keep being a secret.

She deserves more. She tells herself over and over, just to be sure.

I am more than this.

I
am
more
than
this.

Chapter Four

Rathlin

Glasgow

Rathlin has been sitting still, her head resting on the back of the sofa. She has pulled her legs up to her side. Her bags are on the floor beside her. She has been visiting the past. Molly is next to her, nudging her nose into her waist, her paws entangled in Rathlin's legs.

. . .

Rathlin
Ballynoe, 2003
Rathlin tastes the sea on her tongue, feels sand on her teeth. She smells her mother all around her, her familiar perfume cocooning them. She hears her father cackle like a chough. She's closing her eyes, tentatively, not sure whether she wants to wander backwards any further. She sees the strand; the wind's up and she's watching the run on the shores, towering waves breaking and pulling back mid-roll, decreasing their speed but still landing on the beach with momentum. She's shivering, the south-westerly wind snaring her, whipping up a frenzy under her jacket. Skye is there with her arms round her daughter, circling her waist, hands clasped on her stomach. Her hair falls forward and Rathlin doesn't swat it away. She's breathing in the scent, cherishing this moment. Skye's talking through the strands, her words tumbling gently.

'Rathlin pet, come on in and get some soup, it's freezing. You're always out here watching the sea horses charge the shore.'

Rathlin's turning around, kissing her mother, snuggling into the taller, broader warmth of her.

'Mummy, why do you and Daddy always say the breaking waves are horses?'

'Rathlin, for a ten-year-old you're pretty intense.' She's leaning into her daughter's head, kissing her daughter softly. 'Listen, you can hear the hooves, even from up here on the hill, and look,' she's pointing, her arm straight, her finger stretching into the distance, her flesh as white as a winter wave, 'see the way the water is breaking, spilling over into a white froth? That's a horse's mane, the hair rising and falling as the water rolls. It was Poseidon, the king of the sea, that created horses, but ye know that.' She's turning Rathlin around so she can see her. 'There's so many stories about Poseidon, some of them not so nice and maybe we'll talk about those when you're older, but the important thing for now is that he loved a woman who lived on an island and she had five sets of twins. Five. Can you imagine four more sets of you and Breacán racing about? We'd never get a minute's peace.' She's laughing, tickling Rathlin and she's giggling and squirming, but not in a bad way. She's back there in the moment and she knows she's having fun.

'But, Mummy, I don't see a horse when I look at the surf on the sea, I think they are white werewolves, racing to the shore. I can hear them howling. Sometimes I nearly cry cos I think they sound so sad, like something really bad's happened tae them.' She's holding her mum's hand now, her own feeling small and cold inside the tight clasp. 'Those two there, can you see them?' She's looking up, checking Skye is following her finger. 'That's me and Breacán, chasing something, or being chased. I don't know but I think we

34

look scared, Mummy. Why would we be scared? Are we drowning?'

Skye's on her knees. Rathlin can feel her arms on her shoulders, even though she's at home on the couch. Her back's rounding and she's sinking into the essence of her.

'Listen, baby girl, you and Breacán, you come from the sea, you're stronger than the giant waves, than even Poseidon himself. You're not running, you're racing to change the world. Look. Look at the way the wave is pushing into the sand, moving the shells, carving a shape in the silt. That's you and Breacán, being whatever you want tae be. My beautiful twins, in control.'

. . .

Rathlin tries to respond but she's back now, the room cold and damp. Her knees are stiff and when she stretches from the chair, the memories drip down her back. She walks to the kitchen and is startled when she opens the tap and the boiler burps loudly, its water cold and thin as it leaves the brushed metal. She swallows a drink greedily, erasing the essence of sand from her throat. She rinses her cup, carefully putting it away in the cupboard beside the upturned baby bottle. She tries to close the cupboard quickly but it draws her back. It always, always draws her back. She presses her fingers on the cool plastic and strokes it gently. She doesn't last long and when she removes her hand, her throat contracts. The cupboard door closes behind her and amplifies the awkward squeak she's swallowing down. Molly brings her back, nudging Rathlin in anticipation of food. Rathlin responds immediately, picking another treat from the pocket in her jeans.

'Right, girl, let's go and see if we can try and sort out this mess at Ballynoe.' She strokes the dog's head, bending down to kiss her gently on the bridge of her nose. 'That said, ma lovely Aunt Ellen is turning out to be even more of a nutcase than I thought so we may have our work cut out for us.'

Molly barks, loving the attention, so Rathlin sits on the floor beside her so she can cradle her face. 'Aye, exactly, she's hard work, there's no doubt about that but we're a tough team eh?' She looks at her watch, knowing she needs to get on the road if she's to miss the rush hour traffic coming out of Glasgow. She lifts her holdall, taking its weight in the crest of her arms, hauling its strap over her shoulder. She picks up her rucksack and instead of placing it on her back she grasps it tightly by the little handle at the top. Molly jumps in excitement, watching Rathlin as she lifts the car keys from the table in the hall.

'Okay, I've got ma phone, the wee bit of money we have, and more importantly I've got ma wits about me so let's go and metaphorically kick the shit out of all this hassle ma aunt is creating.'

Rathlin locks the front door, nodding in thanks to Molly while she waits for her. She slips the keys into her bag and encourages her to walk on, laughing when Molly's wagging tail whips her softly on the back of the legs. Rathlin stops when she reaches the pavement and takes a look at her block of flats. She doesn't know why she's suddenly compelled to look but she does. The burgundy paint on the close door is peeling. Its graffiti has been stolen by the widening cracks and is no longer readable. She tries to remember what it once said, not that it even matters. The narrow window on the door is buckling, its metal inset smashed by vandals and pushing out like a prolapse. She flicks her eyes from her own flat on the bottom until she reaches the top floor three flights up. Her neighbour, Jean, is there outside her flat, smoke billowing from her hand as she shouts at someone rushing past her. She can't make out what was said, the words lost under a slamming door that has captured their currency. Rathlin watches a person circle down the stairs, only seeing snippets of their journey as they briefly come in and out of view on each landing. The footsteps are echoing. Molly is on edge.

Rathlin can see that it's Jean's teenage son. He approaches her, pushing his face in hers, demanding to know what the fuck she's looking at. She draws back in retreat, muttering 'nothing' as she raises her eyes towards Jean. She's still hanging over the veranda, making her presence felt. 'Hoi you, leave her the fuck alone, it's no her fault you're a good for nothing waste of space'.

Rathlin spins on her heels, her heart racing, her flight impulse telling her it's time to leave. She walks purposefully to the wee concrete inlet where she parks her car at the end of the road. Rathlin can see the chaos when she gets there. She's expecting it. Jean's son is running away, his arms outstretched triumphantly, 'get it right up you' bellowing into the sky. Her car windscreen is smashed and the glass is protruding from its frame like a spider's web framed in morning dew. The guilty party, a faded brick, is resting on the bonnet. Some of the fragments of glass have travelled further and spilled onto the road.

Rathlin sinks onto the pavement, 'fuck fuck fuck fuck' penetrating the floor. Almost immediately she sees Frank, Frances's husband, approaching from the opposite direction and she breathes a sigh of relief. He is shouting at her from across the street, his donkey jacket larger than it needs to be, stretching out beyond his shoulders. His collar is turned up, his white hair bobbing on top like a blackbird with leucism. He pulls his hands out of his pockets and his bus pass takes flight alongside his flapping arms. He stops to pick it up and shouts to Rathlin, his head rotating.

'What the bloody hell, the wee bastards, I'll break their

necks when I get them. Are you okay, hen? They didnae touch ye did they?'

Frank grasps Rathlin's hand and eases her to her feet. She knows she has accepted it more eagerly than she sometimes might have.

'I'm fine, Jean Sinclair's son decided I wiz looking at him the wrong way. I should've known better. It's ma ain fault, I was somewhere else in my head. He went running up the street like he's Maradona after scoring a goal. Prick.'

Frank scans the horizon behind him and turns back with nothing to report. 'I'll kick his wee skinny arse when I see him, hen, and I'll tell you something else, I'll have a word wae his maw, that'll scare him more than anything, Jean doesnae take any prisoners. Better still, I'll set our Frances oan him, she'll run rings round him wae her tongue. Horrible wee shite that he is.'

'True, your Frances is a one-off. I wouldnae like tae have been you going home wae an open pay packet over the years.'

'Are you kidding? O'er the years? I did it the once, hen, and that was lesson enough.'

They're both smiling. 'Here, I met Frances earlier when I was out wae the dog. Looks like she'd had a few sherries so don't be expecting a cooked breakfast coming in fae your nightshift.'

Frank laughs and the lines in his forehead mark the journey he's been on, the crow's feet around his eyes settling confidently on the same flight path. He's seventy-two and still working the night shift at the hospital, a porter the person he still needs to be.

'Aye, like that's ever gonnae happen when she's been out on the lash. I'm glad she had a good time though, she needs a blowout, we both dae. I suppose she told you about Catherine?'

'Catherine? No. She didnae say a thing.'

Rathlin examines his face for tell-tale signs. He's giving nothing away so she keeps talking. The sentences are churning, like her head's stuck in a pencil sharpener and the words are shavings.

'She didnae say a word, Frank, but she wanted tae say something. She asked me in but I couldnae be bothered, you know whit it's like when someone's pished and wants tae chat, you can see it far enough. Shit, I'm sorry.'

Frank shrugs off her concern, shaking his head like all of a sudden he's the one that's apologising.

'Here, don't stress about it, hen, c'mon in the now and see her. She'll no be sleeping. Besides, you're no going anywhere in that motor. What an absolute prick.'

Rathlin clasps her bags tightly, following Frank as they approach their block. His flat is adjacent to hers and she doesn't need to get any closer to feel the memories that are curling around the wooden frames of Frank's front door. Frank fills the space and when he bends to put his key in the door, he drops his shoulder to make room for Rathlin.

Frances is sitting by the fire, the single red bar penetrating the room even though it's still summer, the room not dark enough to put on a light but not bright enough not to need one. Frances raises her chin towards Rathlin.

'Hen, c'mon in out of the doorway.' She momentarily turns her attention to her husband, conducting all the proceedings. She has changed her clothes from when they met earlier. She's wearing dark blue jeans and a grey polo neck jumper, her slippers worn and tatty. Rathlin always imagined her mum dressing like this, rocking jeans in her seventies, her hair still long but silver instead of fire-red. Or maybe she'd have kept the colour strong. She doesn't know, she has no sense of the kind of choices her mother would have made. She tries to picture the Skye of the future but she can only see the one image she's certain of, the one she's familiar with, the thirty-year-old mother who never had the chance to be thirty-one.

Chapter Five

Rathlin

Glasgow

Frances has washed off her going-out lipstick and mascara. Rathlin can see that she is tired, but she also looks sad. The whites of her eyes are strawberry pink, her lids heavy and swollen. Although it is obvious she has been crying, Rathlin knows that she won't be looking for sympathy. Frances is always more concerned with worrying about everyone else.

'Frank, get the wee dug a drink and gie her a bit of that ham that's in the fridge. And don't even start saying it's for your piece. Molly's one of the family, eh Rathlin?'

She guides Rathlin firmly towards the chair on the other side of the fire, not considering no for an answer. It's a Parker Knoll. Rathlin knows this because Frances tells her every time she sits on it.

'Take the Parker Knoll, hen, it's dead comfy. And Frank, make Rathlin something while you're at it. There's some of them cheese slices in the fridge, and don't be frightened tae throw on a wee bit of tomato.' She turns her attention back to Rathlin. 'That okay for you or would you prefer something else?' Rathlin opens her mouth to refuse but Frances straight in. 'And Frank, there's a couple of bananas in there an' all, bring them and a bag of those Salt and Shake crisps.'

Rathlin is still hovering above the chair and Frances directs her to sit, more firmly this time. Rathlin does as she's told.

'That's it, hen, you'll be comfy there. It's nice of you tae pop in. Did you need something before you head up north? Or is it west? I can never mind what direction your home place is.'

Rathlin is about to explain the geography of Ballynoe but she's interrupted by Frank bellowing to Frances from the kitchen. Frances slides forward in her chair to listen, the two of them interacting like chattering oystercatchers.

'Sorry, hen, I need tae hear what he's shouting. Something must have sneaked in the back and cut his wee legs off or he'd come through and speak tae us like a normal bodied person. It's a terrible tragedy.' Rathlin rolls her eyes in mock horror.

Frank is still shouting. 'That wee bastard, Ronnie Sinclair, tanned the windscreen on Rathlin's motor. Just there the now.'

Frances is leaning across to Rathlin, her mouth open, her head shaking in disbelief. 'She's no going anywhere until we can get it sorted.'

He emerges from the kitchen, his long arms hanging by his side and Rathlin and Frances are looking him up and down, exchanging a quizzical look. Frances mouths, 'It's still got legs' behind his back.

'I'm no even gonnae ask what that look's about.'

Rathlin and Frances grin at one another, their warmth as intense as the bar in the fire heating the room.

'Gies your AA details, hen, and I'll phone them up for ye while you catch up wae the good lady.' Frances is still smiling but Rathlin catches the slight turn in her eyes. The movement is familiar. Rathlin sees it in her own mirror. She can understand that Frances is in pain.

'Whit's the matter, Frances? Frank says there's something wrong wae Catherine?'

Frances takes a sharp breath and Frank leans in firmly behind her, picking her hand up, squeezing it before placing it back on her lap. Rathlin is consumed by the intensity of their love for one another. She has shared the same kind of moment a hundred times with her parents. They were always there for one another, even at the end. Rathlin closes her eyes and squeezes Skye and Joe from her mind. Frank helps by snapping his fingers at her.

'Details first, Rathlin. I'll sort out the car for you and then we'll tell you what's going on wae Catherine.'

Rathlin has moved on from her car. She knows it should be a traumatic inconvenience but she's shrugging her shoulders. It's not as bad as losing her parents' home and that's the real danger she's facing. 'Frank, it's a waste of time. I gave up the AA and see tae be honest wae you, I've no paid my tax and I'm about two months late wae the insurance. I guess it will be kinder tae let my wee rust bucket go to tae the big car park in the sky.'

'Rathlin Doherty, have you been driving that motor without any tax or insurance? You could have got the jail.' Frank's reply is an anxious one, his voice rising.

'Calm down will ye, it's no the crime of the century, I just needed the money for other stuff. My wages never seem tae last the month. I honestly don't know how folk manage tae dae it. I'm always totally skint.'

'Bloody ridiculous the crap money they pay you down at that supermarket. They take the piss they really dae. You never seem tae know one day fae the next whether they need you or no. It's a bloody disgrace and the sooner this country is independent the better we'll all be.'

'Tell me about it, Frances. But on the plus side, it's only down the road and it means I can get back in my breaks tae see ma wee pal.' Rathlin pats Molly's head but she's staring at the kitchen and the ham that always miraculously appears when they visit. 'And besides, there's no way I'm giving it up and then being stuck trying tae get benefits that they'll probably say I'm no entitled tae anyway.'

'True, hen, I keep hearing nightmare stories about folks starving cos of this universal benefit crap. It's a bloody sin. There's a load of folk in this scheme, Rathlin, that couldnae dae without that food bank down the road. It's heartbreaking that folks are living like this. Thank god our Frank's still got his shifts at the hospital or we'd be joining them.'

Rathlin's stomach rumbles loudly and she tries to hide it, pushing her arm hard into her belly to smother the roar. She knows that Frances is pretending she can't hear it, too kind not to.

'But here, there's no shame in using it, hen. Food is food and we all need it, especially when we're working hard tae make ends meet.'

Rathlin doesn't want Frances to know how tough things are. 'Actually, I'm no too bad this month. I got loads of shifts cos that lassie fae Glencairn Street did a moonlight flit.'

Frances is nodding, well aware of the gossip attached to the girl's disappearance.

'I had my twin's birthday present tae buy so it worked out well.' Rathlin crosses and uncrosses her legs, not able to stop talking. 'Breacán's been struggling a wee bit wae his health and if he doesnae work he doesnae get paid so I send him what I can. It's more important for him tae pay the bills and eat than for me tae run that shitey wee car.'

'Rathlin, of course you want tae look out for your brother, that's only natural, but ye need tae look after yourself too. Just look at your wee peely wally face, hen, you're aye pale no matter if it's winter or summer. Breacán's a big boy and your health's just as important as his. You're like a rake. I'm surprised you didnae fall down a bloody stank on your way in. Frank, where's her sandwich? And see while you're at it, make another couple for later on.'

Rathlin laughs. She loves the rawness of Frank and

Frances. The chaos of their love. They've been part of her life for a long time. Nearly ten years, not quite but almost as long as she had with her parents. She's been living in the flat next door to Frank and Frances since she was seventeen and she's long since forgotten how she used to laugh at the weirdness of them being called Frances and Francis. She called them the nosey old dears next door until she learned to care about them.

'I do look after myself. I'm fit as a fiddle. I walk miles wae Molly every day. I couldnae put on weight if I tried and ma face just doesnae tan, ma shade is just milk bottle white. My mum used tae say tae me that I was the colour of a gannet when I was wee and instead of black-tipped wings I had a big tufty of black hair.'

'Well, there's no danger of you eating like one, that's for sure.'

'Ha, that's funny, I'll give that you one. But, seriously, I'm fine. I'm a bit stressed out about all this crap wae Breacán and the house, but there's no way I'm gonnae feel settled until I know he's going tae be alright.'

'Aye, I get that, hen, of course I do, but whit about you, it's no supposed tae be a one-way street. He's supposed tae be there when you need him too and in all the time you've lived here I cannae mind a time when he's come tae visit you. No even when everything happened wae wee Isabella, and I'm sorry tae mention it, hen, but it's always played on my mind, it really has.'

The rage is sudden and intense. At the sound of Isabella's name Rathlin is on her feet, toppling the chair in her urgency to defend. She takes a moment, calms herself, giving Frances time to reach out to her. Rathlin pulls back. Her voice is angry but controlled.

'Frances, I don't care how kind and caring you've been tae me all these years, especially after Isabella, but listen tae me, never, ever, ever mention her name unprompted again cos if ye do, me and you are finished. I don't give a shit if you see yourself as a makeshift mother. I cannae breathe when I hear you say her name out loud when I'm no ready for it.'

'I'm so sorry, hen, I'm really sorry, it's just with what's happening wae Catherine, everything you've already been through is forefront in ma mind.'

'How? What is happening wae Catherine? Maybe if you tell me I might actually know?'

'Sit down will ye, just for half an hour, and then Frank'll take you up tae the bus station. I assume you're still going home?' Rathlin nods. 'And bugger the car. You're right, it's just a piece of metal and it probably would have broken down on the way up the road anyway.'

Frank agrees, nodding as he hands her a plate of sandwiches. 'Aye, you leave the car, hen. I'll mibbae see if James McHale can have a wee look at it fir ye, just as a wee favour, no charge mind. And of course I'll gie yous a wee lift to town tae get the bus. It's about time I gave the car a wee run out.'

He sits down on the edge of the chair beside Frances. Frances has spread her weight so she can rest her shoulder into his side. Rathlin thanks him and places the plate carefully on the floor. Rathlin drops to her knees in front of Frances.

'What is it? I'm getting worried here.'

Frances leans forward and strokes Rathlin's hair. Rathlin does little to resist, allowing Frances to push a long strand behind her ear. When Frances settles her hand on her shoulder, Rathlin raises her face towards her to listen.

'So Catherine, our Sandra's eldest daughter?' Rathlin can't understand why she suddenly needs a breakdown of Frances's family tree after years of hearing every family story several times over but she stays quiet. 'She's pregnant, well you know that, obviously, and she's due next month, my first great-granddaughter. We told you it's a wee lassie, didn't we?'

'Aye, only about a hundred and fifty times.'

'Well, they induced Catherine late last night. She's going into labour.'

Rathlin breaks free from Frances's hand and climbs back onto the chair. Molly moves with her, settling by her feet. 'There better be a good reason for mentioning Isabella in this context. Two minutes ago you're having a go at ma brother for no being here for her, even though he knows *nothing* about her, and now you tell me you're a great granny. What is it you want me tae say? Congratulations? Absolutely, congratulations, I'm genuinely happy for you all but try and be a wee bit more sensitive. For fuck's sake, Frances.' She's on her feet again, a yo-yo without any of the fun.

'Rathlin, wait. Don't leave the now, I've no finished. The wee lassie, Catherine's wee girl. She'll be stillborn. Catherine wasnae feeling much movement and…'

Rathlin is sinking and she can't do anything to stop it. Frank is there, catching her. He helps her onto the seat.

'…I don't know how anyone deals wae this kind of thing, hen. My heart's bloody breaking.'

Rathlin folds her arms around Frances. She tells her sshhh, her voice as gentle as she can make it but it's hard to keep calm, not now, not when she thinks there's an expectation for her to speak about Isabella. Frances accepts her embrace and the silence softens the edges of the harshness. Frank's phone beeps and he passes it to Frances.

'Frankie, hen, there's a message fae Sandra. She wants you to call her.' She takes the phone from him gingerly, letting it sink into her lap.

'I'll ring her in a wee minute. Maybe you could get Rathlin

a cup of tea tae wash down those sandwiches. She's had a bit of a shock an' all. We all have.'

'Sorry, hen, aye, I'll get a cup the now, no bother. I should have thought earlier but we're just a bit all over the place this morning.'

'Frank, honestly, don't bother about tea, I really need tae get going or I'll miss the morning bus. It takes forever and I want tae get there when there's still some day left in the day.'

'Rathlin Doherty, you're no stepping a foot outside that door until you've eaten those bloody sandwiches. And here, I've got something else for ye.' Frances lifts one from the plate, standing in front of Rathlin until she begins to eat. 'Frank, grab a couple of bottles of that wine fae the larder will you?'

'Frances, I cannae take wine fae you. That's too expensive.'

'Don't be daft, it's for you and Breacán for your birthday. And don't you worry about the cost of it. Frank and I get it as part of the Marks and Spencer's dine-in-for-a-tenner deals but we don't drink the stuff, cannae abide it. We only dae spirits.'

Rathlin can hear Frank clattering about in the hall. He arrives back in the living room accompanied by an unrecognisable piece of music. He's clutching a milk bottle crate. Rathlin realises it is full of bottles of wine.

'Red or white?'

'Jeez, it's like an off-sales in here. Listen, whatever. I'm embarrassed enough. This is so kind of you.'

'Frank, gie her a white and a red, and also go and grab a couple of they wee mini bottles from the fridge an' all.'

'You keep mini bottles of wine in the fridge and you don't even drink it?'

'Ach aye, hen, it's tae offer the lassies a wee drink when they're visiting. They use tae be able tae take a glass even when they were driving but they're all too scared of losing their licence now tae bother. Quite right too.'

'Bloody hell, you two, you're always looking out for me.'

Rathlin is ready to leave now. The sandwiches are eaten and the dog is licking her lips in satisfaction. 'I cannae thank you enough for all this stuff but I really need tae go. The bus is a good five hours. I'm so sorry about the wee baby, I really am.'

Frances takes her hand and peels it open. She pushes a twenty pound note into her palm, mouthing to her to just take it.

Chapter Six

Ellen

Home alone. Glasgow, 2004

My nose wiz scratchy but I really didnae want ma fingers tae wake up so I let the itch nip away at me until I couldane bear it any longer. When that happened ma plan was just tae wake up one of my fingers, the long wan next to ma thumb, but as soon as the wee pesky thing was scratching away at my nostrils the rest of them joined in like a marching band and before I knew it my shoulders and elbows were oot of the covers. I kept my eyes closed though cos then my sight wouldnae be awake and I wouldnae have tae see if my ma and da still hadnae came hame.

It's no that easy lying there hiding your sight. Especially when the sun's got its big cheery hat on and sending its wide-awake fingers through the curtains tae yank my curls and tease me out of my sleep. I tried my best tae ignore it but I just gave in and let ma sight out of the dark, opening my eyes wan by wan as though as I was writing Morse code.

So that was ma eyes, ma fingers and ma elbows back in working order so I thought I may as well make a wee start oan my legs. I stretched them as long as I could, my toes wriggling like as if they were oan the sand that I'd been tae once so long a time ago that I couldnae really remember what it smelled like, just whit it felt like and that was all scratchy but hot and nice too.

When I did stretch ma toes they broke out oav the covers

and landed oan a wee bit of sunlight that was tickling ma bed an' for a teeny moment it wiz as though I wiz on the sand beach again. I'm no a wee lassie but, ah'm five, and I know fine well the difference between pretend and real. But I wanted it tae be pretend when I gave ma legs a wee shake and tiptoed through tae my ma and da's bedroom telling the inside ma head voice that they were gonnae be all curled up under the duvet. But the other inside ma head voice was saying tae me they wouldnae be there an' even though I didnae want it tae be right, it was right and I started greetin' like a wee lassie.

My ma an' da were gone. They'd been missing for about a million years, said inside-ma-head voice, until another inside ma head voice said I wiznae tae be stupid as I'd seen them after school the day before when they'd given me a key, MA AIN KEY and told me I wiz a big lassie and could go hame and pour some cold milk fae the fridge ontae the wee bowl of cereal they'd left me oan the table in the kitchen. I'd said 'aw no, whit if wee Hamish has eaten it' and ma dad had tugged the wee pigtail at the back oav ma heid and said 'na, he's no the kind oav cat that's interested in Rice Krispies, he prefers cornflakes' and I breathed like a dozen sighs of relief cos ah wiz starving, or Hank Marvin as wan oav the wee voices in ma head said in the exact same voice as my da speaks in.

Ma da wiz dead right 'spot oan' as he would say and Hamish wiznae interested in ma Rice Krispies, he just wanted a wee cuddle as I ate them, us both holding our working ears close so we could hear the snap crackle and pop song. I say my working ears cos I'd chosen to turn them oan. Sometimes I don't bother switching them oan when I'm in the school an' the teacher's gaun on and on about something that's no that interesting. Like god. Well, I quite like the stories about the manger and the three kings an' presents for the wee baby Jesus, I mean the god bit when we're having tae learn prayers word for word an' have tae keep saying the same thing o'er and o'er and o'er. Sometimes when I'm daein that I switch off ma ears so they're no working and then I switch my tongue off too so I don't have tae say anything. I get ma lips tae stay on though so it looks tae my teacher that I'm joining in but I don't let my outside voice do any work. Sometimes I don't know if there's any point in keeping my outside voice in cos my inside voice is saying all the words anyway.

Me and Hamish, we got hungry again during Grange Hill so I climbed up oan the chair an' I got the Rice Krispies an' the cornflakes down oot of the cupboard. I poured Hamish his cornflakes first an' I used my outside voice in a big shouty way tae tell him tae wait for me tae pour my Rice Krispies but he had turned his ears oaf and started eating. He used his outside voice tae purr while he was lapping up the milk but he didnae eat the cornflakes and I wondered if I mibbae didn't have my ears turned up properly this morning when ma da said that was the cereal he liked. He didnae seem offended an' he came and curled up oan my bed. Then all my things must have turned off aw by themselves because me and Hamish fell asleep.

Then ma nose itched and that's me back at the beginning standing at the bedroom door looking at a big empty bed wae that stupid inside ma heid voice telling me that wee Ellen wiz abandoned.

Chapter Seven

Rathlin and Breacán

Ballynoe, 1993

In the beginning, the twins are separated for twenty minutes and twenty seconds, an absence in their lives that hangs as crisply as a shirt on a washing line in winter.

Rathlin presses forward first. She seals her entrance to the world with the faintest hint of a smile rather than a powerful inflation of lungs and for a brief moment Rathlin's mother soars above the pain. The knowledge is carved deeply inside her, as neatly as cut peat; her daughter will take the world by the scruff of its neck and fly.

For the moment, on that first day, Rathlin is as silent as a freshly dug rock. Her hair is as black as a raven, the fluffy down as soft as a nest of island mist. Her skin is like a whiteness of swans, her face pale and narrow, large dark eyes taking centre stage as they scan new horizons. She quickly senses her brother's absence and in preparation for him joining her, tenses her arms.

Mamie Jackson, the woman from the village who is helping Skye give birth, rests Rathlin on a soft pillow on one side of the bed, close to her mother's unsettled hips which are bucking and thrusting with each contraction, strong waves of love meant to guide her son out into the world and towards her swollen breasts.

The twins' mother, Skye Isabella Doherty, has fire-red hair that reaches the small of her back, its curling edges like the bracken that mats the forest floor, its tresses now cloaking her shoulders, its vibrancy darkened with sweat.

Skye Smyth was eleven-years-old when she saw Joseph Doherty for the first time. She had arrived in Kintyre from Ireland with her mother, the village her new home. Joseph was on the strand, almost a man, a boy of fifteen, in another world. She called him Joe and declared to herself there and then that she would marry him and here in the final thrusts of childbirth, Skye was little more than a child herself.

They married when she was seventeen and on the eve of her eighteenth birthday, the final night of her honeymoon, husband and wife risked their blushes on a headland on the island of Islay with the arms of the island of Rathlin in the distance. Skye had been born on Rathlin and its blood ran in her veins. The island was sharing the wildness, the landscape reforming as the boundaries shifted and life gave in to life. Somehow they knew, albeit not scientifically, that they had just conceived not one but two children.

Afterwards, as they lay naked, shaking with cold in a headland wind that buckled and bent its way into the most sensitive of places, there was a sense of magic in the realisation that they had conceived. Joe, a shy young man whose protective shell evaporated in Skye's company, suggested names for their twins there and then. His hand clenched tightly in Skye's, his lips brushing the soft skin of her belly, he bellowed out like a cattle in labour to his new daughter and son.

'Listen. This is your father speaking.'

Skye pushed his head away and laughed, the sound slightly odd and unnatural, the damp chill in the air making her teeth clash. She gently pushed Joe to the side, stretching her arms so she could grab her pants and jeans. She pulled them over cold flesh, shivering as her clothes refused to roll smoothly over her skin. She left the zip open and drew Joe's lips back to her belly.

'Believe me, Joe, our children real or imagined, are listening. How could they not with you hollering at them fae a matter of inches away?'

He ignored her, words dripping from his lips in quick succession.

'Skye, let's call the weans Rathlin and Barra. Look at this world. We're surrounded by a sea and sky that moves and shifts and brings something different at every point of every day. The islands, they are solid, they centre the sea and sky... us too.' He straightened his knees, rising to his feet, his steps certain on the soft curved earth. A buzzard was watching from above, static in the sky, its cat-like meow circling their shoulders.

Skye was less sentimental. She was born on an island and had eighteen years named after another.

'Really, Joe? Should we no think of something a bit more normal?'

'Why would we want our children tae be normal when we already know that they will be exceptional?'

'Jeez, Joe, I think the cold's getting tae you. We don't even know if I'm pregnant never mind that I'm having twins.' She's sitting up, laughing, ruffling Joe's hair. 'But dae you know what, I guess I dae like the idea of calling our daughter Rathlin. Mum loved that both she and I were born over there.'

Skye's on her feet, her hand cocked on her forehead, scanning the island in the distance.

'That's a sign then, Skye.'

'It's a bit of a mouthful. She'll spend her life explaining it.'

'Well, isn't that better than having nothing tae share?'

. . .

And here, on the occasion of her coming together with her daughter, Skye is running her finger along Rathlin's slender cheek, the white of her palm caressing the underside of her daughter's long thin jaw. She's rolling her body to the side, the mattress rippling like an oncoming swell and tipping Rathlin's nest momentarily into the air. As one takes flight, the other sways and a fraction away from a loving kiss, their path changes mid-air. Barra is going nowhere, and coming nowhere even faster.

Rathlin is calling out, her cry a high-pitched squawk, an explosive shrill to alert her mother to the fact that her twin is penned in and thrashing around, drowning in his own self-doubt. Her brother's continuing reluctance to join her is threatening to permanently blur the edges between his new life and his old world. Instinctively Rathlin can sense the danger.

Mamie is calm and cheery. With her finger poised in the air as if she might cast a spell, she is mocking Rathlin's twin from above, asking Skye's swollen belly if the child submerged inside is a seal pup, somersaulting in playful twists and diving for cover. But Rathlin knows that her other half is in trouble, that if they don't get him out he will never suck on the air that she is sharing, without him, with her mother.

With Rathlin's warning circling recklessly, they begin to haul her brother from the depths. Flapping and gasping, he's fighting against the cold metal forceps hooking his temples. For just a moment he lies still, understanding that he can't escape the chilling crunch of the midwife's pincers. He's willing them to slice his slender neck and take his head, anything to continue to swill in the warm ocean of his mother's womb.

When the forceps crash into the tin basin positioned precariously on the wooden chest at the end of the bed, they bring something amazing with them. The wave of blood rolling furiously is stunning, thick and dark like a forest of underwater kelp, but it is Rathlin's twin that is the thing of real beauty. Twenty minutes and twenty seconds after the birth of his sister, Rathlin's brother is thrust reluctantly into his new world.

The shock to his system, and his lingering determination to enjoy a bit of independence from Rathlin, hits him hard.

When the forceps withdraw, he flops lifelessly onto the bed, his mother pulling her legs towards her chin in response, pushing her back against the oak headboard engrained with voyages of other lives on other journeys, her sticky hair clinging to its stories.

His skin is as blue as a summer sky and as clear and still as its reflection on a calm sea. For a moment they all do nothing, as if they have paused to frame a photograph. At the opposite end of that impossibly long moment Mamie is rubbing his chest vigorously, the second finger of her right hand sitting on top of her index finger as she urges him quietly in Gaelic to wake up and be with the world that is awaiting him.

'Come on now, little seal pup, dùisg, that's right, dùisg, waken up so we can all meet you.'

Rathlin is the next to move, her arm unfolding from her chest, her body gliding forward. The baby boy is entwined with his sister in an instant and with that motion he opens his lungs, his skin pinking and his fingers and toes curling as he reluctantly cries out to announce his arrival.

Joe arrives at that moment, slipping his jacket from his shoulders as he walks across the room, his entrance strong and yet without deliberate presence. He's holding his lips together, his fingers uncurling on both hands as he turns his gaze from daughter to son to mother. He smiles, the upturned corners of his lips catching salty tears. In silence he's kicking off his boots, black wellingtons caked in the mud of the

57

furrowed fields he has been working since dawn. He's climbing onto the bed, his hands prising Skye's back from the headboard so he can mould into the space behind her.

Whilst kissing Skye's neck, he's pulling her onto his chest, reaching out his arms, placing the palms of his hands on his children's heads, his fingers stroking his daughter's thick black hair and then his son's fine strawberry blonde curls that glitter in the evening sunlight. His fingers are moving back towards his son's face and neck, his hand caressing its speckled skin, like oystercatcher eggs on a pebbled beach.

'What's happened tae Barra's face, Skye?' He's peering over him now, looking intently at the mark that is stretching from his neck to his jawline, creeping beyond it and settling on the line of his cheekbone. 'Is he alright?' He's drawing his hand back, grasping Skye's and drawing them both towards their son.

'Ssh, you'll wake him, he's tired after his journey, he had tae fight hard tae break free of the Coire Bhreacain. He was lost for a bit but Rathlin guided him out, she made him safe. The midwife also had tae use forceps so they've left their mark for now.' She's caressing her son, gently, running her finger along the edges of his speckled skin.

'Coire Bhreacain, that's the whirlpool beyond the shoulder of Rathlin Island isn't it?' Joe's keeping his voice down but it is so low it is booming. Rathlin's opening her eyes, looking at him, responding as if she already knows her name. Joe's smiling, shaking his head at the intensity of the moment.

'It is, and as you know, breac means spotted and speckled in Gaelic so you can forget about Barra, this wee boy has tae be called Breacán. Both he and Rathlin have demanded it. And there's something else too. Remember I told ye all about the magical Breacán's Cave on Rathlin where the water heals everything? This wee boy has already healed my heart. There was a moment, Joe, when I thought we'd lost him.'

'Breacán. It fits him perfectly.' Joe's leaning into Breacán, gently kissing his cheek, murmuring his name before turning to his daughter and doing the same.

And there they sit, sharing time and one another until a blanket of midnight blue sky wraps their senses in what feels like a warm, far-reaching future.

Chapter Eight

Ellen

The field between Ballynoe and Kebble

The sun is high in the sky, delaying its reluctant meander towards the west and its inevitable drowning by the ever-chasing night. Ellen is staring upwards, wondering if today will be its big break, the day the sun raises its fists triumphantly to the flush cheeks of the moon. The silver sphere is ready to duel and Ellen can see that Breacán is part of the scene, in his shirt sleeves, his joints gnawing hungrily at the last of the warmth from the sky.

Breacán is sitting on the mountain beside the house where he and Rathlin were born. The hill is soaring into the multi-coloured sky, ribbons of gold and orange and candy pink towering protectively over Ballynoe. Its bricks and mortar were constructed by their great grandfather but that hasn't stopped Breacán from repeating this story to Ellen. At first he told it with love, as a way of sharing his past with her, but now to add a dig. It's a bad move on his part. It tells Ellen that his history is more important than the present he shares with her.

The farmhouse sits on a shelf in the mountain, like a cuckoo clock on a mantelpiece. Local tourist information, on the other hand, describes the unusual geographical configuration as a stepping-stone for the fabled Scottish giant, Benandonner, as he prepared to go to battle with his Irish counterpart, Finn McCool. Breacán has firm views on this, repeatedly telling Ellen that he doesn't buy into the hopscotching giant theory. She agrees with him on that, but she's not always with him when he's enthusing about water wraiths and selchies, and the fairies in the hawthorn tree. Barra loves it though. She laps up all the stories that once upon a time he learned from his parents.

Ellen is sitting on the gate at the edge of the hollow, her step midway between giving in and staying strong. She can see that Breacán is breathing deeply. Instinctively she knows he's in pain. He's looking down at the only real home he's ever known and for a moment she feels a surge of guilt.

Stop that right now. Do not let that man keep walking over you.

She listens to the voice and is happy to be reminded that she is threatening to take it away from him for a reason. She has to be more than nothing. He can't keep secreting her out of existence.

She can see what he admires about the house though. It is one of only two homes on this side of the mountain that sits in peaceful seclusion. Below is busier, the white cottages along the single village street like foot soldiers in its shadow, each uniform home shouting out its own identity in the form of a garden of different shapes and colours. From Ellen's perspective, the houses are shouting at the shoreline, warning the tide not to come too close. She wonders if the people that live in them hear voices too.

The afternoon air is cooling and the sky is fading like fabric on a garden seat that has been resting in the sun. Ellen knows that Breacán is waiting patiently for his twin sister, wondering who to love more. She's watching him, her own voices telling her what he's thinking. She tries to calm the voices telling her that he really has had enough but they race to the fore. She listens for a moment, their loudness sending her right foot in Breacán's direction. She's going to

61

him, giving in. Why does anyone need to know? It's their business that they're together. They've kept it quiet for all these years and they've just got stronger and stronger. People are so fuckin nosey. But then she hears the voice asking her why she always has to be the abandoned one and she presses her foot firmly into the earth. She's going nowhere.

She hears an engine drawing that bit closer, its enduring purr clearly audible and she's watching for his reaction. It comes as soon as the syrupy mix of oil and diesel trickles up the hill and teases his nose. He looks towards the horizon in anticipation but the road is empty, the scent drifting up the hill from a boat drawing life into its engine in the harbour below. Ellen stifles a laugh. He can't even get that right. She waits for the smell to pass, and, in its place, the yellow blossoms of the hillside gorse casually loiter, the whin relaxing at having recaptured its space. Ellen kicks her heels against the gate, knowing it won't be long. Rathlin will come and a decision will be made.

She rubs the bridge of her nose and notices that Breacán is doing the same. Ha, she thinks, now *that's* special powers. She can see him fiddling with something in the palm of his hand, raising his fingers to his mouth. Shit, he's in a lot of pain. She says it out loud and then holds her breath tightly until she's satisfied that the words haven't travelled to him, letting him know she's watching.

Breacán is pressing his fingers into the hollow just above his cheeks, collecting the fallout from the stabbing pain that Ellen knows will be pushing east and west, its flight as troublesome as a ravaging seagull. He sinks his head forward and his bright red hair glows in the bracken like the embers of a winter fire. Ellen follows his every move, noticing that he is reaching into his pocket, pulling out his mobile phone. He's holding it up in front of him, checking the signal status for any sign of life. Ellen takes her own phone from her pocket and waits for it to ring. It doesn't. Instead she hears him say, 'Annie'.

Ellen stretches her body millimetres closer. She can hear Breacán but she has to imagine the other side of the conversation. *It's his ex. He's spending time talking to his ex and not you. He doesn't even like you. He likes her. And Rathlin. He hates you.*

Breacán's voice is loud and strong.

'Hiya, it's me. You okay tae talk for a second?' His deep syllables are flying long and hard into the distance. Ellen is snaring them, interrupting them and knocking them temporarily off their busy stride. Silence. Then.

'I'm totally grand, I'm just sitting up on the hill waiting on Rathlin coming. It's a beautiful day and the gorgeous light in the sky made me wonder what you're up tae.'

The real-life silence is drowned by the voices in Ellen's head. She can hear Annie giggle, flirting with the man she loves, telling him that she wants them to get back together. Then she hears Breacán provide the sting in the tale.

'I've had a shit day. Pity you're no here. Mibbae you'd know how tae cheer me up.'

Ellen sniggers. Breacán is trying to flirt, but she knows him even better than he does. There's zero sentiment in his words. He turns his head to the east, to her house at Kebble, to the upstairs gable window. She stands tall in delight. He's hoping that she will be watching, absorbing his movement, wishing that he hadn't left things the way he did. Ellen follows his gaze, knowing that he lived in that house for a while too, deposited there with Rathlin to live with their grandfather the day their parents died.

Ellen shifts her gaze back to Breacán, following his eyes as he moves from her house to his own. *Well, technically they are both yours, Ellen.* He is looking across to the narrow lane that stretches between both houses, its white limestone pebbles crashing like the tide, its surf having spat out the house and placed it at the end of the road. The roof is blue-black, a chimney stretching into the sky, pale grey smoke climbing and then falling away with the birds. Ellen follows the chitter chatter of the turf as it burns into the skyline. She wonders why he's lit a fire. Hmm. For Rathlin, of course. Anything for Rathlin.

Breacán still has the handset to his ear but his lips are pulled tightly shut. Ellen's stomach is churning, imagining Annie cooing like a pigeon, puffing out her chest as she tries to steal back her man. She relaxes when she hears his raised voice, his pitch out of control and beautiful to her ears.

'Jesus, Annie, don't start being all melodramatic, will ye! I shouldnae have called. I'll tell Rathlin to gie you a call when she can.'

Breacán hangs up and Ellen knows it's because his heart doesn't want safe and normal. He's drawn to her, empowered by the way she accepts him as he is. She knows he can't resist the way she loves him, the way she makes him feel like nothing else matters. He's coming back to her. Rathlin has nothing over this. She takes her phone from her pocket and texts her friend, Anita, setting her plan in motion.

Jump into the shop when you get here. You cannae miss it ;) It's right beside the bus stop. I'll meet you in there. I need to get some fags and vino. Loads tae tell you. x

Chapter Nine

Rathlin

The bus home to Ballynoe

Rathlin boards the bus swiftly and moves towards the back. She perches herself and Molly in front of the last row. She slips in her earphones, looking anywhere but up when the other passengers join her. She narrows her eyes, ensuring that all she can see is shapes.

The engine sparks into life and startles Molly. She barks excitedly. Rathlin's mood is more sombre. She's thinking of the space in front of her, the place she calls home, even though she left when she was a teenager. She closes her eyes so she can see it.

Home is peering from a jagged hill above the shore. The farmhouse's pearl face has been scoured by the wind. Rathlin knows she won't need to stretch her neck to see its permanent scowl and she also knows that when she draws closer she will anyway, her chest tightening as its threadbare walls reach out to her, tossing a blanket of memories over her shoulders.

. . .

There's a five hour journey ahead. The bus will twist dizzily through Loch Lomond, its waters foreboding and intense. Then there's the slow hike towards Lochgilpead before the long stretch that brings the sea and the beautiful sight of the islands of Gigha and Islay. The real road to home. She diverts her attention to social media, flicking through Twitter updates, looking but not seeing what's on the screen in front of her. She finally pauses to absorb its content. It's her own. Her finger is hovering on her own profile. The header photo is one of her and her twin brother, aged eight, their arms wrapped around one another, their mouths mid-laugh. They are standing in front of the porch, the photograph taken from the garden. She clicks on the image and it springs into life. Ballynoe pops up behind Rathlin and Breacán on the screen. She pinches her fingers and zooms in on their faces. She smiles instantly at their mischievous grins. She notices that her parents' window is open, that the curtain has been snared on the outside sill by the wind. She imagines Dad behind it, watching Mum, smiling at her, getting ready to make them all laugh. She clicks the cross on its edge and the image shrinks back but it remains stamped to the screen like a statement of intent. She and Breacán are the same height. They can see the world from the same vantage point, a place of familiarity and warmth. She presses the phone tightly into her palm and looks beyond the technology, searching for that old sense of worth.

A message arrives from Frances and stings. 'Sandra's text said come to the hospital. We went after Frank dropped you off. Cara had been born, such a beautiful wee wean, hen, but she wasnae alive. So sad and unfair, it breaks ma heart. I can send you a wee photo we took of her. You'll understand, pet, since you know this pain.'

Why would anyone want to send a photo of a dead child? Anger rises but just as quickly dies. Frances is only trying to do the right thing. And she's hurting too. *There's so much pain in this world.* This isn't the first time Rathlin has thought that but it's the first time she has said it out loud on a bus. She doesn't wait for a reaction, throwing her head down so she can only see the floor. She thrusts her phone in her pocket, pushing it deep inside so she doesn't smash the screen with her fist. Molly jumps up on the seat and Rathlin lets her stay. Perfect cover for her face. She pulls her close and pats her head but Molly wriggles free, stretching across Rathlin's knee so she can nuzzle her nose into her bag.

Rathlin gives in, drawing the package of sandwiches from inside. As her wrist twists, she glances at the time and realises that there's only an hour and a half left of the journey. She checks again, wondering what has been stealing the passing hours. She rubs her eyes, wondering if she somehow slept. She lifts her head forward, disappointed that if she did sleep, it didn't produce a message from her mother.

She's feeding Molly when the bus stops abruptly. She shoves the dog out of the way so she can look out the window. Her heart is racing at the fear of the unknown. And there it is, the known, right in front of them. There is a deer on the road, its misadventure in front of a car the result of its venture into the unknown. It was still young, a roe, its dusty fur compromising the sharp blue of the sky. Rathlin can see that her large brown eyes have stopped searching for a better outcome and the poor creature's instinct is telling her that there is barely a breath between her and the end.

The deer is badly injured, but it isn't immediately obvious from its calmness. Its legs are tucked underneath its body and its strong neck holds its angular head so still it is statuesque. The automatic headlamps of the guilty car are slinging a dipped light behind it, the ground silent.

A girl in the seat in front interrupts Rathlin's vista, leaning into her. Their elbows grate together briefly while she carves herself into the scene.

'Now there's something ah don't get tae see every day.'
Rathlin doesn't add to the statement.

Her hair is as black as night, flashes of blue strands tumbling into view as she stretches up from her elbows, its dye long since swallowed by the creeping moss of her natural strands. The colour mirrors the tattoo staining the brown skin of her neck. A blue rose, its preserved petals full and blooming, and a long green stem staggers down to her shoulder before disappearing under her t-shirt. Rathlin imagines it roaming for miles, unfettered, its roots sucking the very life of her. She lingers on its edge, allowing herself to wonder.

'That poor wee thing...', the girl nods towards the window then turns to Rathlin. She's staring at the edges of Rathlin's mouth and Rathlin bites her bottom lip, suddenly self-conscious. The girl seems oblivious to her discomfort and returns to the deer. 'It's a shame isn't it?'

Rathlin is looking at the deer. Her hands are placed tightly around her dog's neck. She caresses her fur imagining the pain she would feel if it were Molly and not the deer on the road beside them. She turns around, her response husky in its breathlessness. 'It must have taken a right whack. Hope it's got a big mammy or daddy that'll come back and ram that stupid prick in the arse.'

The girl raises her phone to the window, framing the deer in the glass within the glass. Rathlin uncurls her shoulders, the city collapsing like a demolished high rise behind her. Her words tumble. 'It's like she's been waiting on this moment of drama her whole life. I don't imagine I'd be as chilled if I was about tae pop ma clogs.'

The girl is still staring at the miniature version of the deer she is clasping tightly in her phone. Finally content, she pushes her knees up onto the seat and grasps the handrail firmly, turning her back to the front of the bus.

'God, me neither. Ah'll probably bottle it like everyone else wae any sense about them.'

They turn in unison and stare at the deer, their cheeks in line.

'Whit's waiting for you at the other end of this journey then. Anything exciting?'

Rathlin unfurls her tongue from behind her teeth slowly. 'Ma wee brother. Although I'm no sure if exciting is the right word. He's pretty laid back. He lives just up the hill from the bus stop in the village. You?'

'*The* bus stop?'

'Aye, the bus stop, there's only one. What brings you tae the back of beyond?'

'Ah'm going tae help a pal. But it's no a great hardship. Ah could honestly do wae a change of scenery and ah think *beyond* sounds like it could be interesting.'

Rathlin laughs but replies quickly, defending home. 'Actually, it's a really beautiful place. If you like a nice view you've come tae the right place. We're on the sea and the Atlantic's pretty special. So are you fae Glasgow?'

'Now there's a story. Family legend has it that ah was born in India, the secret child of a famous Bollywood actress but the social work version tells me it was plain old Govanhill. Ah guess ah can get away with the former so sometimes ah just stick with that version. Depends who's asking really.' She pulls a face, smiling.

'That doesnae sound complicated at all.'

The girl responds, running her right hand through her hair. 'It is an' it isnae. Maybe we'll see each other again, beyond yon beyond place we're headed, an' ah can tell you more.'

Rathlin clocks that the girl with the rose tattoo has turned her attentions to the sandwiches beside her.

'Here, dae you want one of these? My neighbour made

them up for me. She's always worried I'm no eating enough.'

'Ah wouldnae mind, ta.' She reaches across, accepting it gratefully. 'How long have we got tae go, dae ye think?' The bus is on the move again, picking up pace and twisting around the narrow road, the sea in clear view.

Rathlin glances at the time again, comparing the clocks on her wrist and her phone to be sure. 'Less than an hour now, no long until you see the heady heights of my wee town.'

'Oh it's a *town* now, that spiralled quickly.' She laughs loudly at her own joke. 'Right, ah'm gonnae grab that row of seats behind you for a wee kip. Ma pal will be full on when ah arrive. Ah'm Anita by the way.'

Rathlin's eyes lock with Anita's, looking at her longer than she needs to and not pulling away until her cheeks begin to burn.

When the journey ends, Rathlin feels a hand on her shoulder and turns, already knowing it is Anita.

'It wiz good tae meet ye. Hopefully ah'll catch up wae you at some point.' She's yawning but Rathlin can make out what she's saying.

'Aye, nice tae meet you too, Anita. I'm Rathlin by the way.'

Rathlin is expecting the quizzical look. Next up will be the *what kind of name is that* question. Anita has a different response.

'Cool name, like that wee island in Ireland. It's on ma bucket list. Ah've got a burning desire in me tae go an find Robert the Bruce's spider.'

Anita pulls her hood over her head, her bangles jangling on her wrist. Her shape slips slowly towards the front of the bus. There's a purple rucksack sinking low on her hips and pushing her into the yellow light uncoiling from the window. As she presses into the distance, her shadow bleached, Rathlin remembers she's home to fight. She's distracted for a moment by the rowans standing to attention, still there, exactly where they were when she last visited. She doesn't know if she has the strength.

Chapter Ten

Rathlin

Back on Kintyre peninsula

Rathlin notices Mamie Jackson as soon she stands up. She's getting up from a seat closer to the front of the bus, her back more buckled but still familiar. She sinks into the past and slips an arm around Mamie's back, leaning in to kiss her.

'Mamie, I didnae realise you were on the bus, all this way and I didnae get a chance tae chat tae you.'

Mamie pulls away from the embrace, looks confused, unable to place her. Rathlin takes a step back, remembering Breacán telling her Mamie is a bit forgetful. Typical of her brother to underplay things. She curses Breacán under her breath, making a mental note to have a word with him.

She changes her tack and becomes the stranger Mamie thinks she is. She asks Mamie if she needs help with her bags. Mamie responds warmly and Rathlin searches her smile for some recognition. She tells herself she can see it, that Mamie knows who she is. The past has paired them like a platform and a train. Rathlin pushes Mamie's fringe from her forehead, offering her a wee titbit of gossipy nonsense she's heard from Breacán. Mamie accepts it heartily and Rathlin smiles at the vivaciousness of her response, her words as fresh as sliced peat. It lifts Rathlin forwards, towards the bustling hydraulic doors.

The world outside is welcoming them boldly, the sea air

immediately enveloping them in its saltiness, its coarseness pushing their heels onto the metal step. Rathlin obliges, despite knowing she is treading on memories that will make her laugh and cry. She helps Mamie over the hurdle, resisting the powerful urge to rest her head in the curve between her shoulders. She remembers its space as emblematic of a time when the taste in her mouth was less bitter.

Mamie accepts Rathlin's help, unable to understand that she is the little girl she helped birth nearly twenty-seven years before, the wee lassie who clung to her when the lives of her parents were reduced to ashes. None of it matters because nothing of this version of Rathlin remains for Mamie anymore.

Rathlin would love to slide into her memories, to pin herself to the scrapbook that has been ripped apart and taped back together out of sequence. The new Mamie is here, completely three-dimensional, but the old Mamie is somewhere else, a place where Rathlin may not have existed. Perhaps in Mamie's new world she was never born and her mum and dad are still alive and beautiful, a digital presence that Breacán shares with the loving family she has never been a part of.

She stretches her fingers into Mamie's, willing her to remember. She whispers 'I love you' in Gàidhlig, but knows that Mamie recognises only the chill of her fingers as they curl loosely around hers.

On the narrow road beside them, Mamie's grandson Niall emerges from the jaws of his old Capri. Rathlin leans back, remembering the chill of its leather seats against her back as she lay beneath him on her seventeenth birthday. Niall lowers his chin when he sees her, his eyes closed to her memory. Rathlin unhooks her fingers from Mamie's and warms their sudden chill on her stomach.

She's remembering Isabella. She's feeling her swimming

deeply inside her, twisting and tumbling, the bond between mother and daughter impenetrable. Her kicks grew from the low gurgle of a distant stream to deep waves that surged between the moon and the sun. Isabella only stopped momentarily to sleep and build strength for their long life together.

Rathlin gazes intently at Niall, searching for something of Isabella in his jaw. His features show no resemblance of their daughter. She swallows hard and for a moment she can only hear the sound of the wind, its fertile breath brushing treetops. She waits, holding completely still, until a bird catches the moment and carries it on its wings. She exhales, watching it flying into the distance.

Rathlin's attention is drawn back to Mamie. She is settling into the car while Niall shuffles around to the driver's side. His head is low, his neck straining, perhaps from the responsibility of caring for Mamie. He has had his own shit to deal with. Meanwhile she carries the weight of their daughter's death alone. Always, always alone. Inside she cries out for her mother, knowing she won't come.

She has seen enough and turns her back. She sinks her roots into earth. The bracken is swaying, her physical connection with it cementing her return home.

Chapter Eleven

Rathlin

Ballynoe

At the foot of the hill Rathlin squints up at the house. She is running her fingers along her ribs, pressing her fingers deeply into her skin in response to her quickening breath. She closes her eyes, straining to hear her mother's call to come inside. When she hears it, she lets her twelve-year-old legs carry her past the door and into her mother's arms. She's holding herself there, briefly, before demanding to know what there is for eating. Her mother is laughing, holding her playfully and planting tiny kisses on her cheeks and forehead. Rathlin's remembering the hint of tea escaping from her lips, her mother's hand as it passes her a biscuit but only one biscuit in case it ruins her appetite, her brother entering the kitchen and snatching the biscuit from her hand, her legs taking her after him as they chase each other down the hall, the foundations of Ballynoe snaring the screeching and laughing.

. . .

She comes back from almost *Then* and steps back, one step, then two. She can see the house clearly. Despite the passing of years, it never really changes. It is tall and white. The paint under the window frames and beneath the guttering is flaking but Ballynoe is still glistening. The blue-black tiles of the roof have captured the west light and the colour is anchored, ancient voices settling into its mast. Rathlin knows the chatter will intensify when night falls and the lighthouse sweeps towards it, swaying on the edge of a ruthless sea.

The house is two and a half stories high, the attic windows protruding like watchful eyes, the border of the house painted a foot high in green paint that matches the frames of the window ledges and the wooden slats of the porch. Rathlin pauses, remembering a lengthy discussion between Mum and Dad before the paint was added. Mum had said it would be pretty; Dad said it would be a pain to maintain. They were both right and she wonders if she and Breacán will ever replenish the paint to its previous richness. She rolls her eyes, knowing that there's more than paint to sort.

She can't understand Ellen. Why is she threatening to sell the house. It doesn't make any sense. Yes, technically she owns Ballynoe, but only by default. It's never been *her* house. She never showed any interest in it, even when Aonghus left it to her. Even when he died she told them it would always be theirs because that's what he wanted. Not now though. All fuckin hell is breaking loose and not only is she declaring it to be *her* house, but she's selling it.

She is stealing the little bits of her parents that remain – the smells, the sounds, the memories both light and dark. Rathlin thought she had nothing left to lose but the past can be ripped away twice. She wonders why the shit just keeps coming.

But more than that she wonders why. Why is the wee boot doing this? Rathlin curses her lack of clarity and hopes that Breacán will have insight to share. She looks across the field and growls under her breath. *For fuck sake, Ellen, have you not got enough already?* She's looking at Kebble, Ellen's house. Well, one of her houses. Kebble and Ballynoe are almost identical. They differ in the watchful eye of the attic windows. They are missing in Kebble and make Ballynoe stand apart.

Mum and Dad carved them into their house so the twins could have more space. Rathlin flicks her eyes between both houses, her hair lifting gently in a sudden burst of wind from the sea. She feels her stomach wretch and she swallows the water at the back of her throat but it doesn't change anything. Her parents are still dead and they never had a chance to watch their twins grow into their lives at Ballynoe.

How the fuck can a twenty-one-year-old create so much grief? Rathlin feels her muscles tighten. She stretches her arms, ready to take flight.

She takes a deep breath. She can see Breacán sitting on the hill, watching for her arrival. His left arm is outstretched and strong. Rathlin squints at him, trying to see if he is wasted on Tramadol or having a good spell with the arthritis that menaces and smothers him.

She forges on, excitement building despite everything. She attacks the hill with as much gusto as she can gather, thrusting her heels into the thick bracken, her determined steps towards home efficient and deliberate. Her focus is fixed firmly on the earth that is lifting her into the softening sky. Molly is running alongside her, free of the city restrictions, darting in and out of the long grass. She can see that Breacán is still watching, his frame resting on the basalt rock high above the house. He has pushed his spine tightly against the hillside and he looks majestic, as if he was resting on a stone throne carved into the backbone of the mountain.

When she gets closer to the house, Rathlin knows that she and Breacán are about to share a memory about their father. She fills her lungs with a life lost and throws her brother a salute. She unhooks her bags from her neck and drops to the ground. Molly copies her, hunching down, settling on all fours like a lion in a city square.

. . .

77

Once upon a time, Joe Doherty shared this space with his children, his voice like a train on a track, its metal edges clipping loudly as it raced to the point of no return.

Now, Rathlin is scanning across the bay to the caves on the coastline, searching for the spiritual magic of the other world he always promised. The sea is on the move, its spray trailing behind the waves like a bride's train. Joe would have shared a story about a sorrowful wedding. She's connecting with him, watching the veil, its intensity smothering her as she imagines the legacy her father would have created for this moment. She's listening for his voice, finally hearing it in his story.

He had told them that once upon a time, the village had come under siege from water wraiths, evil female spirits who appeared from the caves and dragged two young children playing unsuspectingly on the shore, down into the depths. The brother and sister were rescued by a selchie. The seal in human form tore into the waves and set the children free, tossing their breathless bodies on to the strand where his wife rubbed their tiny chests with such intensity that they were compelled to find new breath. Being a selchie, a seal in the water and a man on the shore, the brave villager lost his human form and was resigned to spend the rest of his life at sea. His haunting call to his wife and children, the twins' dad said, was heard for many years afterwards.

It is a story with legs and every time their dad excitedly told them the narrative, the outcome was different, more vibrant, more extreme, frequently evocative and tragic, and then sometimes comedic with a tone so deliberately funny that Rathlin's and Breacán's uncontrollable giggles raced down the hillside like rabbits chasing the early morning light. Often times, the selchie in the narrative died, other times he was saved by the sweet music of a beautiful mermaid. It was nothing, but it was everything. Memories are all they have.

. . .

At the front gate Rathlin draws the metal bolt from the concrete post. It screeches and the echo races across the open field between the twins like an eagle in search of a small mammal to feast on. Rathlin waves at Breacán, snorting comfortably when, like a reflection in a mirror, he waves back. Rathlin doesn't know if it is her or him that has willed him to his feet but she knows that for them both it signifies the beginning of a painful descent towards their twenty-seventh birthday and the fifteenth anniversary of their parents' death.

The twins arrive at the front door of Ballynoe at the same time. Their embrace is needy. They collapse into one another as if the lumberjack has called *timber* from deep within the forest. The house behind them is still and quiet. Rathlin moves away first, leaning back so she can look at Breacán. Molly is seeking attention but Rathlin gently pushes her aside so she can concentrate on her twin.

'How goes it?' She wraps her arms around his neck, clinging on for a second before releasing her grip. She kisses him gently on the cheek, the contact bringing a rush of blood. She is home. The feeling is both warm and chilling. Breacán responds with a smile and then a worried glance.

'I'm good. But are ye sure you're okay? I got your text about your car, wee shits doing that to ye.'

'Aye, but could have been worse, I could have been in it. Don't fancy being smashed on the heid wae a brick. And you can stop lying, I can tell when you're in pain.' Rathlin smiles, extinguishing any tension before it can settle. There is a dull ache filling her chest. Its flush is familiar. The Breacán pain.

She was barely four the first time it happened and it struck with such force she thought the sky was moving backwards until she realised that she was falling, the crush in her chest lifting her, her legs rising from the earth like a feather caught in a spring breeze. She can't remember what Breacán had done, only that her father's voice, bellowing low in her little brother's direction, was more than she could possibly bear. She has felt its enormity several times since.

Rathlin can see that Breacán is standing with his weight on his left side, meaning his right hip is grating too much to allow his foot to root into the earth and let him stand tall. He shifts his weight to the porch window, lowering his bum onto the thick sill with the swiftness of a wave crashing onto the shore. His shirt is rustling against the glass, a single wave kissing the shingle strand.

Molly nudges Rathlin's bag in Breacán's direction and Rathlin laughs loudly. She bows dramatically and lets Breacán pick it up, even though she knows he might struggle with its weight. Breacán rolls his eyes, making a joke about how heavy it is.

'Jeez, didn't realise you were moving back.'

'Very funny. Just a wee while, you'll be glad tae hear. A welcome escape fae the boredom of work. Has Annie been around?'

Breacán shrugs, no, and Rathlin wonders why he seems surprised she's asked. He looks away. Hiding something. 'I think she's away, on a hen do or something. You'll be pissed off you're missing it.'

Rathlin laughs sarcastically. 'Bummer, my invite must've got lost in the post. Pity, I'd have loved a night out wae a bunch of pished hysterical lassies talking about weddings.'

'Aye, right enough, you and your ripped jeans would have looked the part.'

'You should have told me you'd joined the fashion police.'

Rathlin stares at her brother intently, her shoulders rising and falling. What a weird thing for him to say. He's filling gaps with whatever comes to mind. Yip, definitely hiding something. Breacán shrugs back, her reflection his, and his hers. Rathlin carries on. 'And never mind me, you'll be looking the part when Annie brings all the bride magazines home that just happened tae mysteriously fall into her bag.' She searches her brother's eyes for a reaction but there's none. She's not even sure if he was listening.

The silence that follows though is comforting. They stroll quietly into the house. Their surroundings are yawning, waking up to greet them. The siblings part company in the hall, their inner selves directing them to their own spaces to gather strength for the days ahead. Molly watches as the twins siphon off. She circles, lying down in the hall, creating a bridge across their forever.

Chapter Twelve

Rathlin

Ballynoe

The bath is steaming hot and the residue of the searing heat is clinging to the tiles. Single drops of water are finding confidence and merging with others, forming rivers of condensation on the tiles. The walls are holding Rathlin safe but they are also closing in on her so tightly that for a moment she can't find the energy to breathe. She's thinking about a night in Glasgow a few weeks earlier.

James' parents are away, the house empty, a cue for the inevitable. At twenty-six, Rathlin's trying to feel like the teenager she never had the opportunity to be, a half-hearted attempt to be carefree. But beneath the flirtation she's on a mission. At last orders in the pub, there's a welcome silence. She's sitting at the bar, next to James. She's tightening her lips, saying nothing, holding the same tongue behind her teeth that had teased him into submission many times before. He's breaking the silence as Rathlin drinks whisky.

'We cannae dae this anymore, Rathlin. It's got tae stop.'

She's placing her glass on the wooden counter, holding her gaze. She's nodding, her lips closed, her tongue curling and finding solace in a ridge on the roof of her mouth, its lines muddled, like she's been sucking too many strawberry sherbets.

'I mean it, Rathlin, let's face it, I'm no really that intae you and you're no really that intae me. There must be more tae life than this.'

She isn't responding. Instead she's turning away from him, gazing beyond the window and the world that is diminishing in size and substance through the mottled glass.

Rathlin washes carefully. She sinks a sponge into her muscles with purpose, sweeping the night with James from her bones in long, deliberate strokes. She lingers at the top of her thighs, enjoying the numbness, the feeling of a dull sense of nothingness when her hand finds a place of rest between her legs. She closes her eyes and tries to remember the surge of desire, the uncontainable need to be wanted spiked by James and his proclamation that it has to stop, that they can't do this thing anymore. There is nothing left of that surging fire and she breathes a sigh of relief, slipping her head underwater. Her hair swirls freely, like seaweed, swaying around her neck. She sinks into the strands, feeling their grip tighten but she goes with it, hoping it will remind her that she doesn't desire James.

Rathlin knows that it should be the end. She wants that too and she's nodding when he's sitting beside her at the bar, telling her it has to stop; it has stopped. He's telling her that she's nothing to him, just someone to dance on when there's nothing else on offer. He's saying it to her face, his lips wet with spittle, but that doesn't matter. Rathlin doesn't need to see him to know he is right. She thinks she hates him. She recoils when he's touching her, feels sick when he's thrusting inside her but she thinks that's fine because she's not worth anything else.

She doesn't want him either. Having James in her life is pointless, degrading, but the shock of his rejection is worse than the misguided warmth their pretend relationship offers so she's raising her eyes, working hard on him in response, irrational fear driving her to prise his lips open with her tongue, challenging her to push her hips into the small of his back as he turns away from her in the pub porch. It is needy, and meaningless but it's part of her unplanned plan. Rathlin doesn't know how to deal with power, to exert any kind of control. It gives her comfort to feel so worthless. It's worth it to try and replenish her womb. It won't replace Isabella but it might fill some of the empty space in her heart.

Chapter Thirteen

Rathlin

Ballynoe

'Bloody hell, are you warm enough doon there?'

Rathlin is mocking Breacán, albeit playfully. He is on the floor in front of the grate, his back pressed against the armchair where their mother had nursed them. His checked shirt is unbuttoned from the sternum down, opening up his bare skin like a ski jump. He pretends he's shivering, exaggerating the rigour. The twins are in familiar territory, duelling in sarcasm.

It is August but they are tending the fire as if it were December. The coal is burning fiercely. It is at its most powerful phase, the rich orange quiet and strong. Confident flames stretch high into the chimney. Rathlin sits on the floor beside Breacán, needing as well as wanting to be close to her brother. Neither sibling speaks. They're watching the colours change and the fingers of fire mould into handshakes. The flames connect. Their conversations start, stop and move on.

Breacán reaches back, picks up a box from the table beside the chair and opens its edges. Rathlin watches him, wondering what he's doing. He curls his fingers round the box and tugs at the cardboard with his short nails, finally prising it open. Retching, he shakes out its contents. Rathlin reaches out and touches the back of his hand.

'Is that your jag?'

'How'd you guess?'

Rathlin's instinct is to be sarcastic, but she holds back. Breacán is upset. 'I've had enough of this shit, Rathlin, I just don't want to do it anymore.'

Rathlin lifts the syringe from his fingers and places it back in the box. She places the box on the table and turns to face her brother. She swallows hard, keeping the tears cool in her head not hot on her cheeks. This moment can't be about her.

'Breacán, stop, you're freaking me out.' There are dark circles under his eyes but she holds back from touching them. How did she not know it had got this bad. How did she not not know he was falling too. She's his protector. 'How long have you been feeling as low as this? There's no shame in it Breacán, there's loads about mental health on social media the now. It's nothing tae be ashamed of and it's okay not to be okay.'

Breacán straightens his shoulders. Shit. Rathlin has put her foot in it already. She has challenged his masculinity. His sense of worth. You can't be a *real* man on the farm if you're sick. Weakness won't do. And definitely not mental *and* physical weakness.

'Fuck sake, you being a drama queen isn't going tae help. I'm no about tae jump off the pier, Rathlin. I've just had enough of that shitey drug, enough oav my useless body and if truth be told, enough of feeling there's got tae be more than this. This is it. Our lot.'

Rathlin scowls, mumbling her annoyance at being called a drama queen.

'You've just perfectly illustrated my point, Rathlin. That look was all drama.' They both laugh. 'Look, I'm getting through it, it's been a crap day and the thought of taking this methotrexate jag isn't helping. I'll be sick the night and then fucked all day tomorrow when I'd much rather be annoying ma big sister.'

'Breacán, my lovely kind brother, that's so considerate of you, but it's no this shit that's making you ill.' She holds the syringe in front of his face. 'It's working as a farm labourer. You cannae dae manual stuff the way you used to.'

'Cheers, sis, thanks for confirming I'm useless. Can you also tell that tae the pricks who refused me sick money cos apparently there's nothing wrong wae me.'

'Eh, who's the dramatic one now? Of course there's something wrong wae you. The Tories are just a shower of bastards with all that assessment bullshit. They don't give a flying fuck about driving folk into poverty. What are they expecting you tae live on when you cannae get out of your bed?' Rathlin is shouting now, the Breacán pain sending her to her feet. 'And while I'm at it, you shouldnae have tae work for someone else on another farm for pennies. We should have Dad's land. You should be paying people tae work for you.' She clenches her fists, the rage continuing. 'Donald Doherty selling the land before Mum and Dad were cold in their graves was just unforgivable. Dad loved that farm.'

Breacán butts in and Rathlin holds her words between her teeth to let him speak. 'What was the point in Aonghus having the land? He had no interest in farming. Granddad did him a favour selling the farm and giving him the house. At least he couldn't mess that up.'

'Oooooh, "Granddad was daein him a favour". Have you lost the plot? He was being a total bastard. Maybe the farm would have sobered Aonghus up and you'd be working for yourself just now, not some clown up the road.' Rathlin stops to take a breath, the onslaught of words taking all that she had.

Breacán is preoccupied, fighting with his arthritic fingers to secure the buttons on his shirt. Rathlin's watching, wondering why the simplest things have to be so difficult for both of them. He hauls himself up onto their mother's chair and she kicks her heels on the floor, not sure where to go or what to do. Finally, Rathlin bends her knees and sits down on the rug, her back to the fire. It's too fierce and she shimmies forward, closer to her brother. He's calmer than she is, less inclined to shout to make his point.

'What is the point in going on about this? We don't own the land and even better, we don't even own the house now because Aonghus died and ta-da, he left it tae Ellen.'

Rathlin has stopped shouting but her voice is loud and strong. 'Aye, exactly, but this nightmare all started wae your precious *Granddad.*' Rathlin can see her grandfather's face. She can smell his body odour and it makes her feel sick. Everything about him and Aonghus make her sick. 'Can you no see what a horrible human being he was? He rented the house tae Mum and Dad when they got married, even though they were working the whole farm for him.' She pauses, giving Breacán a chance to break his silence. It isn't forthcoming. 'He was quick enough tae sign it over to Aonghus when they died though. And then our dickhead of an uncle doesnae sign Ballynoe over tae us, even though he said he would. It's our inheritance, Breacán, yours especially. You've been living here all this time and now you're going tae lose it. Donald and Aonghus were both arseholes, but for some reason you cannae see it.'

Breacán is shaking his head. 'Gonnae stop flying off the handle for a minute. I'm exhausted wae it. I just want tae be able tae work, and not tae be homeless. It doesnae really matter who did what when, it's happened.'

Rathlin composes herself. She needs to calm down because the stress is making his flare-up worse. She grabs his Methotrexate injection, exaggerating her movements.

'Breacán, don't take this crap the night. Give it a wee miss this week. This shit is built up in your system anyway.' Rathlin is holding the syringe precariously in front of the fire, ready to toss it into the flames, teasing Breacán as she edges it closer to the grate. 'You know you want me tae dump it. Let's just pretend life is normal, just for five wee minutes. I did a first aid course at work so I'll tape yer shoulder up, practise my lifesaving skills.'

Breacán smiles. 'I suppose you being a first aid expert is the one and only benefit of having you as a sister.' He pushes forward in the chair and buttons his jeans, covering a belly bruised by weekly injections of chemotherapy toxins that make him sick and well. 'Fuck it, go for it, I could dae with a drink after Ellen's latest outburst. But, wait a minute...' He pulls Rathlin's arm back from the fire. 'Don't throw it in there. Jeez, if we don't blow up, the smell will have me puking for Scotland.'

Rathlin disposes of the injection and settles back down on the floor.

'Now that's over can we turn the big light off now? It's like Blackpool illuminations in here.'

'You're so weegie now, Rathlin.'

'What dae you expect? I've been living in Glesga now for almost as long as I lived here so it's bound tae rub off on me but I've still got some teuchter traits.'

Breacán turns off the light and settles beside his sister and the glow of the fire.

'I take it fae your mood that our loving aunt Ellen was in good form then?'

'Aye, she was indeed, and full of ultimatums as you can probably imagine.' Breacán's words are crackling up the chimney. Rathlin can feel the distance returning.

'I thought maybe she'd have calmed down a wee bit given the wean's starting nursery but...' He pauses and Rathlin waits for more. 'No such luck.'

'I honestly think that lassie forgets that she was homeless and living under a bridge when Aonghus picked her up in

Glesga. She's an absolute chancer. Does she really want tae come here on Wednesday? On our birthday?'

Breacán's voice is low. 'Yip, that's the D-day she's given. Mum and Dad's anniversary too. What is it they say? It never rains but it pours?'

Rathlin sighs. 'No chance she's coming in here. We can talk down at Mum and Dad's grave. Maybe that'll help her see what an arsehole she's being.'

She picks the poker up again, trying to convince herself that it won't happen. She won't allow it to. She stabs the fire and a rush of brilliant flames rouse into life, a final burst of energy before their embers fade and fall silent.

'What's happened tae make her want tae do this? She was happy enough tae say we could stay after Aonghus died. She even said she was going tae sign the house over tae us as that's what he wanted. I don't get it. Something else is going on.' She stares at Breacán. 'Has she hinted at anything at all tae ye? Maybe she's discovered there's oil under the garden.'

'There's no point in trying tae be all Sherlock about it. Maybe we'll never know what it's all about.'

'Eh, like that's gonnae happen. I'll find out, even if I have to force it out of her.'

Breacán furrows his brow. Rathlin's watching the lines travel across his forehead and her heart skips when she realises they mirror her father's. Or at least her memory of them.

'Fuck sake, that's a bit extreme. She's mibbae dealing wae something we don't know about and you being nasty isn't going tae help.'

Rathlin smooths the lines on his forehead, the connection with her dad too strong. 'Me being nasty? Are ye forgetting she's about tae make ye homeless? I know we're trying to keep it light but we need to wise up too. We need tae sort this pronto.'

'Aye, but legally, no by kicking fuck out of her. We're no Bonnie and Clyde.'

They laugh, their limbs briefly crossing the space between them. Molly wants in on the fun and rises to lick Rathlin and then Breacán, taking care to share the moment with both.

'Ach, I don't know, I quite fancy myself as a bit of a rebel.' Rathlin sidesteps the dog and picks up a discarded toy. She throws it at Breacán. It stops short of his hand and Molly snatches it, retreating to the corner with it. 'Look, I'm just ranting. We'll get a lawyer. Surely we can get legal aid given we've no got two pennies tae rub together. We'll sort it, this house is ours. She knows I'm not going tae sit back and make this easy for her.'

'You havenae threatened Ellen in writing have you? That's the kind of shit that the lawyers could use against us.'

Rathlin sighs. 'Na, I'm no that stupid. I told her on the phone she was done for if she didnae stop her crap.' She yanks her phone out of her pocket and scrolls to Ellen's name. The message is simple and still there. *Do this and you'll regret it.* She deletes it anyway and thrusts her phone into her pocket.

'Whit are you looking at on your phone then?'

She finds a laugh. 'Hoi, retreat little brother. Nobody likes a nosey parker.' She's shooing him back, laughing as she remembers the time she and Breacán were trusted with putting the sheep in the pen but they decided instead that the sheep should be free and ferried the flock home to enjoy the garden and their mum's vegetable plot. They weren't asked to gather the sheep again. 'I've no said anything stupid tae her. Here, dae ye think she'll bring the wean tae this meeting? It'd be nice tae see her, even if she is, literally, spawn of the devil.'

'Jeez, Rathlin, that's no funny. And yes, she probably will, they go everywhere the gether.'

Rathlin wonders what Breacán would be like as a father. Good, she sums up, then the guilt hits her. Hard. She didn't tell him about Isabella. Breacán is still talking, enthusing about Ellen's daughter, not hers.

'Barra's so grown up, the other day she was asking me such big long questions. She's too smart by far.'

Rathlin is not thinking about Barra. She's yearning for Isabella and the questions that are silenced. She is thinking about her ghost child.

Chapter Fourteen

Rathlin

Ballynoe

Rathlin needs to leave the room so she can breathe. She has to push through the *what might have beens* when it comes to Isabella. Breacán's presence makes her want to imagine another life with her beautiful child and that's not possible. Nothing she really wants or needs is possible. No parents, no daughter, no life worth living. Not in the way other people live. She's alive, but she doesn't live, not really. She's on a journey of existence. It's unbearable not seeing her brother every day, and sometimes not for months at a time, but sometimes it's even more unbearable when she does see him because in every blink of his eye she wants to live those other lives. The kind of life that Aonghus obliterated along with her parents. The one that died forever with Isabella. It's true. You can actually love someone so much that it physically hurts.

Rathlin is standing at the window at the end of the corridor, by the kitchen, the staircase and the downstairs *good* room that is still full of things that belonged to Aonghus. Why didn't his grieving widow collect them. Still hasn't collected them. Maybe she always planned to take the house from them.

She goes back again, remembering the excitement of the unveiling of the new window. Dad put it in so that Mum could see the sea without having to go outside and stand at the gable. It was a prolonged reveal. First, Dad erected a curtain around the whole area so no-one, especially Mum, could see the work as it progressed. He fended her off, laughing, whenever she went near. He could sense her approach, feel her without seeing her. It was her perfume that announced her, filling the tallness of the hall and lingering in the pale blue wallpaper they put up *to go with* the window. Rathlin laughs hard, she's hearing her dad over and over again asking if anyone's heard the like of it before, *new wallpaper to match a window*. Not just the window, Skye would say, *the extraordinary view from the window*. Dad's no entry zone was operational for two whole days, a gaping hole in the wall covered only by a tarpaulin that let the wind whistle and sing about the excitement beyond it. When Mum cried, Rathlin cried too, not because she felt like crying but because it was the right thing to do.

Joe... How did you...This is the world, it's amazing.

Listen, Twins, Dad's beautiful window means I can see all the way over the sea to Rathlin... and look at the glass.... come here, closer now. She's pointing to a shape etched on the glass. *That's my mother's house, your grandmother Isabella's house where she used to live on the island, where my story began.*

Breacán's already away, shrugging his shoulders. *Looks like this one.*

. . .

Rathlin is in the kitchen and she's shouting to Breacán. 'So how's Ellen finding the money tae pay for a lawyer?' She emerges from the fridge caressing wine and chocolate. She slings her shoulder towards its door, pushing it shut, the disappearing light plunging the kitchen back into darkness.

Now her mother has left the scene, the hall is cold and she runs across it quickly, the draughty wooden slats breathing the night air onto her bare ankles. She stops at the wooden sideboard, twisting on her hunkers as she bends in and hauls two glasses from its depth from memory. She bustles back into the living room, breathless from her adventure. Breacán is smiling, laughing at all the commotion that had been coming from the hall.

'Great, ye made it back but true tae form you disappeared fae our conversation mid-sentence. What were you saying before you had a fight wae Mum's sideboard?'

Rathlin throws herself onto the rug in front of the fire. Holding her toes like marshmallows in front of the grate, she hands the glasses to Breacán. She untwists the metal cap on the bottleneck, screeching when she nearly drops the bottle. 'Shit, I could have spilt some of our precious nectar. Eh, whit was I saying? I was just wondering how Ellen can afford tae get a lawyer when she's no working. I'll tell you what though, it's gonnae be awkward for this lawyer having tae deal with us being as wanky as we can in unison. However, enough of that for now. I need tae talk tae you about James.'

She pours the wine, easing a glass into Breacán's fingers, clicking the top with her own. It sings in retort, its rhythmic music providing a background to the slàinte mhòr they deliver in sync. Breacán drinks slowly, refusing the chocolate pyramid Rathlin tries to thrust into his hand.

'Not the now. I'll maybe have something later. So, spill them then, what happened wae James. You didn't go and see him again, did you?'

Rathlin laughs sarcastically, its drama meant to shield her embarrassment. She knows that sex isn't always empowering, and when it comes to James it definitely isn't.

'Rathlin, you didn't, did you? You don't even like him. He's using ye.'

'Steady on, you don't even know him. Aye, he's a prick, I know that, but you only know that because I told ye.' She lifts the wine bottle and replenishes her glass. 'Maybe I should pair him off with Ellen. James is around the same age as us so he's only six years or so older than her. A bit better than the hunner years older Aonghus was. That was just creepy.'

Breacán raises his voice, the dynamic making Rathlin jump. It's such a new sensation for her.

'Rathlin, just shut up will ye, we're supposed to be trying tae sort this but it's just a big joke tae you. I've got everything tae lose here but that doesnae seem tae matter tae you. It's no as if you come home very often anyway.'

'Aye alright, Ginger Heid, you're right, I was making a wee joke, remember those? Guess what, Skye and Joe were my mum and dad too, you're no the only person who lost them tae that maniac of an uncle of ours and if I want tae deal with their anniversary and the potential loss of our family home wae a bit of fuckin humour then I fuckin well will.'

Breacán's retort is immediate. 'This place isn't more important tae you than me. You left. You didnae even come back for three years, and even then you only stuck around for a night. Remember how that worked out? All you were interested in was shagging Niall in the back of his car. On our birthday too.'

'Stop being so pathetic. We were seventeen. You've got no idea what was behind me being with Niall that night and what the fuck did it matter that it was our birthday?'

'What did it matter? It mattered that we'd hardly seen each other in years. Do you seriously think Mum and Dad would have been happy about that? I didnae even know if ye were alive or dead half the time cos ye didnae even bother tae call me unless you were pished. Years without giving a shit about me or Ballynoe and now you're acting like this is the most important place in the world.'

Rathlin stands up and places her glass on the table.

'Fuck up Breacán. I didnae choose tae leave here when we were fourteen. Your precious grandfather got shot of me. Dae you think I liked being in shitty foster homes, away fae you, my only friend in the world? Mibbae you could have tried to get me back and don't even start about what happened ten years ago. I fucked off again cos it's what I needed tae dae. You might have been happy to live in Ballynoe wae the person responsible for killing our mum and dad but I certainly wiznae.' Rathlin's hands are in tight fists, their movement controlled and deliberate, her knuckles as white as snow-capped mountains. Molly jumps up and licks Rathlin's left hand. She withdraws it coldly, thrusting her hands firmly into the pockets of her jeans. 'But I came back after that, didn't I? I came back and helped you sort this place out when you got sick, even wae Aonghus still being around, or have ye chosen tae forget that small fact? Don't mind me, Breacán, I just spent a year driving up and down that bloody forever winding shitty road in between working crap hours in a pish job cos you and this place don't matter a fuck tae me.'

Breacán grasps her tightly. She bends her head back and kisses his right cheek. He responds, kissing her left cheek.

'We'll find a way through this, Rathlin. We've got each other, that's the main thing.' Rathlin sinks into his embrace, keeping it tight until the morass is replaced by a sentiment only they share.

Chapter Fifteen

Ellen

Kebble

Ellen is swinging on the rocking chair in Barra's bedroom. Her back is straight and her legs are pushed long in front of her. Her shoeless feet are resting on the narrow windowsill. Her inside-her-head voices are cursing her for looking. The sharp edge of the windowsill is digging into the thin skin of her Achilles but she remains steadfast, pushing her knees up and down like the inside-of-her-head voice is telling her to. The chair is gently rocking and as she bobs back and forth the cold plastic of the binoculars chills her eye sockets. Barra is asleep in the bed behind her, the soft words she is murmuring mapping the journey she travels.

The window is on the gable end. It is small but the glass is clear, a portal between her and Breacán at Ballynoe. Their homes are separated by a progression of small green fields and a single-track road peppered with upended chalky white limestones. Each house is a goalmouth, defending she from him and he from her.

Ellen knows that Breacán knows that she will be watching him. Her inside and outside voices are confirming it for her, all chattering at once in a broad Glaswegian twang. The loudest inside-her-head voice reminds her that she had watched Rathlin arrive at Ballynoe and that the porch door had swung, its hinges whistling. Even a piece of wood was happy that the twins are together. She closes her eyes, remembering the way Breacán had given in to her, (the real her, not any of the nosy inside-of-her-head hers) just the day before, in the bowels of that same porch, his passion more potent than a concern about who might wander up the road and see them, locked in one another's arms.

Ellen hears the bell tring and she leans over Barra to make sure she's settled before beginning her descent downstairs. Her body turns at angles as she methodically makes her way down each step towards the door. She's telling herself that she's glad Anita is staying, grateful for all the help and support, but at the same time she's wishing she was alone so Breacán could visit and say *sorry*.

I didn't mean it, Ellen, of course we're going to tell Rathlin, I want everyone to know how much I love you.

With each step her inside-her-head voices are screaming how much they hate Rathlin and the disruption she's causing. Her mind keeps replaying it, over and over, *the arrival scene of Rathlin embracing Breacán*. This is one relationship that is difficult to penetrate. And yet she knows that she can smash the bond with their secret. She doesn't want to do it, she doesn't hate Breacán, she wants a life with him and he wants the same. He just needs to shake off whatever it is from the past that's holding him back. If he doesn't the shit is going to come at him and his sister, full steam ahead. She has to stand her ground for Barra. There is more than one bossy voice telling her exactly so. Another pipes up and tells her she has to be strong for herself too but there's a high-pitched laugh from elsewhere in her head reminding her that she's worthless. Girls like her don't deserve the happy ending.

In the excitement she forgets her friend is at the door and pulls a chair out from under the table in the kitchen, the heavy oak grating against the concrete floor. Its audio spirals up the open staircase to Barra's bedroom above and she pauses for a second, listening to the quiet that follows, only sitting down when she is satisfied that her little girl continues to sleep. As soon as she's in the chair she's back to her feet, pacing the floor. When she stops she rests on the range towel rail, its warmth immediately calming her. Hamish wanders into the room, his shrill meowing sounding painful as he makes his way to Ellen's ankles. He curls between each foot, repeating a noisy figure of eight as he sways coyly to his own music.

She diverts her attention to Hamish, turning her ears up and letting a smile tease the corner of her mouth, its audacity encouraging her to give in and let it embrace her lips. Her mouth opens and she can feel her tongue tickling her front teeth, talking without speaking in an outside voice. Hamish is dancing on and Ellen is allowing the smile to broaden, remembering the first time she met Breacán. She was sixteen, newly married to Aonghus and brimming with the confidence that moving to the village brought with it. Breacán was older although nowhere near as old as Aonghus. He was twenty-one and already shaped by loss. They are a perfect package, says her inside voice.

· · ·

'How ye doing?' she says when she sees Breacán for the first time. It's his grandfather's wake, her husband's father. 'I guess me taking the plunge an' marrying yer uncle Aonghus kind of makes me yer auntie.'

He's saying nothing in retort, his eyes following Aonghus as he moves across the room. Breacán is almost smiling at Ellen before he walks away. She can see it in eyes that are hiding nothing. The silence is stark after he's gone. There's an emptiness yanking at her insides, its intensity cranking bit by bit towards the kitchen ceiling, like a pulley indebted by its wet washing.

Ellen is watching the full of Breacán's height as he's strolling towards a chair at the back of the room, the fire-red hair curling around the nape of his neck, the brief moment she has shared with his green eyes still flickering in her own, making her voices chatter more vividly than she can ever remember. She's gazing at his shoulders, broad in the way Aonghus's might have been before the drink curled him and cursed him, his back strengthened and matured from working on the farm. But she notices the limp too, the way Breacán is compensating for it by holding his weight to one side, jinking from side to side to make it look like he is skipping with purpose, pushing forwards towards his goal.

She's watching him clambering onto a stool, using the weight on one side of his body to steer himself to his destination. Once there, she follows as he circles his right wrist with the fingers of his left hand, soothing something that is making his lips grimace at the corners. She's still watching when Rathlin is reaching out to him, placing her own hands over his. The bond between them is like nothing she has ever seen, stronger even than the protection she feels for Aonghus.

Ellen is turning away from the twins, searching the room for her husband. She finds him in the kitchen, his promise to stay sober obliterated by temptation. She goes to him, slipping her fingers into his.

'Here, I thought you definitely werenae having a drink? This is a new start, Aonghus. That old bastard is dead. We're gonnae bury him the morra and then it's time for you tae dae something wae yer life instead of drinking yersel intae the ground. You need tae forget him. He's no allowed tae have a space in your head anymore. Agreed?'

Aonghus is pulling Ellen towards him, propping his own body against hers. She's laughing, warmly, her feelings of friendship and protection genuine.

'Whoa sailor, you'll have all these folks thinking you're being inappropriate with a teenager at your father's funeral. Mind you, if only they knew, eh?'

She doesn't mean for her words to cut him but they do. Aonghus is shaking his head, digging deep to find the very few words that have the strength to climb over the wall of his closed throat.

'You're right, Ellen, he's definitely dead, there's no debating that, but nothing's changed. I'm still a useless piece of shit.'

Ellen is pushing hard on her tiptoes, pulling his head towards her chest so she can whisper in his ear.

'We've got our demons, you an' me, but we'll work them out.' She's kissing him softly, on the cheek. 'And listen tae me, you're no useless, you take care of me. Are you forgetting what a privilege that is? I'm quite the catch, am I no?'

They're acknowledging the moment, leaning in, for a brief moment, their lips are touching. Rathlin cuts into them, glaring.

'Jeezo you two, have a bit of respect, this is a wake. Get a room or whatever, take a hike into the woods for all I care. By the way, I heard ye fished yer new bride out of the Clyde, or did I just hear that there wiz something fishy about the whole thing.'

She's turning around, walking forwards, sneering. Ellen feels the weight of her as she deliberately bumps into her, pushing past her hard, catching her square on the shoulder, her scowl laced with intent. Ellen's sharp and she's already back in front of her, standing her ground.

'You might just regret that attitude wan of these days.'

'Regret what exactly? Saying tae my ancient uncle and his just over the legal limit teen bride that I think they're so much in love that they should be taking their sweet loving somewhere a bit more private, especially seen as we're all here tae mourn are we no? Sounds like bloody good advice tae me.'

Rathlin is heading towards the door as Ellen is turning to Aonghus. 'She infuriates me. You're thirty-four and I'm sixteen and sharp as a tack. It hardly makes you a paedo. What is it you're no telling me about her. She's always as frosty as fuck.'

'There's nothing tae tell, Ellen. She blames me for Skye and Joe dying, that's all, but it's a pretty big all when you think about it. She hated being made to stay in this house wae ma dad when they died. Fuck sake, they were only weans but they got no sympathy fae him. I hate being in this house, even without him in it. Rathlin had a really hard time dealing wae everything and ended up in a foster home. She was only about fourteen when they took her. She cannae stand me and it's okay, I get that.'

'Fuck sake, Aonghus, as if, you're ten times better than her.' She's looking up at him, trying to encourage him to respond. 'And what's up wae him?' Ellen's watching Breacán limp across the room. 'The twin brother. He seems a bit unsteady on his feet and I don't think it's cos he's pissed.'

'I don't really know the details, some arthritis thing. He finds it hard tae get about sometimes and he's struggling tae work. Has been for a while now. Before I met ye in Glasgow and ended up staying there wae ye so some lunatic wouldnae murder ye on the streets...' He smiles and Ellen does too. He kept her safe. And still he keeps her safe. 'Rathlin had been coming back and forth helping him tae work on that rented land we were farming on. That wiz a nightmare. She hated me being wae him in Ballynoe and she didnae hide how she felt. She hardly ever stayed over though, drove back all that way overnight just so she didnae need tae see me in the mornings.'

'Actually Ellen, I was going tae talk to ye about this the

morra but now that we're moved into Kebble, I'd like tae formally give Ballynoe tae my niece and nephew. I've always told them it's gonnae be theirs anyway and so it should be. It would be if Dad hadn't been such a sick fuck and left it tae me.'

Ellen is sighing, hooking her arm through his.

'See Aonghus, I told you coming back here would dae you good, that's a lovely idea, you should dae that so you should. But no for her specifically. Rathlin's a fanny, that's blatantly obvious, but Breacán, he seems sound and I know you two lived the gether and worked the gether for a long time.'

She's moving closer, whispering in his ear. 'What a bloody good coincidence that your da died and we were able tae come back here and help everybody get a new start on life, eh? I'm so glad you told me everything cos that means we can make it better. You'll see.'

. . .

Ellen hears her name being called out and she turns around slowly. Anita has startled her even though she'd welcomed her in the back door just moments before.

'For fuck sake, Ellen, will ye stop padding about the floor an' offer me a cup of tea or something stronger? Ye've hardly said two words tae me since ah got here.' Ellen shrugs her shoulders and sits down at the table. She follows Anita when she stands up, her feet pitter patting on the floor all the way to the fridge.

'If you're looking for the wine, I havenae had a chance tae put it in there yet. It's still in that bag on the floor.'

'Gie me it over an' ah'll stick it in now.' Ellen tuts at Anita's clicking fingers but she reaches to the floor and hands the bottle to her anyway. Anita hauls open the fridge door, the wine clattering as she places it on the shelf. 'An' for fuck sake has someone broken in an' robbed all the food fae yer fridge? It's like a bank holiday Monday in there. How did ye no say when we were in that wee shop at the bus stop?'

Ellen ignores her, stretching up and leaning into a cupboard. She throws a share bag of crisps in Anita's direction, moving back to her seat when she's satisfied that she's caught them.

'Dae you want something tae wash them down?' Anita nods at Ellen as she places a gin bottle on the kitchen table, two glasses clinking when she sits them neatly alongside the green glass. 'Here, you pour. I just need tae keep my eye on something outside.'

'Here, let me see an' all. Are the twinnies outside the house?' Ellen feels Anita pushing in front of her so she can see out the window too. They budge up together, their elbows touching, their backs rounded as they stretch over the windowsill, their stomachs cutting into its edge. Ellen relaxes and surprises herself by winking, a huge grin tearing across her face. 'They are indeed. I'm keeping my eye on the prize, Anita.'

Ellen accepts the crisps Anita is offering her and they crunch loudly, their hands intermittently slipping in and out of the bag. Breacán is standing outside the house across the field. Ellen slaps Anita's arm telling her to shoosh as she crams another fistful of crisps into her mouth. 'Shut it a minute will you, I need tae hear myself think.' She watches Rathlin wander past him, stopping at the garden wall, calling the dog back. The wind carries her voice into the kitchen but she can't make out the words.

Ellen places her fingers on the edge of the sill and straightens her back. Breacán is standing on the threshold of the door, neither coming nor going. She watches his fingers settle on his hips, his hands lowering when the dog comes running.

'They're heading back in, they're just letting that dog of hers out. I don't know why she couldnae dae that herself.'

Anita ignores her, watching Breacán's back as he disappears behind the green door. 'So that's the prize. Ah'll tell you what, he's no as good looking as his sister. She's hot as fuck. If ye'd told me that, ah'd have goat here much sooner.' Anita's voice tails off into a wolf whistle. Ellen waits for her lips to settle so she can be sure she's listening.

'Oh my god, you better no start. You're here to help me, no find a plaything for yourself. I mean it, Anita, I cannae afford tae run two houses. I'm relying on you and your law degree to sort this out and get them to fuck out of Ballynoe. I want tae sell it so me and Barra don't need tae stress about money.'

Part Two

Chapter Sixteen

Rathlin

*The Forest behind Ballynoe, 2005
and Ballynoe, 2020*

Rathlin is back there. She wants to go and yet she doesn't, so she never quite allows herself to travel all the way to the journey's end. She dips in, leaving when she needs to. She's asleep, in bed, but she's moving beyond reality, off to spend time with them. She's hugging her mum and dad. Skye and Joe are warm and laughing, excited because it's the twins' birthday. They have turned twelve and are on the crest of a wave. Rathlin is waiting for her birthday present, impatient but trying to be mature, sourcing a calmness that is, apparently, somewhere deep inside her now that she's twelve. But maturity is boring so she's squealing, the pitch high and shifting, its pattern an imprint on the glens before it surrenders to the skyline. She's all ready to feign surprise because she's already guessed what her present is. Rathlin long ago planted her desire in her parents' minds with her incessant chatter about the benefits of cycling. She had cut a picture of the bike she loves from the catalogue and pinned it to the kitchen notice board. She feels it's better to be safe than sorry because her mum could so easily pick a girly one with a pink frame and matching fuchsia seat and a wee bell ding ding dinging on the handlebars.

Once upon a time Rathlin might have liked something cute but times have changed. She needs a racing bike, something with speed so that she can beat Breacán, even though he goes out less and less, preferring to stay in his room. When he does venture out, it's not even as far as the garden. Maturity is making him different and Rathlin wants her brother back.

Even though Rathlin is hoping with all her might that the perfect bike is on its way, she's not absolutely sure. She's thinking about her mum saying, 'What's for you won't go by you' and she's wondering if it applies to bikes. Rathlin is definitely excited but feeling a bit sick.

Skye and Joe are wheeling the bike into the kitchen, the spokes catching the morning sunlight and reflecting on the wall like a Catherine Wheel, spin spin, spinning, the chain clink clink clinking, the wheels click, click, clicking on the concrete floor.

Rathlin is crying, both in her sleep and in her dream, and when she's wiping her face with her sleeve her mother is there, stretching forward to kiss her, her hand on her forehead, a caress on her cheek. Molly is there too, pushing Rathlin's arm from her face, licking her cheek, swallowing the salty tears. She's snuggling in. She knows what's coming next.

In the other place, Rathlin is on the floor, her hands stroking the beauty of the bike. The wheels are the purest white. She stretches her hand to the leather seat, working backwards and forwards, consuming everything. 'Mum! Dad!' She's jumping to her feet, momentarily letting go of the prize, immediately grabbing it again when it begins to topple. 'This isn't just a new bike! This isn't just any old new bike. What we have here is nothing short of perfect. Look here. This is a Raleigh, a top-notch racer with the kind of speed that needs all these fancy gears and well-oiled brakes. This is a bike that was made for me.'

Rathlin is pausing, just for a moment, her excitement

suddenly pierced by the pink bow Skye has tied to the back of the seat. Like she does every single time she travels back, Rathlin is rolling her eyes, sighing, her mortification released in a series of short sharp breaths which make it difficult to speak. Joe is laughing, leaning into his stomach, bending over like a Swiss army knife when he sees Rathlin's dramatic reaction. He straightens his torso, kisses her on the forehead, and reminds her softly that she is twelve not twenty and that there will be plenty more embarrassing moments from Mum. 'Enjoy them,' he says. 'You'll be wishing she was here to do it one of these days.'

Now Rathlin usually surfaces while she can still see her mum's smile and hear her throaty laughter as it's swallowed by Joe's kiss, but she's hanging on this time. Maybe it's because she's in the old house, in her parents' bed. She doesn't know but she wants to stay with them. Waiting. Then she realises why. She wants to see Breacán. It's his birthday too.

Rathlin is listening to her twelve-year-old self, hearing her laughter, listening as she's teasing her dad for being dramatic. 'As if Mum's for the grave anytime soon,' she's shouting to him. Rathlin wants to stop the words, to pull her *now* hand across her *then* face but it doesn't go further than Molly who ducks, leaving Rathlin's fingers grasping at thin air. In the other place, Rathlin is escaping the clutches of her older self, carrying on, saying the words that the dreaming Rathlin is desperately trying to steal.

'You're so dramatic, Dad. I know my granny's long dead but look at my beautiful mammy, she's going to be here forever.'

Every single time she's saying the same thing and every single time Skye is hugging her tightly, just for a moment, but she's in there and Rathlin is clinging to it, her face buried in her mother's hair, her perfume taking her back to every single day of her whole life with that scent following her. Rathlin knows it's going to end, this moment, this destiny in motion, and she's trying to cling on but her mother's words break in.

'Right, beautiful daughter, you've nearly used up your special twenty minutes and twenty seconds, let's go and see this bike in action and then see Breacán turning twelve.'

And then she's gone, the seal broken, the warm space cold and empty. But Rathlin's staying in, forgetting the significance of the moment. She's slipping back to being a child with ease, sinking deeper, pushing a distance between her *now* and *then* self.

Despite herself, Rathlin is allowing herself to be bugged by the way her dad is always reminding her that around the corner the world will be a different place. She knows. She isn't completely stupid. She knows that the world is changing and she's changing with it but it shouldn't mean she has to put a foothold on growing up and it certainly shouldn't mean she has to keep liking the stupid girly bows her mum still sticks on presents.

She is growing up faster than they are noticing. 'I'm twelve,' she's mumbling to herself, 'practically a teenager, almost old enough to drive a car.' The *now* Rathlin would have shirricked her for that but she's too far away at the moment to have any sort of influence. *Then* Rathlin's moaning is making her remember a promise Dad made. He said it not so long ago, when she was hanging about the field when he was kicking the hay in it and she was going to make sure he delivered on it.

'Hey, Dad, don't forget you promised me and Breacán a tractor lesson after our birthday picnic.'

Now it's Joe who's rolling his eyes. Rathlin is finding this hysterical.

'You're like an elephant. You forget nothing.'

'And it's just as well or you'd be losing your Superdad title.'

Rathlin's laughing, truly excited. She's keener on the tractor lesson than taking the bike out on its virgin voyage but she isn't letting on, and she doesn't want to lose sight of her mum's big broad smile. She knows that Mum is worried. She's feart that Rathlin will go piling into the field gate on the tractor but she won't say because she's too lovely to spoil this one special moment on Rathlin and Breacán's birthday.

'C'mon, Mum, you know you love it when Dad teaches us stuff. It makes you go all warm and fuzzy.'

'Ach away with you!' Skye is shooing her away. It's all so lovely and nice. Rathlin is back again, watching, shouting that she should have known as the moment is just too painfully, sickeningly nice and leading to nothing other than disaster.

Rathlin loves doing stuff with Dad, especially out on the farm. She knows he loves it too, the twins helping him and listening to how he does everything, his chance to shine and be the centre of their world. Rathlin is watching him, remembering him as the dad who can do everything, the dad who is the strongest man in the world. A dad who loves his children to the moon and back.

But things are changing. Rathlin has her period, the cramp in her stomach is intense and she's drawing her hands across her middle. The cramps in her stomach are griping, the blood-letting harnessed in the sanitary towel between her legs, its setting as discreet as Santa at the summer fayre. The pain in her belly, the weight of the disgusting thing between her legs, the embarrassment of feeling it rub against her thighs as she walks exhaust her. She feels like a prisoner, her body snatched by the water wraiths, their tiny teeth tearing it apart bit by bit.

The significance of the white leather seat hits her. She clenches her legs together, wondering if the dam will hold the flood and decides no, and then yes, and when she sees her mum's face she knows she can't spoil the big moment. She prises the bike from its place against the kitchen table and pushes it outside into the sunlight. She's not going to let anything spoil the big reveal. Back in the real world, or at least somewhere between the dream and here, Rathlin wonders if she knew, if she had a sense of how important it was to let her mum and dad see her happy. She falls back into her birthday scene and climbs onto the white saddle, anxiously, circling the small field in front of the house like a horse being led around a paddock.

Rathlin is happy. Mum and Dad are laughing, their arms entwined, pride racing across their faces like the second hand of a clock. Rathlin looks at them, wondering if this is a scene from always. She hops off her bike and hunches down on the ground to check her pedals but really she's looking to see if there's any blood on the seat, any stains on her clothes. All clear. Time to get the birthday boy.

Breacán, she thinks, is still in bed. Rathlin imagines him huffy, bored with the thought of being dragged outside to see her in all her glory when all he wants to do is play with his PlayStation or whatever it is called. Rathlin has no time for such things. She's still yearning to run off in search of 'camp runamuck', their own little secret den where they have fun, alone, together. Computer games are boring. But no, there he is, Breacán, standing in the doorway, making the effort to watch Rathlin show off her birthday prize. She's waving enthusiastically when she sees him, her lovely little brother.

It's his day too after all, Rathlin thinks, reminding herself that whilst they sometimes argue and even fight, claws in and feet never raised, Breacán is Rathlin's best friend. He is

114

her everything. The kids at school are fine, but they're not one another so the twins keep their distance. Or at least they did. Breacán is changing and Rathlin doesn't understand why. They have one another, and the farm with all the animals, and the freedom to do (pretty much) what they please. Boys are just weird, she concludes.

In bed, *now* Rathlin watches and giggles, a smile breaking across her cheeks as she watches the other Rathlin turn and swagger, all Shirley Temple in her drama.

In the birthday scene, Rathlin is jumping back on her bike, circling for a while, showing off her cycling skills; using no hands, knowing that Breacán is laughing while Mum is shouting in sheer panic, screaming at her to hold on. Going around one more time for dramatic effect, Rathlin eventually climbs off and places her new bike carefully on the wall beside the porch. She is ready to give Breacán his present. Her twenty minutes and twenty seconds are up. It's Breacán's birthday too. Rathlin has bought him a gift. They don't always give each other birthday presents because when they were younger the telepathic messages would sometimes get confused and there were times when Rathlin bought Breacán a gift and he didn't have anything for her and vice versa. Today is different. They are twelve. Rathlin looks back in. Did they know? And what could they have known?

Rathlin still doesn't know exactly what happened. She never, ever goes that far.

Rathlin and Breacán have placed their gifts for one another in the hall. Breacán's gift to Rathlin is wrapped beautifully. She's caressing its neat paper, knowing that Mum has shared the moment with him, planning the surprise. There's no way Breacán can have achieved such perfection on his own. Rathlin's gift for Breacán is wrapped in her own way and in its organised chaos, it looks like a burst ball. She's nodding at her hard work, feeling a sense of pride, knowing it is all her own doing. She is excited about giving it to him because she thinks it will bring him back to her and their imaginary adventures out on the road.

Rathlin, Breacán and her parents are inside the hall, the light from their mum's special window casting a halo-like glow over them. Grown up Rathlin is watching from the edge of the scene, urging Breacán to hurry up and open his present. Molly rolls into her side, snuggling in. The dog knows that Rathlin of *now* and Breacán of *then* are cheek-to-cheek and it's all going to come tumbling down.

The summer sun follows the birthday girl into the hall. Keen as she is to unwrap Breacán's gift to her, they have to wait. It is a tradition for Rathlin to give her gift first. She's the eldest and it's her duty to welcome Breacán into his birthday. When Rathlin was younger that was so much harder to deal with. All she wanted to do was rip the paper off her present but Skye was insistent that it was Rathlin's responsibility as a big sister to be kind and give her brother his moment. Both Skye and Joe like to remind Rathlin that she had her big moment all to herself on the day she was born, before Breacán joined the scene. *Now* Rathlin is talking in her sleep again, 'Aye, but he soon got all the attention when he came out all wispy and blue.' Will she have to spend her whole life feeling guilty for spending an extra twenty minutes and twenty seconds with her mum?

In the hall, Rathlin is hugging her brother, tightly at first then loosening her grip, unclear if this is still something you do to your brother when you have both just turned twelve. Breacán is pretty clear. He's folding into the embrace, tickling Rathlin hard in the ribs and she's play fighting with pretend follow up punches.

They don't sing Happy Birthday though. They do that at the picnic in the forest. The annual family tradition of Mum,

Dad, the twins and enough food and birthday cake to feed a small army.

In her bed, Rathlin is screaming, 'Don't go, don't go' but the twins can't hear her because the wrapping paper is too noisy.

Breacán is finally ripping off the paper in one go. When he sees what's underneath he's laughing and laughing and Rathlin is angry, sure he doesn't like what he has found but Skye's rushing in to calm her.

'Breacán isn't laughing at you, Baby. He's laughing wae you but you've just no started yet'.

Rathlin is clenching her fist, in the *now* and the *then*. She doesn't understand what Skye means but she does when Breacán hands her her present. She's peeling off the paper, slowly, in protest. And then Rathlin is laughing too. It's the same gift. It's nice to have matching binoculars to discover the world. Rathlin and Breacán embrace, sharpening the edges of a moment when they are one in the same. Two halves of a whole.

'Runamuck?'

Rathlin is asking Breacán if he wants to go to their camp, to try out their new presents. He's nodding, not looking, not committing. But he's fun again when they leave their presents in the living room and head to the kitchen for breakfast, making monster faces and doing disgusting things with the food in his mouth. Rathlin is watching Dad but he's laughing. Mum's trying to be strict, asking them if this behaviour is appropriate for a boy and girl who are almost teenagers. There is no harshness in her voice so she doesn't really mean it. Their mum is not the type to lose her temper. She has a stern mood, a no-nonsense-don't-mess-with-me face, but it never erupts.

Rathlin and Breacán are tidying up the dishes when Annie arrives, as usual pretending she is here to see Rathlin when really she just wants to hang out with Breacán. They disappear into the living room to play his stupid game. Mum is worried Rathlin is feeling left out but she's fine, *now* Rathlin shouts to confirm. 'I'm fine, I just don't feel much like talking to Annie today.' She hasn't started her periods so Rathlin is in another place now, she'll need to catch up before we can be proper friends again. Rathlin is on her way to becoming a woman which is a scary thought but Mum seems so relaxed in its company she supposes that it can't be all bad.

Rathlin is asking her mum if she has time to go down to the beach before the picnic, and she's nodding aye, asking if she wants her to come along too. Birthday Rathlin is saying no, she'd really rather she didn't, she doesn't want any of the other kids in the village to think she needs a child-minder just because she fancies a wee dander out in the world without Breacán. *Now* Rathlin is shouting at Skye to go, fuck it, just tell her to shut up, you're the boss and you'll decide what happens but she's nodding her head and saying, sure thing, but don't be late back for the birthday picnic.

Birthday Rathlin decides not to take her bike. She's walking, the heat from the sun warming her legs and turning them pink by the time she gets to the strand. It's quite a long way and she's feeling a little breathless. *Now* Rathlin remembers how that feeling is going to get worse soon and tries to get out of the scene but she can't because Birthday Rathlin keeps her in, tight, and before long she's imagining herself back up the hill, looking down on the world far below with her just a wee speck on the sand. She brings herself back to the beach, applauding her decision not to bring the bike because she'll have to face the long climb back, especially with a white saddle and an in-use lily-white sanitary pad.

Rathlin stays where she is until she sees her mum waving

from the garden wall on the edge of the hill. Rathlin knows it is her mummy even though she can't see her properly without her binoculars. She's cursing herself for not thinking to bring them. She can take them out later.

Birthday Rathlin reluctantly begins the walk back up the hill to home. She is enjoying her wee spell alone on the beach, to a point. This solitude thing is all new to her. Normally Breacán and Rathlin are within spitting distance of one another but things are changing a wee bit and sometimes Rathlin likes to be on her own too, to sit and look at the oyster catchers and peewits playing on the strand, imagining their conversations, creating lives, much as Breacán is doing with his computer games.

Birthday Rathlin is dawdling up the hill, minding her own business when Dad comes flying down on the trike, his hair curling up behind his ears. He's pulling the brakes on hard, stopping noisily by her side, his face a mix of anger and worry.

'Did you pass Breacán on yer way up the hill?'

She didn't so she's shrugging her shoulders, shaking her head. Joe is annoyed at her retort.

'Don't be cheeky, young lady. I'm asking you a question so just do me the courtesy of answering.'

Rathlin is shrugging again, but she answers because she can see he is worried.

'No, I've no seen anyone since I left the farm this morning, think everyone's playing hide 'n seek.'

She doesn't ask him why, despite the wee niggle that is washing over her when he says Breacán's name. *Now* Rathlin stays quiet too, too frightened to speak.

'Jump on, I'll bring you back up tae the house.' Rathlin wants to say she'll walk but it doesn't feel right to be on her own anymore.

Back at the house Skye is pacing the floor, all the stuff

for the birthday picnic unpacked on the kitchen table. The cake shouldn't be out of the fridge, the icing is melting but like everything else that morning it would be wrong to say, not then, not at that moment. Dad's wandering outside to the hall. Rathlin can hear his voice. He's talking on the phone, then he's crashing into the door with a bang when he comes rushing through it, the hinges crying out in pain. He's looking at Rathlin and then at Skye.

'Any chance of giving me a wee minute with yer mum, Rathlin.'

She says no without thinking because she wants to hear. It's something to do with Breacán. Her gut is telling her so. Skye is edging in alongside her, taking her hand.

'Don't worry, Joe, just tell us what's going on.'

'Annie's in her house. She and Breacán had started tae walk down to the village when they saw ma father coming over the field. She said Breacán told her tae go back home. There was something he needed tae dae with his granddad.'

Rathlin's watching them, their eyes moving from one to the other, paleness, colour draining from cheeks, worry gathering in wee folds under their chins. Mum isn't speaking.

'Annie said Breacán looked a bit upset.'

They tell Rathlin nothing else other than to stay put. 'We'll be back soon, pet. Don't you eat any of that cake while we're gone.' They're trying to soften the moment but Rathlin can't relax and she can't eat. She wants to be sick. She doesn't stay put. *Now* Rathlin is screaming, yelling at her to stop, 'Stay where you are and everything will be okay' but Birthday Rathlin is walking out of the back door, picking up her bike. She's ignoring her, can't hear her shouting.

'You selfish bitch, stop. You're going tae kill Mum and Dad'.

Molly is there, waiting.

Chapter Seventeen

Ellen

Glasgow, 2015

It's a week since the wedding. Aonghus is inebriated, the drink loosening his tongue. His words are clambering for freedom and Ellen is greedily accepting them. She is encouraging him to come to bed. His gait is unsteady and she's walking behind him, helping him navigate with her hands wrapped around his waist, watching as he makes each of the fifteen steps in their tiny rented house. He's staggering from side to side, his weight leaning backwards, his hips arching into Ellen's arms as she's gently pushing and guiding him.

Ellen's sitting him on the edge of the bed but he's unable to stay upright and he's falling backwards onto the pillow. She's removing his boots, stopping for a moment before unbuckling his belt and wrangling with his jeans, yanking them over his hips, navigating knees that are bending and straightening as she works. She leaves his t-shirt intact and stands up and watches as his body tilts, heaves, and rolls onto Ellen's side of the bed. She's standing still beside him, reflecting on what's happening, wondering if this is the moment it all changes between them. She's turning out the light, climbing into the bed, nudging his heaviness so she can find some space. She's on her back, unfamiliar with his breath on her shoulder, his heat warming her bare flesh. She's repositioning her arm so her sleeve is covering the hottest spot. In this space, Aonghus is a stranger to her, his body having never crossed an imaginary line in the middle of the bed.

She's sixteen, a married woman of more than a week, and she hasn't slept with her husband. An inside voice, its tone authoritative, teacher-like, is telling her that it's because she is worthless. And maybe it's right. Her parents didn't want her so why should her husband want to touch her. Aonghus is sobbing gently into the deepest part of the pillow.

Her voice is compassionate, willing him to share. 'What's happened tae you, Aonghus? Being drunk and sad all the time isnae right.'

He's responding to her question quickly and fully, his body lilting into her side of the bed, his head turning towards her. Ellen's on her side, being careful not to touch him and break the spell, ignoring the voice telling her to take him in her arms.

'Jesus, Aonghus, when did it start?'

He's saying, I was ten, at least she thinks that's what he's saying, the words sometimes hard to hear through the sobbing, the sentences chewing up in the back of his throat. She's listening hard, guiding him back when she can to the moments when it was difficult to hear.

'It's no your fault, Aonghus. He's a monster and you were just a wee boy for fuck sake. You didnae do anything wrong. Your da was supposed tae have been looking after ye.'

He's sobbing, the words tumbling now, a chaotic mess stuttering to an end when she still doesn't understand the extent of the destruction. She ignores the voice, stretching into his space, talking to him in the darkness, building a jigsaw with the details.

'He's evil, Aonghus, no wonder you feel fucked up about it. He's making you his everything when you're a child mourning his mother and then he's tossing you to the wolves and ignoring you four years later. I could kill him.'

Aonghus is calmer, his breathing more settled but he's still hunkered down under the quilt, the cover reaching his chin, his hands tucked inside, holding his body close, keeping a distance.

'One minute I wiz just a wee boy and everything was fine. Joe was ten years older than me but I was still his wee brother and we had some fun. Da… he wasnae really part of anything. Me and Joe and Mum, we'd be doing stuff and he was never with us. Even when Joe brought Skye round, he ignored us all. And then Mum died when I was ten. I missed her so much, miss her so much.

'Skye, she was kind and let me walk down the aisle beside her at their wedding even though I wiz only twelve. It was the best day I'd had since Mum died. I was watching Joe, wanting so much tae be like my big brother and a man just like him. I didnae want tae be the kind of man my da wanted me tae be.'

'Aonghus, sssh now, you don't need tae go on, it cannae be easy talking about this.'

'At first Joe was still living in the house so it didnae happen too often but after the wedding he and Skye moved tae Ballynoe and it was just me and him in Kebble.'

'I mean it, stop now, you don't need tae tell me anymore. I know he's a monster.'

'But I didnae think he was a monster when he stopped. I was fifteen and he just struck me off, stopped talking tae me, stopped doing all those awful things tae me. It made me feel alone and I couldnae handle it. So I drank and now I cannae stop drinking.'

'Aonghus, stop. Think about it. If it wasnae for the drink we'd never have met. A sober Aonghus wasnae going to stumble on me.'

'Small mercies.'

'A miracle, that's what it is.'

He's leaning over, kissing her gently on her cheek, pulling back quickly so she knows there's nothing else behind it. She feels the wetness of his face as he momentarily presses against her.

'I'm sorry about this. You're beautiful, more beautiful than I could ever have imagined my wife tae be but I cannae. I just don't want tae be any closer than this. I'm sorry.'

'Bloody hell, don't be sorry. I'm no in any rush tae do anything so you're doing me a favour.'

Aonghus is talking, calmer, sharing, the detail of his clarity cutting her insides. She rolls with him, helping him share, her questions non-judgmental and kind.

Later, Ellen's sitting up in bed. Aonghus has fallen asleep and she's crying, her inside voice screaming at her so hard she's closing her ears, holding them tightly, the palms of her hands pressing against her lobes, her head throbbing at the force of her connection. She's waiting until the messages stop competing with one another. It's her own voice, her outside voice, deciding what she needs to do. Aonghus, she thinks, needs to go home, and he needs to feel no fear when he gets there. When he wakes in the morning, she's dressed and waiting. She tells Aonghus she's going to stay with Anita, feeling bad at leaving him on the crest of such a catastrophic crisis but she's being kind. She's going to see Donald.

Ellen is scared. Donald is dangerous. Stay away from him. Go home. She can feel the knife pressing against her through her clothes, ready to handle him if she has to.

She arrives at the farm unannounced. She goes to the back door. Aonghus told her it would often start in the kitchen and end with his silence as he's frogmarched through to the bedroom. At ten-years-old, he did as he was told.

Donald is sitting at the kitchen table when Ellen walks in, content that he has no right to privacy. He is barely able to stand up but he tries anyway, demanding to know who she is. She introduces herself as Aonghus's wife. He's sniggering.

'That good for nothing idiot. Didnae see him getting himself a wife. Seems he got himself a bairn instead. You must be half his age, got tae gie him credit for that.'

'He's eighteen years older than me, Daddy-dear, which is hardly the crime of the century. But having sex wae somebody under the age of sixteen, say like, a relative of yours, a very very close relative, now that would be a crime wouldn't it? Not that you'd know any perverts that would want tae dae something like that.' She only stops to take breath, careful not to give him room to intervene and steal her moment.

'Aonghus was lucky tae have been brought up in a place like this. It's gorgeous. I wasnae so lucky. My ma and da buggered off when I was five and that was that. Care homes and foster homes for me after that, oh and a nice wee spell living under a bridge in Glesga. That's where I met your Aonghus. He's a decent guy, actually.'

Ellen's picking a cup up from the shelf and then she's sitting down, lifting the teapot and pouring the tea into it, drawing it from high above her hand so it falls intently, prolonging the moment. Donald is shuffling his feet, uneasy at her intrusion, too slow in his old age to react with anything more commanding.

'I said tae Aonghus, nothing is ever as bad as you think. I bet if you went home tae your da, he'd get everything out in the open, bare everything over the kitchen table so tae speak and talk about whatever it is that's upsetting you both so much.'

Ellen's grasping the edges of her seat, dragging it across the floor without standing up.

'So, whit's it tae be? Should me and Aonghus come here and have a wee chat wae you?'

Ellen's pushing her hand into her pocket, pulling out a packet of cigarettes and a lighter. She can see Donald watching anxiously, hear him breathing heavily. 'Whoa, what's with the big eyes. Were you expecting something else tae come out of my pocket? Don't worry, I'm not a maniac, well no too much of one anyway.' She's lighting her cigarette, drawing long and hard on the filter, blowing smoke rings in Donald's direction. 'Sorry, I should've asked, mind if I smoke, Big Man? The air's mingin in this room. Smells as if some kind of torture took place in here.'

Donald is standing up, his shoulders curling towards his crotch, his back buckling like a Uri Geller spoon. 'I don't know what you're doing here but I do know that if ye don't get out right now I'm going tae call the police. You can explain tae them how you broke into an old man's house and threatened him.'

Ellen's stubbing her cigarette out on the kitchen table, dragging the tip along the oilskin so it leaves a black line, like a sooty slug trail.

'There seems tae be a wee misunderstanding here. I already told ye, Daddy-Pops, I'm your new daughter an' I just want us all tae be happy. Maybe we can reminisce about Aonghus's childhood. How does that sound?'

Donald is sitting back in his chair, his knees too weak to continue to hold him upright.

'Aonghus, Aonghus...what's all this interest in him? Did your precious husband forget tae tell you that it's his fault his brother's head was pretty much blown off, along wae his wife, leaving two wee weans without any parents?'

Ellen is shrugging her shoulders, indicating that it isn't big news to her.

'Aye, he mentioned that that's the *official* story ye aw told the twins but he also told me why he was in the woods that day. And he told me why he needed that gun.'

Donald's placing his hands on the table. His fingers are thin and bent, the skin almost translucent. Ellen is trying to imagine how something so feeble could have inflicted so much pain. He's lifting his right hand to his cheek, rubbing it vigorously. The skin is crinkling across his face, like a wave lapping the shore. His face is unshaven so the ripple is audible, water rushing through shingle. His hair is long and unkempt, a brilliant white falling down around his neck. Ellen is imagining grasping it and using it to strangle his throat.

'Leave me alone. I'm an old man. I mean it, I'll phone the polis.'

Ellen's slow clapping in response.

'Go on ahead, Mister, I'm sure they'll be keen tae hear more. In fact, I'm definitely sure they'd want tae know all about the special daddy-love at Donald's house. Dae you want me tae dial?'

Donald's face is fading to grey but it's a few seconds before he's clutching his chest. Aha, I've won a watch here, thinks Ellen. A heart attack at exactly the right moment. She leans in, unable to believe her luck. His features are contracting, his face shrinking like a deflating balloon. He is crying out, not words, more a muffled cry. Ellen is wondering if it's reminding him of when he had Aonghus's face in a duvet. He's dying. Quite quickly as it happens. It only takes a few minutes, but for him it must feel longer. The intense pain ripping through his body must be like a tsunami wiping out every living organ in its wake. She stays perfectly still, until she's satisfied that he is gone. It isn't the outcome she expected but it's a welcome bonus.

She spends some time before she leaves, working out what they'll do when they move in. The first thing, she decides, will be to destroy everything that reminds Aonghus of the past, starting with the kitchen table. In fact, she decides, everything in this room will have to go.

Ellen's visit remains a secret. Aonghus will never know about it, although she has to work hard at pretending everything is new to her when they visit Kebble for the first time. All the traces of her visit are there, but it doesn't seem to matter; Donald is just another grave dodger who has finally slipped into a hole. It happens, and life moves on when the dead person is already straddling the grave.

Ellen and Aonghus move into his house before the funeral, burning everything flammable in an almighty fire they light at the back of the house. She loves that house, despite all its amassed badness.

It is where she lost her virginity to Breacán in the very first week after the first night they met.

Chapter Eighteen

Rathlin

Ballynoe

As soon as Rathlin opens her eyes, she remembers the previous night's fuel was alcohol. Her head is throbbing, her mouth dry.

Christ I'm dying. Why oh why dae I no stop after a couple?

A glance at the clock tells her it's 8am so she climbs out of bed, slowly, massaging her temples as she rises from the mattress. Her tongue sticks to the roof of her mouth. She needs water. Her bedroom door creaks loudly as she opens it and she groans at its intrusion. She heads to Breacán's room, part of her wanting to climb into bed beside him like they did when they were kids, playing hide and seek whilst their mum and dad pretended they didn't know where they were. Rathlin sighs. The unconditional ease with which she could jump on Breacán has long passed. The love is still there but grief created a private space between them and cornered it off. She can't enter his nor he hers.

She sends Molly on ahead to do her bidding at Breacán's door but it's open and he isn't there. She should have realised. 8am is like halfway through the day for Breacán. His bed is unmade but the room is remarkably tidy. She eyes the brightly coloured duvet cover and the fluffy rug beside the bed and concludes that Annie must be an occasional visitor.

Her brother. She tries to think back to the night before. Admittedly some of it is hazy. She remembers the wee argument they had and breathes out in relief that it was a tame tiff and quickly forgotten. She has a vague recollection of them getting the record player out and dancing to Mum and Dad's 80s collection. She rubs her knee, grateful that Dexy Midnight Runners haven't finished her off.

She resists the urge to nosey further and heads downstairs to find him. The cross words will have been forgotten. They always are. Neither of them is any good at talking stuff through. Forget it and move on has been their motto since the separation. The Separation. The words make her stall and she turns to Breacán's window. Kebble. There it is. Like a ghost.

She has tried to forget the day the social workers came and the way she marched herself out the door without even saying goodbye to her twin. She was fourteen and she didn't know it was going to be forever.

Rathlin is in her bedroom when they come. The radio is as loud as she can make it. The bedroom is the room *he* has given her. At his home in Kebble. The room he made her take, *after*. The room's walls are cracked and studded with her intermittent roars, her attempts to exhale the false prophecy that once promised her a happy life. Rathlin hasn't bothered to claim this new territory or make it her own. It will never be part of her. She stares at the carpet as if it were a mystery, its stains passive but visible. She doesn't hear them enter the room. Her back is to the door. She is grinding her teeth, trying to contain the rage she directed at Breacán before slamming the bedroom door in his face. The rage burns for her grandfather but she is firing it at Breacán, furious at her twin's reverence for a man she knows is unworthy of respect. Breacán always stands between their granddad and her rage.

130

Protecting her, he says. Taking his side, Rathlin says.

When she realises she isn't alone, she thinks it is him, her brother, and she turns, an apology hanging on her lower lip. Instead she says nothing as the strangers tell her it's time to go. She's taking in every other word: Glasgow, foster home. Something about *we'll see how it goes*. Rathlin knows how it will go. It can't be worse than this. Every day seeing Ballynoe, consumed by grief.

She'll get back here one day. When she finally feels confident enough to speak. She's telling this to the social workers, leading them to the window so they can see. They're helping her pack her things and she's talking quickly, asking about school.

'We'll be in the same classes, won't we? I'll need tae help Breacán settle in because he's a bit more shy than me.' She's laughing, knowing that he'll be more popular than her. He's tall and strong and handsome. Like their dad.

Then she knows it's just her that's leaving and she's screaming and kicking. When she sees her granddad enter the room she aims high and hard at his head and he draws back, swinging into the slope of the roof.

'See, this is why she has tae go. I've had two years of this and I cannae dae it anymare. She's no well. Youse can help the lassie better than me.'

Breacán is shouting over him, promising he'll come and find her. Rathlin's bones grind to nothing on the path as they separate her from her other half. She closes her eyes.

· · ·

Rathlin sighs, moves on, but the headache is making her dizzy so she sits on the edge of the bed. A silver bracelet on the bedside table catches her eyes and she smiles. At least Breacán's not lonely. She'll slag him about it later. She's way too rough just now to engage in banter.

Molly patters downstairs behind her and they stop at Mum's window. The dog climbs up on all fours and settles her toes on the ledge. Rathlin presses her face against the glass, her eyes closed to the view but her forehead enjoying the chill. She chivvies the dog, shuffles to the front door, opens it gingerly and urges Molly to go and pee. Closing it behind her, she returns to the window to watch the dog do her business. Satisfied, she calls her in and makes her way to the kitchen, her bare feet brushing the cool, soothing wood of the floor. She can smell bacon cooking in the kitchen and that creates a contradiction. She can't decide if she's ready to eat or puke. She wanders through the doorway, still shivering from the morning air. She pulls her mum's dressing gown tighter around her shoulders, stopping for a moment to tie the belt. It's trailing on the floor and she tuts, annoyed at her lack of respect for her mum's things.

'I hope that flesh isnae for me, Breacán.' She's peering over his shoulder, screwing up her face. Breacán is at the cooker, one hand on a frying pan handle. He raises it from the heat, tossing sizzling bacon back and forward.

'Are you mad? This is incredible. You cannae beat dead piggy for breakfast.' He lifts the pan closer to his face, inhaling deeply, recoiling moments later when a spatter of fat rises from the bacon and sparks him on the nose. He clatters the pan back on the iron ring and Molly growls at the noise, adding to the chaos.

'Ha, that's god punishing ye for mocking one of his wee pets. It's disgusting, can ye no smell that?'

'Fortunately lack of smell isnae one of my many disabilities, Rathlin.'

She collapses dramatically onto a seat and rests her elbows on the table, dropping her head onto her outstretched hands. 'I need water before I die of thirst. If only someone was standing next tae the sink and in a position to save my life. Molly, can you help...please...'

The dog is hovering alongside Breacán at the cooker, hoping for scraps. Breacán fills a glass with water and slides it across the table to her.

'Thanks. The old twin sixth sense is working again I see.' She smiles but he's already back at the cooker. 'But seriously, Breacán, granted it could be my hangover kicking in, but that bacon is horrendous. I haven't touched meat since I was about fourteen, remember? Well, of course you don't remember because we stopped eating together then.' Rathlin stands up, unable to settle. She leans into her brother, kissing him on the cheek. 'Morning by the way. Hope yer heid's no pounding like mine. Did ye sleep alright?'

'Aye, no bad considering I had to listen to you snoring.'

'Shut it, I don't snore, ya wee dick.' She punches him playfully on the arm and he exaggerates a painful cry.

'I'm only kidding, but I did hear you getting up. Were you okay?'

Rathlin delays her response and distracts him by slowly prising the fish slice from his fingers. He's got two pans on the go, one with bacon and one with Quorn bacon, or facon as Breacán calls it, commending himself for considering her dietary concerns. She kisses him again and he squirms this time, pretending to vomit.

'Any tattie scones? I can make us ma amazing cheesy scrambled eggs?'

'Aye, those eggs sound good but hurry up, I'm starving. You're right about the hangover. We didnae even drink that much, did we?'

'No, not too much, just the two bottles of wine I brought fae Frances and a fair whack of that bottle of whisky we found at the back of Mum's cupboard.' Rathlin laughs loudly, stretching her eyes with sarcasm.

Breacán grunts and opens the fridge. Rathlin watches his head disappear behind the door. When he re-emerges he hands her a plate with potato scones. 'And the answer's yes, I made these wae some leftover spuds.'

Rathlin nods approvingly. 'Well done. They look just like Mum's.'

They pause, peering in on each other's memories, but the food is taking centre stage and they're soon swiftly bringing breakfast to its conclusion.

'Ye didnae answer me. I heard you up during the night.'

'I'm fine. It's just a bit weird. I feel so close tae Mum in her old room and that just makes her feel so much further away. I should probably just sleep in ma own room but I havenae done that since we were twelve. Mum's room is easier somehow even though I keep dreaming about her and I keep trying tae stop myself cos it's so hard tae see her and not be able tae touch her. Like we keep saying, it's shit waeout her.'

'It is. And it's always worse at this time of year.'

Rathlin is looking beyond the house and into the woods. 'I cannae believe it's been fifteen years, Breacán.' She turns to him and he's nodding his head in agreement. 'Sometimes it feels like fifty, then other times it's like they've just died an' we're still twelve. Quite the happy birthday wasn't it, finding our parents lying deid among the trees the way we did?' She's not really expecting her brother to answer but he does anyway.

'Nope, but yet here we are.'

Rathlin is keeping the outside in frame. The forest looks gentle, as if it wouldn't harm a fly. 'Do you ever dream about them?' She lowers her eyes. She will not bloody well cry.

'Depends what you mean. Going to sleep and having a dream about them, no, but sometimes I'll be in the middle of doing something and I realise I've been remembering.'

Rathlin stands beside her brother. 'It's both for me, the dreams and the thinking. When we were kids we were mourning what we'd lost but now I just find myself mourning all the things I'm never going tae have.' She settles her head on Breacán's shoulder and he bends, allowing her shape to imprint on his. 'In some ways Ballynoe is all we've got left of Mum and Dad. I can feel them in every room.'

'I don't feel their presence as much as you. Mibbae I'm losing sight of them.'

Rathlin shakes her head. 'Don't be daft, there's no any right or wrong about it, it's just different. I couldnae bear it if we lost this place tae Ellen.' Rathlin turns to her brother, expecting a response but he's staring at Kebble. 'You thinking about what Ellen's up to too?'

Breacán turns away and grasps the handle of the sputtering frying pan. 'Nope, my hunger is taking priority.'

'Good plan, food first, right the world after.' Rathlin is at the worktop pulling plates down from the cupboard. 'By the way, tae go back tae your original question, I was up during the night but just tae the toilet about three o'clock. I'm pretty sure I heard you going out no too long after that at the crack of dawn. Some secret rendezvous ye should be telling me about, little brother?'

'Think you must be losing it. I wiz out of it. I didnae even wake up until half an hour before you emerged looking like death herself.'

Rathlin hits Breacán over the head with a dishcloth and he pretends he's scared.

'Hurry up and eat your breakfast. I need tae go over to the farm and stack the bales that we kicked the other day. You can come if you want. I need tae earn some dosh tae match that fourteen quid you were telling me about last night cos if I don't, we'll no be eating anything much tomorrow, that's for sure.'

Rathlin is being careful not to speak out loud.

Didn't go out my arse. Sounds tae me like there wiz a wee booty call with Annie on the go. Why tell me though? I'm only your twin sister.

Chapter Nineteen

Ellen

Under a bridge in Glasgow, 2014

I wiz expecting the worst, because that's what happens. No always, I'm no a drama queen who exaggerates everything, but most of the time it doesnae turn out that well for me. The crap just creeps up, especially when you think you're happy. For example – when a ma an' da who love you, and you love them, go and die, or when foster parents, who ye think are kind, turn out tae be liars. More of that later.

First, the *worst*. I wiz, as I mentioned, expecting it, so when I saw him I jumped tae my feet, just like I'd practised. Like a Ninja. My heart was thumping, loud, like a voice without words hammering at me from the inside of my head.

Wake up. Defend. Attack. Run.

I wiz ready for him even though I wiz standing oan my bed, dressed in my clothes. All my clothes if the truth be told cos I wiz wearing everything I have. Which, isnae that much, but better than nothing whatsoever at all. It made me hot and sweaty, and let's face it disgustingly smelly inside my sleeping bag in the wee home I'd made for maself under a bridge next tae the River Clyde. I didnae have a choice. I needed everything tae hand. I also needed tae have a bath but I didnae have wan of those magical things close tae hand either. Not since I'd left home. Home that isnae really home. I mean the place I stayed wae my foster parents. But as I started telling ye it turns out they are almost as shite as the other pair who'd left me as a wean.

I should have expected the worst.

Standing oan my sleeping bag on the ground I wiz thinking quickly, preparing my defence and my exit. You always have tae know your exit. He came closer and I could see his face. I didnae recognise him, I mean he wiznae like us, he wiznae the type oav person tae be sleeping rough. He wiz staggering, pished probably, but I knew he wiz dangerous. They all have the potential tae dae you wrong.

I swept my right hand across my left wrist and pulled the handle of the knife from under ma sleeve intae my fingers. My muscles were tight, like the elastic band hauding my hair tied up in a bun at the back oav my heid. I wiznae daft, I knew men could use hair as a weapon for pulling.

Anita had given it tae me. The wee red knife that is. The elastic band wiz my ain. She didnae want me tae run away. She said our foster ma an' da were the best she'd ever had and it would be a million years before she'd gie that up for the streets. They hadnae lied tae her like they'd lied tae me though an' ah didnae think there wiz any way back fae that.

I think I always knew something wiznae quite right about the car crash *story*. My ma an' dad didnae even have a car but when ye think something will hurt ye badly ye block it out. An' I did, for ten years until my inside-ma-head voice demanded tae know the truth.

I found the newspaper report in the library. Tae be fair tae my foster parents, it wiz a car crash oav sorts. My parents were drug addicts who had been too greedy for their own good. Overdosed on heroin. Lights out, just like that. Who cares about the wean who's home alone? They didnae, that's for sure. So they werenae heroes. They werenae loving parents *tragically* robbed of their lives in a car crash like Ali and Paul had tellt me. It wiz my memory, no theirs, and they didnae have any right keeping it fae me.

Parents number two left me wae no choice. I had tae go.

As I mentioned, Anita didnae agree wae me leaving. I think she thought I wiz being dramatic. She'd only been wae us two years but we were fine the gether, I'd started tae think of her as my sister. Obviously she wiznae my blood sister but she wiz tougher than me an' the kids at school were dead scared oav her so she wiz cool. I called her my sister tae make myself cool too.

When I wiz leaving, Anita tellt me about the dodgy blokes that would try an' rape me.

She wiz right and I wiz ready for him as he came closer. But I didnae have tae be. When he stopped near me I could see that his face wiz sad. He didnae look like an angry thief. He said he wiznae coming any further. He said wiznae going tae hurt me. He said he needed help.

He needed my help.

And despite all the voices telling me tae stab him an' run I didnae. I helped Aonghus and he helped me. He helped right up until the point he couldnae help himself anymore.

Chapter Twenty

Rathlin

Ballynoe and Kebble

Rathlin is sitting on the wall, catching her breath. The warm summer air is adding heat to her cheeks, already red with the exhaustion of helping Breacán with the bales. She's watching him carry on working and she's grateful to be with him, out in the open. The vastness of the fields, the swooping swallows and the waves lapping the strand at the bottom of the hill are giving her strength. Clearing her mind from the pain. The house was taking her too close to her mother, or rather the memories of her mother she isn't ready to visit. Ironic given she is here to fight to keep those same memories, in that same house.

She closes her eyes and listens to the life she's missed. There's a buzzard cat cawing its freedom cry overhead. When it falls silent, she doesn't need to open her eyes to know that it is splitting the air in a dive, talons poised. She imagines a leveret finding safety in the bracken, away from their sharp edges. When she opens her eyes, she wonders if this is the life she and her brother would have had. When she was a child, she had wanted to be a farmer, quizzing Skye and Joe about everything, spending as much time as she could outdoors with them before and after school. She and Breacán would talk about how they'd run the farm with Mum and Dad but then they died and the Separation happened. They stopped talking and life stopped being lived in the way it had. It stopped being their lives. Post-Rathlin and Post-Breacán were different people.

Pre-Rathlin and Pre-Breacán memories are all around her but she pulls herself back. She goes back to watching Breacán at work. She takes in the curl of his back, smiling when she realises that despite his fragility, Breacán's shoulders are as broad as their dad's. His arms are moving at speed, his body stronger than they both give him credit for. He's a man now, a red-haired version of Joe. Rathlin notices that he's wearing their father's black work boots, the long laces wrapped around his calf, the steel on the toe cap protruding through the leather and glinting in the morning light. She remembers her dad pushing his thick socks into them in the kitchen, sometimes his mood light and playful, other times his shoulders curving towards the floor as he slipped his feet in silently.

She allows herself to go back to that place, not in a dream but in a memory. She sits on the edge of it cautiously, smiling just a little when her mind recalls Joe coming in at night, asking the twins to help pull his boots off. He'd sink his toes into the sole and they'd be tugging and tugging and then he'd let go, howling with laughter as Rathlin and Breacán are tossed like pancakes onto the floor.

Rathlin moves away from the scene, its pain slicing too deeply into the softness of the morning. She's far more comfortable looking at Breacán, the baby brother she shared space with in the womb. He's stronger than he was yesterday, she can tell by the way he is stacking the bales, his actions repetitive, his movement delivered without a wince of pain on his face. She tugs at some moss on the top of the wall, her legs outstretched, her feet crossing at her ankles. Breacán calls her to action and she responds immediately, consuming his guidance and leadership without question.

'We make a good team, don't we?'

Breacán pauses before replying, scanning the work they've done and nodding his head.

'Aye, you're doing okay, for a city lassie. We'll build some muscles on ye yet.'

'Don't be a dick.'

'I'm no getting at ye. I can mind how much ye wanted tae be a farmer. *Daddy, I'm gonnae be just like you when I grow up.*'

Rathlin ignores his gentle taunts, deliberately staring with pride at the dirt under her fingernails until Breacán leans over and grabs her hands.

'What's the matter, you chip a nail?'

'Fuck up, I'm no frightened of getting ma hands dirty.'

'So I see, you're pretty manky. C'mon, let's head back tae the house and eat before I die of hunger.'

Rathlin takes a moment. She's deciding what's best. Going home to eat isn't what they need to do right now. 'Na, let's do what we spoke about earlier and go and talk tae Ellen. I promise I'll keep it cool. I can't spend Mum and Dad's day breaking my heart about losing another part of them.'

She runs ahead without waiting for an answer. She shouts *shotgun* but her demand to ride up front is stolen by the sea breeze. She jumps on the quad and takes hold of the handlebars, cementing her command and confusing her brother.

'Move.' Breacán nudges Rathlin's elbow, a gentle encouragement. 'How am I supposed tae drive with you here?'

Rathlin tightens her grip. She knows she's not going to give up her territory. 'It's my turn tae drive. You got a shot on the way up here.'

'Stop being a fanny and let me drive.' Breacán is shouting into Rathlin's shoulder blades and she can feel his breath through her shirt. She stays determined.

'And you stop being a dick. I'm driving.'

Breacán gives in and settles behind Rathlin, wincing when his hip jars. Rathlin hears his pain and holds her breath sharply, only releasing it again when he starts to lecture her about driving.

'Are you sure you know how tae drive this? It's been a lot of years since we were messing about wae Dad on the trike.'

'This will be a canter compared tae the three-wheeler.' She strains her neck towards Breacán. She winks at him, laughing at herself when she realises she's winking with the eye he can't see. 'Stop panicking. I'll no kill you. I'm sure that god aw yours is keeping an eye out for his favourite twins.'

'You havenae believed in god since we were about six and you told the priest that Jesus was obviously a vampire cos we were all expected to eat his body and blood.'

Rathlin laughs and the weight of her brother's giggles on her back is as soothing as the warmth of her mother's hand. She keeps the silliness going, keeping her presence close.

'I'd completely forgotten about that.' Rathlin turns around fully this time. Her face is in line with Breacán's chest and she feels a love so intense her heart dances. Tears spill from the corners of her eyes and she swats them away, blaming the wind. Her heart still and her eyes clear, she lifts her neck up so she can see directly into her twin's face.

'Shit, dae you remember the look on that priest's face? He was horrified. Made perfect sense tae me.'

'And Mum too, but mind how we had tae pretend that you'd seen the light so they would let you into school?'

Rathlin remembers. She turns away from her twin, into the darkness. 'I do but it's bullshit. Whit kind of god would let Mum an' Dad die like that and leave us with the monster.'

Breacán finds a positive and it settles Rathlin. 'Mamie was around. She was kind.'

'She was. What a sweet old lady. She helped a lot in those early days. Fuck, we didnae have a clue what tae dae, did we? Here, did I tell you I saw her on the bus?' She moves her hips into the handlebars. He pushes further back on the seat to accommodate her spin. 'She didnae even know who I was. That's so sad, the woman who brought us into the world and we've lost her too.'

Breacán draws breath to speak and Rathlin interrupts him, grabbing his wrist. 'At least we've got each other, Breacán. And we do still have our lovely aunt. Hopefully she'll welcome us wae open arms when we get over there.'

'I'm pretty knackered. Let's just go and have lunch and sort it later.'

'Oh my god, what is wrong with you? We're running out of time tae sort it. You preserve your energy and I'll dae aw the talking.'

Rathlin turns to the front and accelerates quickly. The quad jumps into action and thrusts forward. She feels Breacán's body weight shift towards her and urges him to be careful. Breacán grips his hands around Rathlin's waist and she settles into the comfort of them. He is supporting her, keeping her safe. She automatically scrunches her shoulders when his breath tickles her ear.

'Mind we can't go on the main roads, Rathlin, no without any helmets on.'

Rathlin mouths a sarcastic *aye* but Breacán can't see her. The wind is whipping her hair around her face, sinking deeply into her spine through the neck of her shirt. She drives around the immediate space, circling the small field twice. She listens to her dad's voice, still loud and clear inside her head, instructing her how to drive the trike. She falters for a moment, remembering that they never did get their promised tractor lesson.

Keep your shoulders back and your head moving. You

need tae be watching everything. There are hazards every-where.

She's doing as instructed, moving her head, listening, turning when she spots the rabbit burrow underfoot. She changes direction, sharply, and Breacán digs his fingers into her sides. 'Watch it, ye maniac, you'll crash.'

'No, I won't, we're fine.'

Rathlin can feel Breacán's silence as she pulls up at the gate but she doesn't attempt to analyse it. She knows he hates confrontation but she doesn't feel confrontational. She's just going to talk to Ellen and try and make things right. She keeps the engine revving, studying her brother as he heaves the heavy metal gate open. He stands at the post, pulling himself to attention as Rathlin drives through, saluting him.

He climbs back on and Rathlin points left, towards Ballynoe and Kebble. At the road end, she pushes the accelerator harder and heads for Kebble.

Chapter Twenty-One

Ellen

Kebble

Ellen and Barra are in the side garden at Kebble, tending to Barra's first vegetable plot. Breacán dug it out for her, preparing the soil so they could labour and grow things together. Ellen's voices were quiet, content, as he patiently let Barra plant individual seeds, laughing as she disregarded expectations of uniformity. As they progressed slowly along the rigs, Breacán explained what was going to happen. He was pointing to the sun, trailing its course over the garden with his finger so Barra would understand what was going to make the plants grow. And then again every week, he would sit on the grass alongside Barra and enthusiastically tell her what was going on underground. When the squeals of delight finally came, Ellen squeezed Breacán's hand in thanks, shrieking in joy as Barra excitedly told her all about the emergence of the first tiny green shoots.

The St Patrick's day tatties have flowered and Barra is on the grass at the edge of the soil, asking the spuds if they're nearly ready. Ellen is lying beside her, her bare legs soaking in the warmth of the sun, the sea breeze cooling the back of her neck. She's tied her hair up in a bun but it's coming loose and Barra, fed up with the lack of response from the potatoes, rolls into her face and tugs at the strands, placing them behind her ears. Ellen snatches a kiss each time Barra's finger circles close.

She hears the quad approaching and jumps up. 'Quick, Barra, sounds like Breacán's coming tae visit his favourite wee lassie.' Her shorts have hiked up between her legs uncomfortably and she smooths them down, her back to the noise of the bike engine. She pulls the bobble from her hair and it tumbles beyond her shoulders, her back a sheer white cliff. Her stomach is tight with period cramps but she still feels a flip of joy knowing he's coming to see them.

'Fuck.' She's muttering but Barra still hears her and scolds her mum for saying a bad word. Ellen mouths sorry. She's looking towards the oncoming bike.

She's here.

This is it. He told her this morning it would be happening soon.

Rathlin is driving but there he is too, taller and wider behind her. Breacán's fire red hair is like the sun setting against the blue sky. Rathlin's hair is lifting in the wind like wings. She's like a crow, Ellen thinks as she examines its feather edges.

A drift of wind blows Ellen's own hair into her face and she grasps it, tucking it behind her ears. A swan, she thinks, as she stretches her neck. She says 'yuck' to Barra, pretending she's almost swallowing the sinuous strands. When she's fixed it, her hands are drawn to Barra's hair and playfully bouncing her daughter's curls, teasing the red edges on her shoulders.

'Look, Baby, there's Breacán. He'll know if the tatties are ready.' She straightens her back, making herself taller, pulls Barra in front of her, resting her fingers on her daughter's shoulders. She tells her voices to be quiet so she can think. She's nervous, despite having waited all these years for this moment. Breacán loves her, and she loves him. A voice goes into rehearsal.

Of course you can keep the house, Rathlin, because we're going to be living in Kebble. Together.

Rathlin halts the bike on the path at the edge of the vegetable gable. Dramatically, of course. *That girl's all about drama.* Ellen ignores Rathlin's pathetic attempt at attention and tries to connect with Breacán but he's looking down, his lids closed to their connection. She's confused. She's not forgotten a word of what he said, early this morning, while Rathlin was sleeping.

Why the fuck's he no looking at you? An inside-her-head voice asks the question but she's ignoring it. Rathlin has come off the bike. She is sauntering towards her, her hair flying again, her arms stretching high into the air. She's bouncing quickly, her feet almost but not quite leaving the ground. Ellen wonders if she is a crow. A voice suggests an alternative and she almost says *perfect* out loud. Rathlin is a raven.

'Hey, Ellen, we thought we'd come and say hi. How's things?'

Ellen decides not to speak. She'd rather hold her counsel. The default will always be to view Rathlin with suspicion, even after everything is out in the open. Besides. She's being too nice. She's going to do something. She can feel her shoulders squaring when Rathlin turns her attention to Barra.

'An' how are you, beautiful girl. I've no seen you forever and ever. Dae you remember me?'

Rathlin comes closer and Ellen tightens her grip on Barra. She almost lets out a gigantic *hoi* when Rathlin accidentally trips Breacán as he rushes to get in front of her.

He's hurrying to get to me first. He's going to tell me something. He better not be changing his mind.

She can't tell as she can't speak to him. Not yet. He's otherwise occupied. Rathlin and Breacán are talking in the stupid sibling voices they adopt and Ellen snorts, finding Rathlin's tenderness a pathetic course of action for a supposed raven.

'Shit. Sorry, Breacán, are ye okay?'

'It's fine, no drama.'

She breathes out, it's fine, he's okay. For now. Ellen makes eye contact, for long enough to remind her that the fight has been won. But then he's retreating. He turns back to Rathlin.

'Maybe we should just come back later. Looks like Ellen and Barra are busy.'

'Whit you on about? We agreed we were coming up.'

Ellen locks her eyes on Rathlin. She keeps her cool, waiting on Rathlin to return her gaze, to tell her what she's going to fly with.

'Ignore him, Ellen. We need tae talk the now. Can we all be grown up for five minutes?'

Fuck, this is it. Ellen lets out a weird noise, a mixture of relief and laughter. She's not embarrassed. She's the winner after all. This is her moment.

'I'm sure we can stretch tae that. Are yous coming in?'

'Sure, why no.' Rathlin nods to Ellen but doesn't start walking. She bends down, passing an outstretched hand to Barra.

'Wow you've got big. How old are you the now? Fifteen?'

Barra tugs at Rathlin's hand and Ellen feels the swing, her hand still on her daughter's shoulder.

'No, silly, I'm a big four. And a half.'

'A big four? That's the best age in the whole world. And is a big four the age you go tae school?'

'I'm going tae nursery school the morra.'

'Lucky you, I used to go tae the school you're going tae. Wae ma wee brother here.'

Ellen knows Barra will turn to her so she's already shrugging her shoulders when her daughter looks at her, screwing up her face as if to say that Rathlin is stupid. They laugh, sharing a mother and daughter moment before Barra turns back to Rathlin.

'He's no your wee brother, silly, he's ma Breacán.'

Barra lunges and Breacán scoops her up into his arms. Ellen's voices are celebrating wildly but she composes herself and watches Breacán look at Barra properly for the very first time.

'Hi, Princess, you having a good day?'

'Uhuh. Mummy's friend was playing with me.'

Breacán ruffles her hair. 'That's great. It's fun playing, isn't it.'

Ellen's loving the moment. She shuffles her feet, her stance temporary, as if she's fallen between two places and she's ready to run to him.

'A bit unusual for you, eh, having someone stay at Kebble?'

What the fuck. Well, that mood changed quickly, lover boy. What a stupid thing to say.

Ellen glares at Breacán, knowing he knows, knowing he knows that Anita was in the house with Barra when they slipped out in the early hours. She hears a voice telling her to shoosh. It's still a secret between her and him. The ring's in her pocket. Breacán's mother's beautiful ring. She can feel the weight of everything it means pressing against her groin. She plunges her hand inside the pocket of her denim shorts, the circle circling for ever and ever. She's to keep it hidden until he tells Rathlin. Tells her they're getting married. He's playing a part for now. Of course he is. She exhales and calms down, joining in with the act, laying it on especially thick.

'Like that's any of your business, Breacán?'

Ellen narrows her eyes. She knows he's watching her. She closes them for a moment, thinking, thinking, thinking. He loves her. When she opens her eyes, Barra has swung her arms tightly around his neck and she's giggling at something. It looks beautiful. She feels herself give in to him, to the *us* that is too secret for her but not for him but the raven's flapping in and stealing the scene.

'Hoi, stupid heid, he's only asking a simple question. No need tae snap at him like that.'

Ellen's right back at her. 'Rathlin, fuck off. You werenae invited here, and you're certainly no welcome here.'

Rathlin glances at Barra briefly before directing her retort back to Ellen. Ellen stops a voice from telling Rathlin to take her eyes off her daughter. She wants to listen.

'Fine. Let's wait and see whit your lawyer has tae say but listen tae me. I'm no as soft as ma brother. You're gaunnae regret picking a fight wae me.'

Ellen laughs. She knows she still has her joker to play. 'Dae ye really think I'm no wan step ahead of ye?'

'Aye whitever.'

She searches for Breacán when a voice asks her what he's making of it all. He's still holding Barra. Ellen can see what should be, the image convincing her that she's doing the right thing. But then he speaks, *fucking it all up again*.

'Can we calm it down? Barra might get upset wae all the shouting.'

'And you can fuck off an' all, Breacán Doherty. Are you really trying tae say I don't know how tae look after ma ain daughter? Actually, don't answer that, you freaky twins probably just assume I'm a shit mum.'

Ellen knows she's hurt him and she feels Breacán coming closer, physically and emotionally. She can feel herself being reeled towards him, her breath slowing. Barra is still hanging on his hip, his voice childlike as if he's having the conversation with her.

'Ellen, ye know fine well I don't think that.'

Ellen lets a smile tease her lips but she reins it in when Rathlin butts in again, always pushing into their circle.

'Aye, what he says.' Ellen looks at Rathlin, taking a moment to decide whether she believes her or not. She decides she does when Rathlin softens, glancing at Breacán and Barra before turning back to Ellen. 'Neither of us have ever said anything bad about your ability as a mother.' Ellen exhales. Right decision. Rathlin agrees with Breacán. Who would have thought she'd have been grateful to hear something the wee witch had to say. She turns off the voices and goes back to listening to Rathlin. 'Aonghus, however much of a prick he was, seemed tae think you were too. I guess we've all got one thing in life we're capable of doing, eh.'

Bang, there it is. Rathlin back to her sarcastic best. Ellen's ready for her, quick as a flash.

'Aye, well he wiz right, I am a good mum and I work hard at being responsible. Better than spending time shagging guys just for the sake of it.'

Ellen sniggers. She's got her. She knows she means *her*. She watches the tightness swallow Rathlin's face. She's glaring at Breacán. She knows he's been talking about her. The ultimate deception. Ellen leans towards Breacán's hips, teasing Barra from him. He keeps talking to her, softly and intently, while Ellen settles her daughter on her waist.

'Sorry wee yin, I need tae go the now. Will ye FaceTime me an' tell me all about your first day at nursery the morra?'

Barra nods and Ellen sees it. Rathlin standing on the outside of the circle. She's hurt her. And Breacán too.

I'm sorry for fuck's sake but ye cannae question the way I treat ma wean and expect me tae just take it.

The voices settle but they haven't changed anything. Rathlin is still angry.

'I need tae get the fuck out of here before I get violent wae the both oav ye.'

Rathlin stomps off but Breacán is still there. *Stop looking at me like that.* He's facing Ellen, talking to her with his eyes, pleading that she make it all stop. Of course she wants to. But she doesn't. She's on fire, punching Rathlin with words, the dark syllables raining down on the back of her head. Breacán's getting it too. And why not. He's treating her like crap, keeping her hidden for all these years like she's something to be ashamed of. She's not anybody's dirty little secret anymore.

'Aye that's right, away and crawl under a rock, Rathlin, cos you're no gaunnae have a house tae go back tae. Unless your brother sorts it. Why don't you ask him what this is really aw about?'

Joker in play.

She feels Breacán push against her as he storms after his sister, 'for fucks sake, Ellen' stinging her ears. The voices have changed again and they're calling out to him.

Stop. Tell her. I'm sorry.

He's already in the distance on the quad, trying to catch Rathlin on foot. Ellen can see him pull level with her. The engine noise is hanging low and loose to the ground so she can't hear but she knows he's pleading with her to stop. That she's telling him to fuck off. Ellen is crying. She brushes the wetness from her cheeks and pushes her neck into the sun. A voice is telling her that she can't watch.

Watch what?

Chapter Twenty-Two

Rathlin

Ballynoe and Kebble

Rathlin is making good headway but she doesn't need to look back to know that Breacán is getting closer. Swallows are swooping around her, closing in to see what all the excitement is about. The breeze is whipping through their feathers as they circle her, waist height, their shadows a sundial. She flies through the false time, keeping tight to the boundary wall. She's heading for Ballynoe. She turns her head towards Breacán when he draws level. He's pleading with her to stop and listen, his words still audible over the thrumming of the engine.

'Jesus, will ye just stop for a minute and let me explain.'

She continues without speaking, gaining ground fast. Her feet are goat-like, manoeuvring through the burrows and tussocks with ease. Her temper is exaggerating her movement, like the peaty burn that's slicing mercilessly down the hillside towards her. She keeps her head high but stops suddenly, turning abruptly so her profile is in focus.

'Understand? I'll never understand anything in relation tae that wee boot. Or you. I honestly cannae believe you did that tae me.'

Breacán can't stop in time so her words miss him. She waits until he slows and then marches beyond him. She breaks into a run, her stride momentarily interrupted as she jumps over the burn, its froth sizzling contentedly and

154

without consideration of Breacán's deception. Breacán is in full sight, revving the bike, trying to outflank her. He curtsies to avoid the water, racing to the gate at the bottom of the field. They are both tumbling to the same place, the path back to the house, their exit from it so very different to the entry that awaits them now.

Rathlin knows Ellen will be watching and feeling satisfaction at her pain. She wants to run back. *I've got a daughter too. She's dead.* But it's unbearable to give Ellen access to even a fragment of Isabella's life. How can she drop that news, as heavy as a rock sliding into water.

Breacán draws level again, fifty yards or so to her right, his hips raised from the seat, his knees clenching the body of the engine. He races across the space between them and for a second Rathlin thinks he's not going to be able to stop and she slows down, holding her breath. Her uncertainty allows him to catch up and he's with her, holding on to the bike with one hand, trying to grasp her shoulder with the other. She recovers her momentum and quickens her pace, swinging her arms, cutting the space in front of her like shears. Breacán lunges forward again, close enough to make contact but Rathlin pushes him back into his own space. She takes a sharp left, ready to vault the wall if she has to but she doesn't get that far. Something inside is telling her to turn.

Deer have gathered on the hillside above her. Two adults and a juvenile. They are set against the daylight sky, yet the scene is dusky. Rathlin imagines a sea fog closing in behind her, a haar on the horizon turning the animals into ghosts, as if she were looking at them through mottled glass. Their shapes shift to new forms and she sees her parents, their arms protecting a little girl. Isabella.

The Breacán pain is piercing her heart. But the engine is darker, more menacing, its roar a sign of danger.

Breacán is further down the field. Rathlin watches him lose control and she loses it with him, her world disintegrating. She runs, screaming at him to pull the brakes, to hang on, to anything. Her words collapse into the soil, panic flooding her lungs. Breacán is clinging on, his knees on the seat, both hands clutching the handles but the bike's raised, on its side, sliding along on two wheels.

Rathlin sees Breacán's back arch into the skyline and imagines it snapping, his lovely bones folding into themselves, a tree shattering in a storm. She runs harder, low branches whipping her face, their flagellation echoing the pain in her heart. Her steps feel slow and dreamlike. She sinks into treacle in a never-ending path but Breacán is falling, in real time. She stretches her hands out in front of her but she grasps nothing. There is just cool air whistling through her fingers. Now the bike threads in her direction, on the same path, knitting together again. She takes a sharp breath. There he is, her Breacán, coming to her. She throws herself across him, enveloping him like she did that first day, twenty minutes and twenty seconds into her life, but this time she misses the point of connection and she's falling, the ground swallowing her. She thrusts her arms out but they can't stop her. She hits the earth with full force.

She can't breathe. The tree stump has struck her full on the chest and her lungs have exhaled their last ounce into the sky. She is left with silence. She struggles to her knees, her lungs are constricting and her mouth is open. She's a salmon on the wrong end of the line. She can do nothing but wait. She is the Breacán of the moment of his birth. Lifeless, cold, blue.

Breacán and the bike are continuing on their journey. The machine spins in mid-air and Breacán flies from the body. They part company, each taking a different path. The bike pushes into the dry-stone wall. In its lop-sidedness it looks almost angelic, snaring the light as it elegantly arrives at its conclusion. In reality, there is a violent crushing and folding of metal as it lands. Rathlin is screaming and when her breath finally comes, it is harsh and deliberate. She stops. She needs to listen to her mother. She's sending her a message from the hillside.

Breacán, quick, tuck your elbows in, bring your knees up to your hips and pull your shoulders up around your neck so your chin's curled into your chest.

He is flying, his movement slow, and he is listening. He's sorting his elbows first, pushing them tightly against his rib cage. Rathlin's asking, 'Like this, Mum?'

'Yes. Now don't forget your ankles and knees. You don't want to come down on them with all your weight. Understand? Twist a wee bit, that's it, bring your knees up and be ready. You want to be able to bounce, not crash. Remember when Daddy took you to the judo classes and all you wanted to do was throw people over your shoulder but you took weeks and weeks tae learn how tae land on the mat properly? Well, you need to remember that now. Bounce and roll and keep your head tucked in tight so you don't bang it on the edge of the wall. Hey, watch out, move a little bit more to your left. That's right. You'll be okay. Now listen, it's still going to hurt, maybe not at first but after a minute or so it's going to feel like the worst pain ever.'

Rathlin's pain has gone to that place it goes when you love someone more than life itself. She vaults the wall, shouting out his name, but he can't hear.

He can't hear anything anymore.

Chapter Twenty-Three

Rathlin

Ballynoe and Kebble

Breacán is silent when Rathlin reaches him. Lifeless. She can't feel that he's dead but she knows he must be. She can remember her mother telling her she was as still as a freshly dug rock when she was born but this isn't the same. She edges closer, her steps soft. She's frightened that her heaviness will inadvertently send him deeper into the darkness. His leg is pushing beyond his hip, his back to front ankle settled at the foot of a crag. Rathlin feels relief. The black boulder is solid, a windbreak sheltering them both from the whipping wind of a new *Then*.

He is, Rathlin thinks, beautiful with the rich purple of the heather protecting him like a shroud. Or a priest's stole. The ritual of the last rites plays out in her head until she must stop listening and look at what is in front of her. But not his head. Don't look at his head.

He's not moving. She imagines his face, as white and pale as when death still held him on the day he was born. Rathlin saved him then. She called out to her mother, forced her to listen, forced her to draw deep into the underworld and haul her baby brother from the depths. She leans into him now because he's still her baby brother and she must be at his side especially now he's so alone, separated from the togetherness of the union of twins.

She wills herself to look. She can't not look, even though

158

she'll never be able to forget the piercing charge of a new recognition. She is face to face with another version of the person she loves. This stranger will stay with her. Not Breacán.

. . .

She has seen those strangers before. She's looking down on Skye and Joe, collapsing into them and feeling the warmth of their blood, her throat capturing its sickly scent, their clothes wet, the redness deep, like bracken in autumn. She's back there, *Then*, her knees opening as she slides into them. She's not sure why she's on her knees, she must have fallen, yes, that's it, she fell down when she saw them and something's pulling her to them, a gravity hauling her in. She's fighting it, trying to drag herself back into the moment just before. *Then*.

She doesn't remember, she never remembers *Then*. The memory is still dragging her and she's beside them now, her body stretched out. She's looking at it, trying to understand why her body is longer than Mummy's, Daddy's too, but she's turning her head and she can see that their legs are bent, her mum on top of her dad, her back to his stomach, his knees tucked firmly behind her. She's thinking about a trick she plays on Breacán, sneaking up from behind, sinking her kneecaps in behind his knee so she can collapse his legs. *Timber* she's crying as she runs away. Breacán shrugging his shoulders trying to pretend he's not bothered that she's done it again.

. . .

She comes back to Breacán, searching for the light that guided her out first so she could save him twenty minutes and twenty seconds later. She touches the fiction of his face and tries to call for help.

Mum, what the fuck do I do?

'I've called an ambulance. Move. For fuck's sake, is he no breathing?'

Ellen's there, taking control and pushing Rathlin out of the way. She's in first aid mode, fighting, pulling at the void that Breacán has fallen into. Rathlin's back, she's here, the big twin, and she's trying to save him too, she and Ellen working together, checking his breathing, compressing his chest, giving him mouth to mouth. Rathlin watches Ellen's lips touch his, the tenderness in the midst of the brutality at odds with everything.

'Wait. I think he's breathing.'

Rathlin swings around to his leg. Ellen is holding his head, whispering in his ear, saying words Rathlin can't hear. She pulls Ellen towards her.

'Here, give me your belt, I need tae try and make some sort of splint for his leg.'

Ellen rips it from her shorts, the length of leather emerging from around her waist like a circling snake. Rathlin seizes it, placing a branch alongside his leg, demanding that Ellen keep her brother safe, that she stop his heart from discolouring like a stone.

The paramedics are here and Ellen asks if she can travel with her. Rathlin tells her she needs to go back to Barra when what she means is she wants to be alone with her brother's too-tight face. But Ellen's defiant, she's coming too, she's going to share the wailing on the winding road. Rathlin holds the scene while Ellen talks to someone on the phone, turning her back from his marbled skin, the life running off it like water from a pebble.

The paramedic is talking to Breacán. Rathlin is breathing hard, listening, taking it all in, her heart soaring when it hears Breacán's voice. It's just a rehearsal.

She stands up, washing the mourning down her back but

before it slips away, his words fall silent and his mouth is painfully still.

Part Three

Chapter Twenty-Four

Ellen

Breacán's hospital room, Kintyre peninsula

Rathlin's body is in an awkward position yet somehow she is consumed by sleep. She is slumped on a high-backed chair that has been pulled close to the bed. Her right arm is resting on the bed and her head is nestling on her other forearm. Her knees are bent and her feet parked tightly around one mahogany leg. Ellen thinks it looks weird, like her legs are an unwelcome intrusion.

Her hair really is as black as black can be.

Ellen is talking to herself, taking advantage of Rathlin's stillness to examine her carefully. She's used to seeing her on the move, her limbs flailing as if she's on the verge of an attack. She looks closely, following the arch of Rathlin's back, her hair camouflaging any suggestion of her spine. Definitely a raven. Rathlin stirs a little and her hair lifts and falls as if she were preparing to take flight. Impressive, thinks Ellen.

She steps gently from her chair and goes around to the other side, getting a better view of Rathlin from the west where one side of her face is visible. Her cheek is high and pronounced. Her nose is long and thin. Ellen's bending over it, pulling back when she's unable to find any bumps.

So what, she's got a good nose, doesn't make her god's gift.

She draws an imaginary trail from Rathlin's nose to the bow beneath her nostril and frowns.

Fuck sake, she's got his lips.

Ellen stops herself from touching them and instead snares a snapshot of first Rathlin's, then Breacán's lips. The corners of both are relaxed and free from sound.

Yip, exactly the same shape, same colour and everything.

She wonders why she's never noticed it before. The shapes must have moved in the same direction when they spoke but this sharing of features has passed her by. She checks again, opening the void she has created between her fingers to see if it makes any difference. It doesn't. It just proves her theory.

Rathlin's face is scrawnier though. So thin it could have been stamped on. Why else would her jaw be so long and curved? 'I told you Breacán, it's a beak your sister's got, not a human mouth.' She's talking to him in her actual voice, stopping for a moment to examine him too. She frames the quietness of his eyes, the stillness of the long lashes. She shrugs, the movement separating her flesh from the sweat-stained t-shirt sticking to her shoulder blades. She shivers and lumbers back into its familiarity. She explores the whole room, looking at it properly for the first time in hours. She checks the time on her phone. 20:02. Seven hours since Breacán crashed. Seven hours of his silence.

The room is painted yellow. Not yellow like the sun when it's showing off on a summer day. It's watery like a sun that prefers to cruise the pavements of city streets whilst smears of bluey-dusk unleash a performance into the sky. There's nothing much to see on the walls. A notice board, instruction leaflets in tiny writing that she's not going to bother to look at, and a clock that has long since stopped keeping time. There's a window. She doesn't know what's outside because she didn't look at the view when her brain was computing the route to the hospital. She remembers only the enormousness of Breacán on the tiny bed, and the blood struggling to free itself from the bandages, rich and red, as vibrant and shiny as a ruby. Rathlin was sobbing, all the time. *Don't leave me, don't leave me*, as if he only mattered to her. Ellen and Rathlin were forced to sit excruciatingly close, their mutual suspicion concentrating the tiny space even further.

The room has a door, ajar so the nurses can observe. She wonders if they are watching her watching him, imagining her wondering where he has gone to, if he is ever coming back, even to share a tiny fragment of life that she can hold in the palm of her hand. She turns her wrist over so she can see the lines. They are jumbled like broken glass at the base of her thumb, the shapes shattered all the way to her fingers. She curls her hands, cursing her imagination for thinking it might have answers.

There's a bed too, metal frames on both sides taut and aligned as if Breacán might escape but the voices are saying he's going nowhere and she knows that they're right. Not now anyway. She doesn't linger long on Breacán or the machines that are hooked to him, or he to them, she's not sure which. Each needs the other to function because there's life in neither when they're not tied together. She realises that. She rubs her eyes, not sure if she can use the word *life* anymore.

Is he alive?

She asks the question but there's no one who can give her an answer. Least of all Breacán. Ellen is looking at his face, thinking that it is rounder than Rathlin's. She glances to Rathlin to check if she's right. She is. His cheeks are as white as the waxing gibbous moon. His colour is usually grey, a pebbly smoothness that sometimes snares the light from his red hair so his cheeks glow ever so slightly. She's sure not to look too closely at his head, not when it so obviously isn't his own. An imposter has taken its place. The swelling has increased its size. No need to look to remind herself.

She also knows he's going to die. A voice told her with such authority she almost fell down dead herself, but she's playing along with the other words, the ones spoken by the cleaner who said *there might be a miracle.*

She wants him back more than anything in the world. She clocks her own thoughts, realising how long it's been since she's allowed herself to want something. Wanting is futile because at the end of the day they still leave you on your own. She remembers desperately praying for her parents to come home and give her and Hamish a hug so tight that she'd gasp for air. She'd know that it was good safe air so it wouldn't matter that for a second she wouldn't be able to breathe.

Want want want.

She wants Breacán to live. She wants him to live with her and feel the love that she and Barra can give to him. They can love him as much as Rathlin can.

More more more.

She is willing Breacán's lips to tremble, to form a shape that says, come here, come and lie alongside me, pull the thin sheet over us both so we can rest and love and live. She can imagine feeling her head on his shoulder, the scent of his hair, crisp and fresh like apple blossoms but she can't see it properly. She can't see it or do it. Not when Rathlin's there.

She glances at Rathlin, seeing her differently for the second time in just a day. She didn't know she loved her brother so much, that life without him would be so unbearable. Breacán never told her that she loved him like this. It's always been the house the house the house. Maybe it's not the house, maybe that's just the glue that holds them together. She looks at him, just his lips again, no further than the lips, and wishes she had some glue to seal the crack on his head and their love for one another. Life, though, she knows, doesn't work like that. She asks him a question anyway, even though he won't answer.

'If you're so frightened of losing her, why take so long to tell her the truth?'

It suddenly seems so obvious to her. Speak. Tell her, then she'll just go back to whatever place she's come from. Then they can be the way they both want. She knows he wants it because she can feel it in the ring she's circling on her finger inside her pocket, hear it in his voice when he's telling her he loves her.

'Fuckin stupid house. It was all fine until I said I wiz gaunnae get rid of it if he didnae tell her. Why didn't he just love me enough tae tell the truth?'

She raises her voice, louder than she should, but she can't help it because the words are clamouring for air and they find their pitch on the wishy-washy ceiling, trapped there, the silence making them louder.

It has made Rathlin restless and Ellen holds her breath, cursing that her question has broken the silence. Ugh. She's moving, flopping her whole weight onto the body of the seat. Its tall leather back is pulsing loudly against her torso. She's stirring.

Fuck fuck fuck.

Rathlin is opening her eyes. Ellen has returned to the chair beside the bed, conscious that Rathlin's movement is the only other thing she can hear. There is an eerie silence in her head, something she'd forgotten was possible. She slices into it with a slow handclap.

'Finally. Breacán's broken in several pieces an' you're taking a nap.'

Rathlin shifts her eyes from Ellen to her brother.

'Give it a rest, Ellen. I'm knackered, and he needs me tae be strong when he wakes up.'

'If he wakes up.'

169

Rathlin pulls herself up, her eyes flicking quickly from Breacán to Ellen. 'Has somebody said something?' Ellen watches her clamber to her feet. She's on the move, stepping to the beat of the breathing equipment attached to Breacán, the softness of the tempo at odds with the tension. 'Why the fuck did you no wake me? I'm his sister.'

Ellen is tired too but she doesn't say *and I'm his fiancée*.

'Calm down. Someone wiz in an' they sorted his dressings an' fiddled about wae all they wires an' that an' said they're still waiting on some results.'

He will die. That's what they were really saying.

Rathlin is staring at Ellen, sensing her taking in her every word. *Finally she's listening to something I've got to say.* When she's finished talking, Rathlin surprises Ellen, stretching both of her arms and pushing them high towards the ceiling. Ellen thinks that the movement is ridiculous, far too relaxed for the crisis.

'Bloody hell ye scared me there. No news is good news. I need him tae be okay.'

Ellen's in the same place, meeting Rathlin in the middle.

'I know ye dae, but he's no out of the woods. He wouldnae be in intensive care otherwise.'

'I know that, obviously, but he'd want us tae be positive, an' besides, people in ma family die on our actual birthday, no two days before.'

Ellen replays Rathlin's response over and over. It's so curious. People deal with stuff so differently. She's making jokes, trying to pretend it's not happening.

It is happening, Rathlin. It really is.

Ellen's hand is hovering over Breacán's and she fights the urge to curl her fingers around his. She waits for Rathlin's gaze to shift and when it does she strokes the back of his hand gently, the moment of skin to skin contact enough to get her through another minute.

'What about Aonghus? He didnae die on your birthday?' Ellen coughs and the unintentional noise unsettles her so she coughs again.

Rathlin is chortling at her. 'I said *family*. He lost any right tae call himself that.'

Bitch. 'I cannae get you, Rathlin. Aonghus wiz decent.'

'Well, ye don't know me so that explains it.'

Ellen holds firm. She knows Rathlin is trying to stare her out, to be high and mighty. Ellen is fine with it. *That's good cos I don't want to know you* but then another voice is changing that thought, and telling her maybe she does. Knowing her might be interesting. She slackens her jaw and lets Rathlin continue.

'And by the way, ye didnae know Aonghus if ye think he's a good guy. The only decent thing tae come fae that prick is Barra an' if she ever asks me about her father I'm no gonnae lie like you.'

Ellen tries to settle the voices. They are screaming. She calms them, reminding them that identity is fragile, made up of what you're allowed to hear. All the same though, what a presumptuous little cow Rathlin is, assuming she's going to be in my daughter's life. Ellen takes a step forward, moving into the words inside her head. They are louder, heavier.

Tell her the truth about Barra, that'll shut her up.

She doesn't though. She stays calm for Breacán.

'The wean is definitely her father's double, in looks and nature. She's as sweet and caring as him.' She uses a matter of fact voice even though sarcasm would have done just fine. Rathlin snorts in retort, rubbing her hand across her mouth.

'Ssshh now, let's no talk shite in earshot of ma brother.'

It didn't take long, Ellen thinks, for Rathlin to be snide again. She stalls her next move, torn between punching Rathlin in the teeth and holding her, pleading with her to listen, making her understand that she's in pain too. She decides on neither, pulling out her phone to message Anita.

He's still alive – if ye can call it that. It's late but can ye bring B tae see him? Thanks for looking after her x

Ellen can feel Rathlin watching her. *What the fuck are you looking at?*

'If you must know I'm checking in wae Barra. I asked ma pal tae bring her here, mibbae it'll dae Breacán good.'

Rathlin is back on the chair beside the bed, her arms bent at the elbow. She's still rubbing her hand across her mouth. Ellen watches intently, following Rathlin's features as they swish back and forth across her face.

'Look, I know Breacán is fond of the wee yin but is it a good idea for a four-year-old child to see someone wae a heid swollen like a pumpkin?'

Ellen says nothing, for once knowing when to stop. She understands how close Breacán is to death. Rathlin breaks the silence with a short cry of pain. She's rolling into herself, pulling her arms across her chest. Ellen leans towards her and stretches her hand out over the bed.

'Jeez are ye awright? Dae ye want me tae get a nurse?'

'It's fine. I'm sure you couldnae have missed the doctor saying it's gonnae be sore tae move for a bit. You've been like a shadow since we goat here.'

'Aye well, someone's got tae keep an eye on you two. But what if you've got internal bleeding or something?' Ellen ignores the voice asking her why she suddenly cares.

'I've no, they scanned me, I'm just badly bruised. But that's enough about me. Breacán's the reason we're here.' Rathlin's shivering and Ellen watches her reach over to her brother, brushing the back of his hand. 'You better not fuckin die on me, Breacán Doherty. I couldane bear a fuckin minute of life on this earth without ye.'

Ellen's response is instinctive. She grasps Rathlin's hand and holds her fingers tightly.

'Don't. Whit happened tae positive thinking? If anywan can come out oav this it's Breacán. He's made oav sturdy stuff. You both are.'

'True, we've been through a lot of shit.' Rathlin steals her fingers back and Ellen can't understand why they've left a void. 'Ye know, when he started talking in the ambulance I thought he wiz okay. I wiz laughing at the utter confused shite he wiz talking.'

He told her. He actually told her.

'You never mentioned he'd been talking tae ye. What did he say?'

'I don't need tae tell you everything just cos you helped tae saved my brother's life.' Rathlin is smiling. Ellen can feel warmth. A truce. Rathlin's shoulders are curling and her neck looks even longer, her features even sharper. Ellen swallows, the moment of kindness so unfamiliar that it pierces her. Her tongue is trapped in her teeth so she nods back, her lips upturned.

I saved his life. Me. Ellen. If it wasn't for me he would be dead. We'd have lost him.

She tries to ignore the *who is we* question that punches her full in the chest. Me and her.

'When you were on the phone tae someone about Barra, he wiz saying that Mum had been talking tae him. Seems she wiz trying tae save him fae the crash.'

'Jeezo, that wiz a moment tae remember.' Ellen is intrigued. She wonders if one of her voices is her mum's. *He hears voices too. He's never said.* Why would he. She never shared that thoughts fall into her head in pictures and voices add the sound.

'I know. I wiz laughing, saying Mum's effort was pretty poor given he's lying there like a cardboard cut-out of himself.

173

I told him it wiz me that saved him.' Ellen lifts her eyes in sync with Rathlin's, blinking when she's sure she has heard the words right. 'Sorry, us that saved him.'

Us. Breacán knows I helped tae save him.

'Did he say anything else?' She knows she's pushing her luck, but she'd love to hear it. Hear her say that he said, 'I love Ellen'.

'Aye, he said that Mum wiz shouting instructions at him, in pure slow motion, telling him how tae hold his body and tae roll like we used tae do in judo when we practised falling. I said I take it ye just ignored her, cos from whit I could see you fell like a sack of spuds, smacked your heid an' busted yer leg.' Rathlin's leaning across the bed, kissing him gently on the forehead. 'You cannae deny it. Big sis has saved your ass yet again.'

'And Ellen.'

'Yes, Ellen. And Ellen. Breacán, let me tell ye again in case ye cannae remember. Our favourite auntie had her tongue doon yer throat an' helped tae save your life.' Rathlin is in line with his face, speaking directly to him. There's nothing coming back. 'Nope. It didnae work. I wiz sure the shock of that would have brought him tae his senses.'

Ellen joins her two hands together in front of her, drawing them closer so she can vouch for where they are. 'For fuck sake, I know ye hate me but how can ye be a complete bastard like that the now. Yer brother nearly died. Might still die.'

Her words fire rapidly and Rathlin falls. Like she's been shot. She collapses into a heap on the bed, her hair tumbling onto the sheets. She's mumbling something. Ellen is struggling to hear. She finally recognises it. 'I'm sorry, I'm really sorry.' She takes it on board, allowing a kind voice to respond, her hand loosely falling on Rathlin's back, brushing her hair before taking flight back to her side.

'I see yer own near-death experience hasnae softened ye in any way.'

Rathlin stops crying but she still winces in pain when she lifts her head to reply to Ellen. 'To be fair, it wiznae a bad effort tae end it. I'm feeling it the now though.' She unzips her hoody, revealing a low-cut vest and bruising so blue it is black, its stain spreading across her torso and disappearing behind her shoulders.

'Fuck, that looks bloody painful. You actually are lucky you didnae end up deid yourself.' Ellen's imaging the blackness of the skin on her back, like the ink stained feathers of a raven.

'Tell me about it, I thought I wiz gonnae die. Remind me never tae get winded again cos that's one of the most horrible feelings ever.'

'No quite as dramatic as flying head first intae a wall.'

'No even close, and of course there's the added drama of satellite navigation provided by our dead mother.'

Rathlin's hand falls from her chest to her stomach and Ellen can see that Rathlin is thinking about something else. She has no idea what. Something she's not sharing anyway so Ellen shrugs it off. Her phone beeps. *Saved*. It's Anita.

Heading now, wish me luck as I don't have a fuckin clue how tae get there x

Ellen swallows a question, immediately forgetting what it was. She's wondering what this moment means. She likes Rathlin. She's understanding for the first time that there are parts of Breacán in her, and him in her. She wants them all to be happy but now she's the one wiping the tears.

She knows she never gets the happy ending.

Chapter Twenty-Five

Rathlin

Breacán's hospital room, Kintyre peninsula

Rathlin is nursing her stomach and despite the pain, being careful not to draw attention to it. It's complicated. *It* isn't in pain, but she is. Metaphorically or not, she's making sure Ellen can't see her hand repeatedly fall onto the barrenness of her belly. She knows she and Ellen are softening to the point that they are almost comfortable with one another, but it doesn't mean she is going to share. Not this. Never this. Besides, the thing with Ellen isn't real. Any fool would see that. It's just fear that's bringing them together.

Her stomach contained that brought fear. A fear that bypassed every emotion and climbed straight to grief. That was her first assumption. Thinking back, she realises how natural it is for her to accept that loss is the only available outcome. Not, however, when it comes to Breacán. She can't. *No*, she won't lose him. There are exceptions to every rule.

She brushed over the significance of the ultrasound scan when she mentioned it in passing to Ellen but it was a momentous moment. Of course she wasn't looking for signs of internal bleeding. She had asked the doctors to search for signs of life. Negative. Zilch. Empty. The foray with James was futile. Her womb is still painfully empty. She lets her hand drop back down and she circles the button of her jeans between her finger and her thumb. She's consoling herself, wondering if it's still too early to tell. Perhaps there's hope of life to come yet, despite the heavy blow to her chest. She straightens her back. Her chest took the brunt of it, not her stomach. She counts the number of days between *it* and now and, completely disregarding the information, decides that yes, there's still time for a teeny embryo to cement in her womb. The fact that she'd had her period before she arrived in Ballynoe is irrelevant. And was drinking like a fish because she was so certain. People have pregnancies and periods all the time. And people don't collapse with force into tree stumps and lose their ability to breathe without taking a moment afterwards to question what might have been.

She finds a smile, and she keeps this thing with Ellen going. And why not? It's better than being consumed by thoughts of death.

'I hope he's already got ma present in as he's no likely to be gallivanting for a while.' She is staying calm. Breacán might be listening. Even though he's not here, he's still here. Ellen is smiling back, a glare of hatred not part of this new thing they have.

'He probably got it ages ago. He bought a wee present for Barra's birthday about three months before the actual day. That's organisation for ye.'

Rathlin's legs are insisting that she walks towards the window of Breacán's hospital room. She looks beyond the blinds for the first time since they got here but it's not the surroundings that she can see. She's picturing Barra and Breacán, her brother hunkering low, a look of excitement on his face as she opens her gift. She breathes in deeply, enjoying the crippling advance of pain in her chest. It's comforting somehow, knowing that she can feel.

She imagines her brother with Isabella. Playing with her. Loving her. It's too painful so she shuts it down, searching for the hardness that's allowed her to keep what she has intact. Don't share it, don't dilute it. Keep her memories close to her heart. She turns to her brother, thinking how small he looks in the bed, how the thinness of the sheet is making him look mummified. She scans him from top to tip, his muscles spent, his bones a skeleton under the cotton casing. Her eyes linger on the protective boot on his leg, reminding her how close she came to losing him. She closes her eyes, but she can still hear the doctor telling her that there's not much hope. She's clinging to the *not much* part of that. She didn't say there was no hope. Ellen's phone dings again and it upsets her rhythm so she decides to really test the *thing*.

'Dae ye need tae get back to the wean?'

Rathlin is hoping that she does. She's genuinely trying to be kind. Ellen did help save her brother's life but enough is enough. She wants to be with Breacán. Alone. Especially if it happens. Fuck, no. Don't even go there, but she does, her mind racing to the scene where they say, *This is it. We're sorry.*

She doesn't want to share that moment of devastation with anyone, least of all Ellen. Ellen's still looking at a message on her phone and Rathlin is willing it's the *that's me going home* response she so desperately needs.

'It's ma pal. She's outside wae Barra. You're right. I don't think she should see Breacán the now. That was a bit daft oav me. I best get her hame tae her bed.'

Thank you, Divine ruler of the universe.

'Ach don't worry. I don't think either of us is thinking straight.'

Rathlin has moved beside Ellen and they're standing adjacent. She can't decide if they will embrace. Surely not, she thinks, and yet she knows that if Ellen reaches out to her, she'll take it. She'll grasp human warmth with everything she has. She waits a moment, wondering if Ellen is thinking the same. She side-glances her brother, shooting him a

178

message that he's going to be responsible for a lot for when this is all over.

Rathlin realises that she's taller than Ellen by a good few inches. Five foot six, at a push. She finds it so strange that she wasn't interested in that fact until now. And why now? What difference does it make? None. But she keeps looking. She's actually beautiful. Rathlin is definitely noticing this for the first time. Ellen's face is just about perfect, symmetric. Like a model in a magazine spread. Not a tabloid model but an editorial one, wearing clothes ordinary folk wouldn't dream of. Rathlin has a closer look and concludes that she's too short to actually be a model and she lets the satisfaction soothe her.

She's pretty sure that Ellen's not wearing any make-up and yet her cheekbones look highlighted. Flushed maybe because it is incredibly hot in the room and Rathlin suddenly feels its intensity. She lifts her hair from the back of her neck and feels the stickiness left behind. It chills her and she shivers into it. Ellen is watching her and she returns the gaze, noticing that her eyelashes are heavy and thick, as if they are laden with mascara. Rathlin drops her hair and rubs her index finger along her own, feeling the fibrous remnants of last night's mascara on her fingertips. She flicks her hair over her shoulders and looks at Ellen's. Her hair is thick and shining, as long as her mother's was, as white as hers was red. She can see some of Ellen in Barra, but Aonghus is the dominant one. Barra has his red colouring. His broad shoulders and full back look strong, not cumbersome on her feminine frame. In contrast, Ellen's hair is light, her muscles taut and her body narrow. Skinny. Like Rathlin. She wonders if Ellen's thinness is a fad. Her own is because that's the reality when there's not enough money for food. She reminds herself that she began this train of thought thinking about Aonghus and not herself and she feels anger rise in the pit of her stomach. She quells it quickly. Breacán looks just like him too. Her poor brother. She shakes her head, disappointed that the uncle she hates more than her aunt is stealing her brother's space in her head. Today of all days.

'I better go. The wean'll be freaking out. Dae you want tae head back tae Ballynoe wae us? Mibbae you can grab a few things for Breacán for when he wakes up?'

Rathlin senses Ellen's head turn to him with her. They both stare, watching his chest rise and fall, rise and fall.

'I dunno, mibbae.' In a split second she wipes out her hesitancy. She's got no intentions of leaving Breacán. 'Actually, no, ma pals fae Glesga are on their way. They're going tae take Molly out an' then I've tae let them know whit I need an' they'll bring it.' She pauses, adding another thought, the *thing* between them real again. 'Thanks, though. That would have been good.'

'No worries. If ye change yer mind, let me know. I could always drop stuff off tae save yer pals a journey.'

Rathlin doesn't know what to do. She's about to say, yes, thank you, maybe that could work, keeping the thing between them going when Ellen adds a blow.

'I've got a key, so it isnae any hassle.'

And it's back, the battle for Ballynoe. Rathlin hadn't thought about it in hours, not even while she has been staring at the face of the devil driving it. Normal service resumed. 'Wow, ye've got a key awready. So you planning on chipping us out the day then?'

Ellen's kind of smiling, laughing, a mixture of sounds that Rathlin can't quite comprehend. 'I'm no that much of a bitch, Rathlin. I've always had a key. Me an' Barra cook Breacán's dinner in Ballynoe every Friday. The wean loves being there an' he appreciates a good dinner after aw the hard work he does.'

Rathlin can't work it out, the bond they have. Can't

understand how they got to be such good friends. How her brother can even speak to Ellen after what Aonghus did to their mum and dad. But she doesn't need to think about it, not now anyway. A doctor has come in, the dark blue of her scrubs feeling enormously intense in the claustrophobia of the pale room. Rathlin cancels the thing with her and Ellen and reminds her firmly that it's time for her to go and get her daughter. She shoos away the pleas to stay for an update, sending Ellen and her intrusion out the door. She closes it firmly behind her.

'Is he going tae be okay, Doctor?'

Rathlin searches for something positive in her eyes but a brief glance tells her that there's no joy there, just a narrowing of the eyelids and a turn of the head towards Breacán.

Chapter Twenty-Six

Ellen

Kebble

Ellen's home, in Kebble. Anita drove while she comforted Barra in the back of the car. No matter how hard Ellen tried to relax, she understood her daughter could sense that Breacán was in trouble. She avoided making any hopeful statements but she steered clear of the truth, too. She's watching Barra, asleep now, having finally released her grip. Her repeated questions about Breacán's sore head, and when is he coming home, remain unanswered. Ellen doesn't know what the doctor has told Rathlin but in her heart she feels a heaviness that can only mean it was bad news.

Despite the overwhelming fear, Ellen is glad to be back. She's safe here. Having put Barra to bed, she tiptoes down the stairs, slowly, hoping the squawking gulls don't waken her. Their chant is heightened, drawing her to the water. She fights an urge to walk into the sea and wash away the discord in the waves. The tide of the unknown is debilitating but she drifts back to the moment. She descends the rest of the stairs, her voices silent, masking her vulnerability. The front door is open and Ballynoe is sitting at the end of the channel between them. She rests her back on the lean-to, her eyes fixed on the house. It looks different now. The bigger thing that she now knows it is.

She coughs suddenly, air pushing from her lungs. She looks down. The haze in front of her is a reminder that Anita is sitting below her, her backside perched on the front doorstep. Ellen pauses, watching Anita's cigarette smoke chart a path to the sky. She follows its constellation, searching for answers even though she's not in any rush to find them. People are always in too much of a hurry. Breacán has stopped the clock. Nothing can move forward or backwards until he decides. She breathes deeply, settling her hips in the space between the then and now that he has created.

She keeps thinking about the mayhem of the accident and no wonder as it's there, in front of her. She can see the outline of the quad where it has collapsed into the wall at the end of the field between the two houses. She cranes her neck, moving her eyes from the bike to Ballynoe and back to Kebble. She circles around Anita's frame, drawn to the chaos. She walks down Kebble path, stopping for a moment to remove some irritating gravel from her shoe. She stays low, listening to the hum of bees on creeping thistles. A grayling is lingering on one of the purple heads and Ellen catches a flash of orange. She is transfixed, as if she's looking at an unusually bright star in the night sky. The view is different from this perspective. She squints and pulls the houses together, the world between them shrunk. They are perfectly aligned, like the wings of a butterfly.

When she reaches the remains of the bike, she hauls herself up onto the wall, grimacing when her legs brush the coolness of the stone. She stands on top of it, a giant of the world. She whistles at the bike, a low tone piercing the sky. And then there's another noise. She can hear a dog bark in the distance. She ignores it and looks back at the bike, her disbelief still there. She closes her eyes, listening. She can't hear a syllable of Breacán's voice in her head. Of any voice. The silence is painful.

She thought he was dead. Felt sure he was dead when she was screaming at Anita down the phone. She could hear the panic in Anita's voice and, even from a distance, she could see the fear in her eyes when she ran out of the house towards them. Her urgent questions were lost in Ellen's demand that she take Barra back into the house.

She can't see this. She won't be able to un-see this.

Barra. Her wee girl was entwined around Anita's neck, her sobs audible across the distance and through the phone. The words settled after she departed, when she climbed into the ambulance to be with Breacán.

. . .

Anita interrupts her. She climbs up on the wall and like Ellen she's looking at Ballynoe. Ellen knows that she, too, is searching for news, hoping that the house has something to share to make it better.

'You okay?'

Ellen knows Anita hasn't asked a stupid question, it's just words to fill the space while she waits for the tick tock. 'Could be better.'

'Dae you want tae head back tae the house?'

Ellen nods. She doesn't need to stand here anymore to relive the moment she found Breacán still and grey and used the power of her breath to bring him back to wherever he is now. Suddenly the air feels damp and her lungs heavy. She hooks her arm into Anita as if she's shouldering a bag and imagines a colourless wind roaring through them, pushing them away from the scene. She stops again, climbing back onto the mossy wall when she sees a figure with a dog walking down towards them from Ballynoe. Anita has spotted them too.

'Who's that?'

'Dunno, Rathlin said she had friends coming fae Glesga. Mibbae she's back an' there's news. Fuck, I'm gaunnae pass out.' She tries to relax but fear dominates, even though there are no voices providing commentary. She squares her shoulders. She can't give in to mourning before the seconds are out. Not yet. It can't be yet. Ellen attempts to jump off the wall casually but she's off balance and stumbles awkwardly. She pauses, pretending she's looking at something, keeping her head low to the ground until she can feel the colour that has drained from her cheeks replenish her skin. When she's ready, she pulls her hair over her shoulder.

'Who's she?'

Ellen is looking around at Anita, not sure who asked the question. Maybe it was her, she doesn't know, it doesn't matter. She only needs to know if there is news. There's a woman approaching in an orange jumper and blue dungarees. As she comes closer, Ellen can see that she's older. Like a gran, maybe. She doesn't know. She never had one. The woman's short silver hair is tucked tightly behind her ears, her lips glossed with a faintly pink lipstick. She walks like a memory, her life echoing under her arches. She's wearing sunglasses despite the sun having shed its heat and light and when she lifts them from her eyes and places them on the top of her head, the metal frame glints against the clearing sky. Anita is tugging at Ellen's sleeve.

'Here, that's Rathlin's wee dug.' She bends towards Molly, scratching her head encouragingly. The dog is wagging its tail, seemingly oblivious to the horror of the day.

'Oh hi, dae ye mind if ah say hello tae the dog?' Ellen's confused at Anita's question. She's already all over the dog like a rash but she's not looking down, she's keeping her eyes on the woman. *She's been sent with a message.* Finally a voice. Rathlin doesn't hate her enough to tell her he's dead on the phone. Or by text. She's imagining opening it, feeling the words burn her fingers.

'Hello, Molly, nice tae see ye again, girl.' The dog barks

in acknowledgement of her name and Anita laughs. 'Well, there's nae danger of ye no remembering who ye are.' She's still patting the dog but Ellen can see that she's also examining the woman in front of her. She's protecting her under the friendly guise. Good. That's what friends do.

'Sorry tae be so blunt but we saw ye coming down fae Rathlin's house. I'm guessing you're family. Is there news?'

'Sort of family. I'm Rathlin's pal fae Glesga. I phoned her there the now but she couldnae talk as the doctor was wae her. Are you Ellen?'

Ellen's transfixed. No new news. He's still alive. Of course he is, she'd know it if he wasn't. *Wouldn't I?* She's asking, but not answering the question she's posing to herself.

'No, god no, that's no me, that's ma pal here.' Anita is pointing to Ellen while she stretches her other hand out to the woman. Rathlin's friend receives it warmly, her fist curling and uncurling. Ellen stays back, observing. 'Ah'm Anita, ah'm staying wae Ellen for a few days. Ah wiz here when Breacán had his accident.' Ellen stares at Anita. She has glanced at the crushed bike and is drawing breath deeply for effect. 'Bloody hell it was pretty horrific. He's lucky he didnae…' She stops, mouthing sorry to Ellen who's swallowing the word greedily. 'This waiting on news now is pure shite. The worry is driving Ellen crazy, aint it?' Ellen ignores Anita's attempt to bring her into the conversation and forces her to continue. 'Can't imagine how Ellen's niece is daein.'

Niece. Ellen hears the word and it stings like lego underfoot. She hates the way it cheapens everything she and Breacán have become. The twins are nothing to her, no relation. She's not some sick fuck going all incesty on her nephew. She glares at Anita but she's shrugging, not sure what she's done wrong.

'Anita, sorry, it's nice tae meet you. And you too, Ellen, hen.'

Ellen looks at the hand the old woman is offering her. The lines on the back are splayed like the spine of a fish. She ignores it, letting it go limp, thrusting her fingers deeply into the pocket of her shorts. Her expression is tight, and aggressive. Definitely aggressive.

'Here, there's no need tae be rude, but if that's the way ye want tae play it, fine. Shouldn't have expected anything different fae you. Rathlin tellt me whit you're planning wae her house'

Her house.

Anita unfurls her arms. Ellen knows why she's doing it. It's supposed to encourage everyone to soften. Ellen ignores the cue and takes a step closer to the woman. 'Her house?' This time she says it out loud. 'That house is mine, plain and simple but given Breacán is where he is, it's hardly the time tae be shouting your mouth off about it.'

The woman is standing firm, her arms now by her side, her jumper stretching over her fingertips. Its orangeness is fizzing, distracting Ellen from her anger. She watches as the woman dips her shoulder and bends to the ground. The sleeve climbs up to reveal the hand Ellen rejected. She uses it to pick up a limestone pebble and turns it over between her finger and her thumb, feeling its cool hard texture. They're all watching. Waiting.

Finally she speaks.

'Hen, we're no doing very well. I'm just feeling that bad for Rathlin. Will ye come up tae the house for a cuppa tea?' Ellen's waiting, aware she's not finished her speech. 'I'm Frances, by the way. I live next door tae Rathlin in Glesga. We're close. I just treat her the same as I dae my own lassies.'

Ellen raises her hand to shield her eyes so she can frame the house. She decides that she likes this woman's warmth, her honesty. She is wondering if her mother would have talked like that, if the sound of her voice was as deep and gravelly. She can't remember anymore. The sound of her has long passed. The smell too. She can't even remember what she used to smell of. She didn't ever give it a name, just a presence, a cloak that protected her. She can remember what she looked like though, the photograph tells her, staring at her from beyond the crease in her purse. Dad's there too, smiling, as if neither of them have a care in the world. She clears her throat, wanting to know more, remembering that she's earned her own space in Breacán and Rathlin's world.

'Aye, let's start again. It's good tae meet you.' She stretches out her hand and Frances shakes it warmly. 'But I don't know if it's such a good idea for me tae go up there the now with the way things were wae me an' Rathlin.' She can hear herself saying *were*. She knows that things have changed between her and Rathlin but she doesn't know for how long.

'Listen, I think ye should come up, we need tae talk, hen. I think you know that eh?'

Your eyes are burning me. Stop. Look away will you.

Ellen turns to Anita and rolls her eyes, telling her she doesn't know what that means. *But wait. Does she know? How?* The voices are back, telling her Frances must know about her and Breacán. Her heart jumps. Rathlin must have told her. Breacán must be awake.

He still loves me.

'Okay, Anita an' I will head up but we need tae go an' get Barra first. She's in bed. Well, obviously at this time.' She looks at her phone. 11pm and there's still light in the sky.

Anita interrupts. 'Aye, good plan. Tae be honest, ah'm dying tae know what that house is like inside.' She nods towards Ballynoe. 'See what all the fuss is about. By the way, that's why ah'm here. Ah'm trying tae help Ellen sort some of the legal stuff wae the house.'

For fuck sake, stop gushing will you, Anita.

Ellen's voices are tapping at her tongue and she's translating the message to her eyes, urging her pal to shut up, stop talking, stop telling her more than she needs to know. Frances responds to Anita but she is looking at Ellen, narrow eyes digging in like a fork in soft earth.

'Mibbae it'll be best if you go back intae the house and mind the wean. Ellen an' I are needing tae have a private chat about Breacán an' Rathlin.'

Anita is waiting for a response. Ellen gives her the nod. *Go. I'll deal with this.*

'Aye nae bother, whatever yous need. Tell ye what though, that house is right handsome. And the setting is mind blowing. Ah can see why it means so much tae them all, even Ellen.'

Frances smiles and turns and walks towards the house, her palette burning brightly against the yellow whin and purple heather. Ellen dutifully follows, asking herself how the fuck a woman she just met got to be in charge in her scene.

There's a man standing on the threshold, his head lowered so he can greet the dog. Frances introduces him, hosting in what is really Ellen's house. 'Thank god you decided to keep your clothes on, Frank, we've got a visitor.' He glances up and moves towards Ellen, smiling at her as he welcomes her into her own house. He seems kind though, his features worn well by time. Ellen continues to think about time, wondering if Breacán is running out of it. She lets her ears hear the beat of the machine that is attached to him. It soothes her. She's satisfied that for now his watch is tightly wound. Whilst that's there, he's going nowhere. He's not leaving her yet. The old man is speaking and she can feel her face relaxing. She clutches it tightly, pulling her features back into place.

'That woman would get me a bad name so she would.

I'd said I wiz getting ready for bed. I'm Frank. Pleased tae meet you, hen.'

'I'm Ellen, but I'm guessing ye don't need an introduction.'

'Aye, hen, ye dae seem tae be at the heart of every conversation around here.'

Ellen can feel Frances gently tugging her arm. She lets her guide her towards the kitchen table. She allows her hand to embrace the small of her back, encouraging her to sit.

'Aye, an' she's about tae be at the centre of another. Stick the kettle oan, Frank. It's time we all had an honest conversation about her an' Breacán.'

Chapter Twenty-Seven

Ellen

Kebble

When Ellen gets back to Kebble she is met with the sharpness of Anita's tongue.

'There you are. Thought you'd deserted me.'

Ellen tuts loudly, still irate from the conversation with Frances. 'Don't be a dick. I'm hardly a missing person. You know I had tae go and talk tae that wummin Frances.'

'Aye ah know, but there's no need tae be a smart arse about it.' Anita is pouring herself a drink. Ellen is preoccupied, staring at Anita as she empties gin into a still half full glass. She lets the alcohol climb to almost the top before adding some tonic. Ellen chews her bottom lip. The bubbles are making her thirsty.

'Touché. Pour us one of them, will you, I'm gasping for a drink.' She sits down, her back to Ballynoe.

'Sure thing, but ah'll make it a wee one. Ah've had two already so ah'm no fit tae drive ye if you decide you're gaun tae the hospital. And don't even start, it's no as if I'd be driving you. I'll no doubt be babysitting cos that's aw ah've done since ah got here. Ah thought you wanted me for ma legal brain, no ma lack of maternal instincts.'

'Anita, stop will ye, that outburst just sounded like a big noise. I'm stressed. Seeing Breacán like that was horrific. I thought he wiz dead.' Ellen leans forward, accepting a fleeting but warm kiss from Anita on her forehead.

'Aye, but he's no actually dead, is he? His heid must be pretty minced up though judging by the state of that bike.'

'That's gory, even for you, Anita.'

Anita shrugs her shoulders, filling the kettle with water. 'Calm down. Ah'll make ye a cup oav tea. Mibbae throw in a couple of Valium.' She takes a biscuit from the tin, biting into the chocolate. 'God ah love a Tunnocks. They're the best aren't they.'

'Anita, for fuck sake, you're just being annoying now, it's no funny.' Anita laughs but Ellen lets her hug her, mumbling an apology while chomping her biscuit.

'So what did that Frances want tae talk tae ye about that wiz all so secret squirrel?'

'Frances, Frances, Frances. Bloody hell, you're acting as if she's the most important person in the world.' Ellen can feel the words coming. She can't hold them back. She's going to tell her she had guessed about her and Breacán but Anita doesn't even know about Breacán so where does she begin. She tries to think of a starting place. There isn't one so she's quiet as a wee mouse, her outside voices zipped tightly shut.

'Fine, keep it tae yerself. Ah'm only the hired help and when ah say hired ah mean free.'

Ellen ignores her and turns the TV on. She sits down at the kitchen table, the remote in her left hand. She's watching nothing, the noise simply silencing Anita's questions. She picks up her phone, her fingers guiding her seamlessly to Breacán's name. She jolts forward. There's a text from Breacán.

Why the fuck have I not seen it before now? He's awake.

She lets out a low noise, her outside voice spitting out a tone she's never heard before. She opens the text, her heart bustling towards the back of her throat.

Rathlin and I on way to yours on bike. She wants to talk. She doesn't know yet but I'll tell her as soon as we get home. Promise. Call you soon. Love you x

She responds immediately, her fingers moving frantically across the screen. I love you too.

We'll get married and Barra can have a sister or a brother, or maybe a sister and a brother.

But then she's stopping, her voices in overload, crashing over the top of one another.

We're on our way. On the bike. How?

Breacán's a machine and a machine's Breacán. The bike's crushed. I'm crushed.

How can you be sending this text now?

Rathlin must be on his phone.

She's in his phone.

She's going to know we're together.

Engaged.

I'm going to be wearing Rathlin's mother's ring.

Ellen's outside voice is mumbling. 'I need tae get back up tae the hospital.' And then bang. She realises that it's an old text. She missed it because she hadn't been looking for a message from him.

He's unconscious.

She clenches her fists and places them between her knees. The shapelessness of her life is making her heavy. She rolls her torso onto the edge of the table, the sound of the machine monitoring Breacán beeping in her ear. She's in the same space she was when her parents abandoned her. Her pain is unfiltered, intense, but she keeps it inside. She can't give away what little of them she has left.

Why do I always have to keep secrets?

She doesn't see Anita looming over her shoulder, reading the text, finding out the score.

'Ellen, whit's gaun oan wae you and this guy?'

Ellen can see that Anita knows but she still releases her fist and flips the phone over, the rose gold frame glistening in the light like a game show prize. 'Nothing's going on, just leave it will ye.' Her outside words are slow and dramatic, like a wee girl in the school playground. Anita grabs the phone and reads the message from Breacán. Ellen isn't trying to stop her. Finally she's found the way to tell her.

'What the fuck, Ellen, he's pretty much yer nephew. And don't even start me on that prick ye married.'

'Fuck up, Anita, he wasn't a prick. Aonghus was really good tae me, you know that.'

'If ye think being good tae ye is treating ye like a mate rather than a wife then fair enough.'

The noises in Ellen's head push her to her feet. She solidifies her stance, shadow boxing her new found shape into position.

'You better shut up about that, Anita. Aonghus had his reasons. As far as folk around here are concerned, he's Barra's dad. Anything else is none of their business so keep yer gob shut because that's how rumours start.' Ellen exhales everything from her lungs, ready for the new world.

'What dae you mean folk think he's Barra's dad? Is Breacán Barra's da? Fuck sake, Ellen.'

Ellen is holding her hands over her ears, the real voices in her head too much to consume.

'Shut up, Anita, just shut up, the wean doesnae know an' if he dies she'll have lost two dads. How the fuck dae I get her through that?'

Part Four

Chapter Twenty-Eight

Rathlin

Ballynoe

Rathlin wakes early, reality tugging her from the little sleep she has managed. She can see that Molly is glaring at her and she wonders if the dog follows her at night, a reluctant companion when the past is trying to steal her back.

Rathlin's cheeks are dry, her fists unclenched. Off duty, the dog yawns and curls up on the bed, slipping quickly into a deep sleep. Frances and Frank are gargoyles, stationed at the corner of the house, upstairs in Rathlin's old room. Breacán is still in hospital. Rathlin doesn't need to be there to know that his breathing isn't his own.

The house is stirring, its tongue wagging in creaking floorboards in the hall, its walls shivering gently, shaking off the dew that is cooling the early morning air. Rathlin's bedroom curtains are open to the darkness. Light from the setting moon is flickering through the window and the dream that shook her in the night is striding back towards her.

She's lying still, waiting until the moment passes. When it does finally shift, it is still dark outside but the world is moving on, taking a step closer towards morning. To the east, dawn is revealing itself slowly, like a flower releasing its petals to expectant insects. Whilst fragments of night linger, the familiar shape of the sycamore has emerged, its branches still full, although its samaras have long since scattered in the wind. Rathlin pushes her back against the headboard. As birds flap in distant nests, she holds onto its post, knowing that her mother placed herself against the same oak, her newborn self at her side as they waited, together, for Breacán to breathe.

Rathlin turns to her mother's photograph, on the chest of drawers beside the window. She leans across the bed, picks it up and holds it close to her heart. She climbs back and pulls the duvet tightly around her. A hug. She hauls her knees towards her chest and places the frame carefully on her thighs.

Skye is caught unawares, one hand cocked on her forehead to block out the sun. She is squinting, her eyelids so tightly shut it is impossible to see their colour. Her hair is curled, smothering her chest and shoulders in a fiery red. Rathlin runs her finger along one of the curls, stopping in the space where there is nothing to hold. She closes her eyes, imagining its softness, remembering how she'd twist a long strand round and round her finger, pulling it free. She'd watched it bounce and her mother would laugh, teasing her not to yank her hair from her head.

Rathlin is smiling, the warmth spreading to her lips. She opens her eyes, tracing her mother's image for evidence of Isabella. It is there in abundance. Her daughter has the same vibrant colour of hair, the rounded jaw line, the pouted lips that are full and decisive. She reaches over to the sideboard and picks up her phone. The picture of Isabella is in her hands in seconds. Isabella is newly born. Rathlin is coveting her in her arms. Her tiny head is cradled between Rathlin's right breast and the fingers of her left hand. Her eyes are closed, long orange lashes curling upwards. Her hair is the same colour, twisting at its edges, a single ringlet pressing against her tiny neck. Rathlin's hair is ragged with sweat, her cheeks flushed with the enormity of becoming both closer and further apart from her mother.

Rathlin and Isabella
Glasgow, 2010

Rathlin has released her grip on her daughter for a moment so the midwife can take a photograph. Frances had pulled the camera from her pocket in the hospital foyer.

'Hen, take it will ye. Ye'll regret it if you don't get a wee photo of the moment the wean's born. We didnae get the chance in ma day. Here, I'll shove it in yer bag. In this wee zipped bit at the front so it's handy enough tae find when ye need it.'

Rathlin is ignoring Frances. She's doubled over in the wheel-chair, mid-contraction. Nothing has prepared her for this pain. When the braxton hicks started she thought, okay, it'll be stronger than this but entirely manageable. She even insisted on a natural birth at her last pre-natal appointment. The midwife hadn't batted an eye. Cow, thinks Rathlin. She knew.

The actual contractions are excruciating. She feels that she is being ripped apart. Her insides have lost any kind of meaning. This contraction has only been at full throttle for a minute or so but for Rathlin it feels like an eternity. It's too much. Everything is too much. Frances and Frank are fussing beside her and that's more interaction than she can stomach.

She wants drugs.

She wants her mother.

She needs her mother.

She loves her mother.

She hates her mother.

She's trying to fill her head with thoughts other than pain but it's pain that's driving everything. Even her memory. As the contraction reaches its climax she's cursing loudly, her mother getting the brunt of her anger for not being around. For not preparing her for this pain.

I fuckin hate you, Skye Doherty.

It's the signal Frank and Frances are waiting for. They know it's time to go. The baby is coming. Rathlin raises her eyes and she watches for a moment as they retreat along the corridor, confusing her by walking backwards. Frances is holding her hands together above her chest to let Rathlin know she's praying. She tries to mouth a thank you but it's torn from her by a roar. Another contraction. It brings a desire to push and an urgency to get Rathlin into the delivery room. What followed will stay with Rathlin forever. Exactly as it does with every mum whose brain has endured its body exhaling another human being.

Rathlin is pulling her daughter closer to her chest, instinctively prettying her wee girl's hair for the photograph.

'Take a few will ye. I cannae wait tae embarrass her on her eighteenth birthday party wae these plastered on the walls.'

The midwife laughs, before gently reminding Rathlin that the baby needs to go to the special care unit overnight. 'It's just a precaution. They dae it wae all the preemies, even if they are greetin as loudly as this wee troublemaker is.'

Rathlin hears the comment and glows with pride. She's *her* wee troublemaker and she's everything she hoped she would be. Feisty. Beautiful. Strong. Like her mother. In looks and nature. She doesn't let herself think about the things she said about her mum as the pain crippled her sense of reality. The only regret she has is that her mum isn't here to share this moment with her.

'And look at her know. As if butter wouldnae melt. I cannae believe she's acting so sweet now after all the drama she caused. That was pretty scary when she wasnae breathing. I wasnae breathing myself. It felt like forever.' Rathlin has forgotten about the photographs and she's hunkering over her child, kissing her forehead, her cheeks, her lips, her ears. Slipping her fingers inside her babygrow to feel the warmth of her skin and the firm beating of her heart. The connection is omnipotent. Just like the pain but more intense. Unequivocally powerful and empowering. She knows her mother must have felt the same when coddling her and for a moment Rathlin feels closer to her than ever until the midwife speaking steals her back.

'Aye, the premature ones create a bit of drama right enough. She's lovely, hen, and it's good tae see you a bit less stressed as well. Are ye doing okay now?'

'Much better, thanks. I'm sorry I wiz shouting at ye but I could feel something wiz wrong. An' I wiz right, there was, but she's okay now, thank god. I don't know how ye do this every day. You deserve a medal.'

The midwife is standing at the bedside. Rathlin can feel that she's waiting for her to pass the baby so she can take her away but she's ignoring it, holding her a little more tightly to her chest.

'Ha, a couple of extra quid in the pay packet would be nicer than a hunk of metal but I cannae see that happening now. I've got a feeling those Tories are going tae win this election and that'll be us descending into the destruction of the NHS again. Ach well, maybe we'll get independence wan of these days. But enough of that. Have you got a name for your wee lassie yet? It would be nice tae write something other than *Baby Doherty* on her cot up the stair.'

'That's a good question. My whole pregnancy I thought I was having a boy and that was easy. He was going tae be Breacán, same as my twin brother. You telling me she was a wee lassie completely threw me but I've worked it out. I'm going tae call her after my mother. Well, no exactly after my mother. For my mother. She's called Skye, but her mum was called Isabella and I think that would make my mum really proud. Hello, wee Isabella, welcome tae your new world.'

· · ·

Rathlin strokes the digital reflections of her mother's and daughter's faces and places her phone down on the sheet. She puts her mother's photograph next to it and slips off the bed. She opens the wardrobe and lifts out her rucksack, peeling the build-a-bear from its safe place inside. She climbs back on to the bed and rolls over. The bear is on her belly, her weight pushing it into the mattress, her womb imprinting the map of her mother's past, the imagined stains connecting mother with mother. The bed, the room, is the epicentre of existence, for both Rathlin and Isabella. She can't allow it to be taken from her. She pulls the pictures and bear in close and sleeps for a while. When she wakes, the world is as she had left it. Her parents have gone, her daughter is dead, and her twin brother is somewhere and nowhere, betwixt and between life and death.

She surprises herself by being able to move, to walk. She tiptoes into the kitchen, not ready to talk to Frank and Frances. She makes tea, boiling a pot of water on the stove, the kettle too loud and intrusive while she craves solitude. Hugging the warm mug she returns to the bedroom and her sacred space. Her treasured pictures are back in their original housings but she knows they are there, sharing the moment with her. She puts the bear back in the rucksack inside the wardrobe, closing the door carefully behind her. She stands by the window, the basalt rock face glistening in the distance. Like fairies. Her mother would tell her that the fairies slept in the cool lava until it was time to sparkle in the early morning dew drops. She follows the trail they would take, settling her gaze on the hill that separates her house from the rest of the village.

At first she thinks they are shadows, from low lingering clouds, but then she sees breath channelling into the sky from long pale faces. There are two, then three, then too many horses to count. She yells instinctively for her brother and the dog throws her head back and howls like a wolf.

'Breacán, hurry up will you, I need ye tae see this.'

'Breacán.'

It's an intimate moment. Like the wraiths and the selchies, this will be a story they share with their children. Would have shared with their children. She's pressing her heart, guiding it to attention. Breacán's still not there so she calls him again, her voice booming louder, her memory blocking her from believing he's not here.

That he can't come.

He's not coming.

There will be a parting and when she stands back, she will be the only one left. She cries out and the horses gallop away with the sound, their strong bodies thundering down the hill, their muscles taut and angled, their manes rising and falling.

She doesn't go with them. The parting can wait. She's not ready. She knows she'll never be ready. She goes back to Breacán, keeping him there in her heart.

'It's like a Guinness advert out there, Breacán.'

She says it out loud even though she knows it will fall only on her ears. She's doing tiny repetitive things, over and over. She checks her phone again, even though she knows the hospital hasn't called. She wouldn't have missed it but she's looking anyway, willing a message that says, oops, there's been a mistake. All is well.

. . .

She imagines that he's back. Home from hospital. Breacán is settling down on the bed, carefully placing his crutches to one side. He's so comfortable he's laughing, gently at first and then so deeply and hysterically tears are streaming down his face. She teases out their conversation, playing it out in full like people sometimes do when they are wandering, their minds charting something that will never happen.

'Whit are ye laughing at Breacán?' Rathlin is giggling herself, even though she has no idea what's so funny. Breacán is trying to speak but every time he opens his mouth, the laughter takes over. He's clenching his ribs, roaring, the muscles in his sides tensing and hurting. Rathlin is climbing onto the bed, aligning herself beside him, joining in, the twins roaring raucously. When calm finally descends in Rathlin's scene, it is Breacán who breaks the silence.

'I can't believe you just said it was like a Guinness advert out there.'

It sets them off again and they are giggling hard, folding into one another. After a few minutes they fall silently into their own memories and Rathlin is pulled back to now. She's looking at the empty space beside her on the bed, wishing her brother was there. She's remembering when they were kids, when they used to climb into bed in the mornings with their mum and dad. Rathlin laughs, for real this time, as it strikes her that they were still doing it when they were nearly ten.

Sorry, folks, I guess we were officially early morning passion killers. No wonder we didn't have any other siblings.

The pain in Rathlin's chest is worse, not from the fall, from everyone's absence. Especially Breacán's. 'He needs to come back'. She's shouting it. She's unable to contemplate the alternative. She's thinking about his shape before his stillness, and creates it and rests her head on his shoulder. She's listening to him talking to her, the words tumbling softly into her hair. He's asking her to listen to Ellen, to let her speak. Not to jump straight down her throat.

'Aye, all right, Breacán, I'll dae it for ye but if she starts any snash, I won't be taking prisoners.' She knows what he'd say in retort. He always said it after every ripple of temper.

'You sure ye don't dye that hair of yers black? You're even more of an angry ginger than me.'

They're both giggling again, but a few moments later the silence is back, drifting in like a sea mist. Rathlin is sawing through it, carefully remembering the last time she visited. When he asked the question again.

'Are you ever going tae tell me why ye left after you'd only just come back?'

Rathlin had shifted her gaze from the ceiling to her brother.

'Aye, one day, when I'm ready. Life won't ever feel right until ye know everything, Breacán, but I'm no at that place yet. You know whit I mean, don't ye?'

Rathlin had gently stroked Breacán's shoulder, the way her mother used to when she was making a statement, not asking a question. She can't remember why she didn't just tell him. Why she didn't tell him that day, the one that began in such terror, ended with the conception of her daughter. Isabella. His niece. The child that breaks her heart each and every day.

Rathlin flicks to a picture of herself and Breacán on her phone and holds it in front of her face.

Mind that time ye said ye'd never ever leave me.

Chapter Twenty-Nine

Rathlin

The beach below Ballynoe, 2004

Rathlin is eleven-years-old, turning ever so gently from girl to the very youngest of woman. Skye's doing her hair, securing two red bobbles on the impossible edge of each of Rathlin's pleats. Rathlin's smiling, remembering instructing her mother to do this, asking her to work quickly while she's prancing up and down, eager to join Breacán at the water's edge. Her mother's words are like sand in her ear.

'You're like a horse that's no had a bite of dinner in a week. Can you hold off on the bolting for just a minute please.'

Rathlin's letting herself go back. She's giggling, her voice still lilted in a childishness that is disappearing elsewhere in her body.

'Neeeiigghhhh chance. If I'm going to beat Breacán then I need tae get some fire in these legs.'

Skye's patting her playfully on the bikini-bottomed bum, and Rathlin feels the wind on her back as she's racing off to join Breacán in the sea, his skinny frame already waist deep in the water. She's forgotten to take off her sandals and she's doubling back, her mum and dad already deep in conversation. Rathlin's hovering at the edge, listening in.

Skye's placing the brush down on the blanket, pressing herself closer to Joe, his bare back resting against the warmth of the rock behind him.

'Joe, honey, why are ye looking so stressed? The twins will be fine. Ye were swimming in the bay yourself when ye were a kid. They'll head to the point an' back like they always do. It's lovely that they're so close. I'm dreading them going off tae secondary school tae make new friends. I don't know...dae you think we're doing the right thing putting them in different classes?'

Rathlin's ready to dip her head into the conversation but she's hauling herself out of the circle, waiting for Joe's answer. *Now* Rathlin's trying to push *Then* Rathlin in but she's not budging. The scene is staying the same.

Joe's lowering his head and his lips catch Skye's, a granule of sand leaving the taste of the sea on his tongue when she pulls back to caress his cheek. He's drawing his right hand over his eyes, casting a shadow on lips that only moments before had shone like the sun.

'These people are experts. They wouldnae have suggested it if they didnae think it was right. They'll be totally fine, Skye, and they'll be inseparable when they're home fae school.'

'I guess you're right and if we keep a wee close eye on them they'll be fine. To be honest though, I'm a bit worried about Breacán. He's a wee bit withdrawn. Dae you think something's the matter Joe? Am I missing something?'

'Aye, ye are.'

Skye's straightening her back. 'What, tell me, Joe?'

'Breacán's getting tae an age where he probably wants a wee bit more privacy if ye know whit I mean. He's nearly twelve.'

'Joe Doherty, exactly, he's eleven and he's no going tae be doing that at his age.'

'Skye, you'd be surprised. You're the one that's saying Rathlin's changed since she got her periods.'

'Bloody hell, Joe, I cannae believe they're growing up so fast. They're ma wee babies.'

'Aye, let's just enjoy them while we still can. They'll be grown up before we know it an' we'll be old gits on our lonesome ownsome.'

'Speak for yourself. I'm younger than you. There'll be a wee spring in ma step long after you've started tripping over wae your arthritic hip.'

The conversation is drawing to a quiet, a silence that's putting Rathlin on edge. She can't reveal her presence now because they'll know she's been listening. She's sinking on to her knees, her frame covered by a beach windshield.

'Sorry, Skye, watch you don't get too comfy there. You'll need to move soon.' He's looking down at her, kissing the top of her head. 'I'll have tae head off in a few minutes. That hay isn't going tae kick itself.'

Skye's sighing, rubbing her hand on Joe's thigh, the motion soft but deliberate.

'I'd offer tae help but I know you've got Aonghus.'

'Aye, if he bothers to turn up. Chances are he'll be pissed as a fart and Dad an' I will be working on our own again. It's getting serious, Skye. He's going tae end up drinking himself to death or killing someone in the process. I've tried tae talk tae him but he's pretty vacant most of the time. He's still a teenager for god's sake.'

'I've tried talking tae him as well, Joe, but he just clams up. He used tae be such a friendly wee boy but I can hardly get a word out of him these days. He's chatty enough wae the kids mind so at least he's communicating with someone. That said, Joe, he better no influence them into drinking.'

'He won't, he knows the twins are just weans. It's just himself he doesnae gie a stuff about. I wish I knew why but I'm fed up asking. Dad says he's selfish an' just tae ignore him but it's hard tae do that, especially when I promised Mum I'd look after him.'

'You do, Joe, you always have done but you're no his

dad. You're only ten years older than him. You need tae be a big brother to him. Maybe you should try talking tae him again, see if you can find out what changed for him. Maybe it's just as simple as mourning your mum.'

'Skye, that's hardly simple. I've been mourning her as well.'

'I know, Joe, but you were older, he was just a wee boy. Imagine losing yer mum at ten-years-old an' let's face it, your dad's hardly a good influence. He's pretty harsh most of the time and tae be honest I think he's quite disrespectful towards Aonghus. He hardly even looks at him.'

'I know, he's as hard as nails but he's always been like that. I don't think I've ever even had a proper conversation wae him in all my life.'

'Which is exactly why you're such a good dad. Chat tae Aonghus, I'll try as well. He could kill himself, or worse, Joe. I've seen him taking the twins on the tractor and my heart's in my mouth. We cannae let him hurt them, or you or me. Our beautiful weans need their mammy and daddy, Joe.'

'For fuck sake, don't even joke about things like that, ma granny was always saying that mocking is catching.'

Skye's pushing herself up, turning around to face Joe square on. He's laughing but she's serious, her lips are loose, but her chin is tight.

'Joe, I'm no joking. Maybe yer da would try tae talk tae him if ye asked him.'

'I don't think he cares about Aonghus. Dad was always saying my mammy couldnae see past his wee red curls and big green eyes. Maybe he misses being spoiled.'

'Maybe, but can ye blame your mum, Joe. Let's be honest, you're no half smitten with ma red curls and big green eyes.'

She's laughing, kissing Joe on the lips, his frame above her as he's rising to his feet.

'Aye, when you put it like that, my ma was obviously as blinded as I am. I'll talk tae him. Right, I'm off before the weans try and drag me intae that freezing cold channel. Keep me dinner, will ye?'

Rathlin's tightening her body, trying to make herself even smaller. She can't be spotted now but she's transfixed, taking everything in, questions fighting to be heard. She takes a sharp intake of breath, knowing she can't ask them.

Skye's still in the conversation with Joe, nodding, her eyes lingering on his frame as he's disappearing into the distance. Rathlin's retreating, running to the shoreline, breathless at the conversation, her *Then* mind struggling to understand, her *Now* mind heeding the warning and wishing she'd taken it when it was offered.

She joins Breacán in the water, and when their fun is spent they stretch their strokes wide and fast and swim back. Breacán pulls in front, winning the water race, but Rathlin is determined to win another battle, squeezing Breacán out of the scene when they run to reach their mother on the strand. Rathlin is wrapping her arms tightly around her mother's neck, her lips smirking as Breacán hunches down wet and alone, his arms falling nonchalantly by his side.

'I wish the summer holidays could last forever, Mum. It's rubbish that we have tae go back tae school soon.'

Skye's hugging Rathlin warmly, rubbing her back encouragingly. Now Rathlin can feel her hand heating her shoulders. She's rolling into it, Molly's back providing the heat she's craving.

'But it's not just going back tae school this time, it's more than that, you're going tae a new school. Just like in a flash, my wee babies are off tae secondary school.'

'But I don't want tae go, Mum, neither does Breacán. We won't even see each other cos we'll be in different classes.

I bet Breacán ends up wae all the cool kids and I'll be in a class wae all the swots.'

'Ach don't be unkind. Teachers' pets are all right, in their own whingey whiney way.'

They're laughing, their backs uncurling for a moment.

'How about you, Son, are you no looking forward tae it either?'

Breacán's shrugging his shoulders and Rathlin's waiting for his response.

'Suppose. Don't really care. Better than hanging out wae granddad on the farm.'

'How come? I thought you liked it up at Kebble doing stuff tae help?'

Breacán's shrugging his shoulders again, stretching up on to his feet. His words are sailing behind him as he runs. 'Last one in's a wee diddy, Rathlin.'

Rathlin's chasing him, their squeals lost to the sea. They're jumping into the water. Rathlin's turning. She can see Skye watching and she feels something crawl under her skin. She's looking towards the caves, trying to shake it off, searching for the water wraiths in the distance.

Chapter Thirty

Ellen

Kebble

Ellen has dumped a mountain of paperwork on the kitchen table. Her heart isn't in the fight anymore but she's going through the motions. It's a distraction from the lack of news. Still. She sighs and rubs her eyes, tiredness clinging like moss on a stone.

'Dae ye want a cup of coffee? By the way, I've found some more bits and pieces for ye.' She is filling the kettle at the sink but the water and her mouth overflow when she turns to talk to Anita. *Fuck.*

Ellen hears a giggle at her feet as she pulls the kettle away from the tap. She tips the surplus into the sink and smiles at her daughter. 'Sshhh, best not tell anywan yer mummy said a bad word. It's just between you an' me.' She kneels down and tidies Barra's hair behind her ears. Barra is jumping on the spot, her head bobbing from side to side. Ellen kisses her and goes to find another hairband for herself. Anita is at the table, pushing the papers out of the way so she can sit on its edge. She puts her feet on a chair and stretches her arms.

'I hear yer a big lassie an' going off tae start nursery the day. Wish ah could come.'

Barra's voice is shrill but coherent as it slams into her mother. 'Mummy, can Nita come tae nursery school?'

Ellen shrugs her shoulders and pauses to tackle her own

unruly hair, using her free hand to draw it all over one shoulder. 'Nah, she cannae, she's too big, and besides, she's got loads of work tae dae here.' She's points to the paperwork on the table and pulls a funny face which Anita ignores.

'Here, you're no going out like that are ye, it's about tae piss down fae the heavens.'

Ellen glances out of the window, screwing up her nose. 'So you're a weather woman as well as a know-it-all, Anita? That sky's as clear as a bell. Sure you don't want tae come along? It's a big day for the wee one.' Ellen hugs Barra, kissing her softly on the lips, whispering that she loves her.

Barra responds with a question Ellen can't bear to answer. 'Is Breacán still coming tae see me?'

No he can't. He can't do anything anymore.

Tears instantly burn Ellen's eyes and she turns to Anita, mouthing a plea for help. Her words are clambering to escape but she holds them tightly between her teeth.

Your daddy is going to die. Again. No, not that daddy, your new daddy.

Anita nudges Ellen out of the way and crouches on the floor beside Barra.

'Hoi, beat it for a minute. Ah want a proper look at this wee star.' She places her hands on Barra's shoulders. 'Breacán and I would love tae come and see ye, but today's just for a mummy an' her gorgeous wee girl tae share.' She lifts her eyes from Barra to Ellen. 'And ah need tae finish my homework. It's like being back at school living with yer mummy.'

Anita clambers back to the table and picks up some of the papers. She lets them fall from her fingers, exaggerating the weight so that they land with a bang and Ellen joins her in an unexpected moment of laughter.

'Funny, hen, but jeez don't get them all mixed up.'

'Oh, my mistake. They're actually in order? All I can see is a ton of shit. Aonghus has kept Ballynoe bills fae years ago.'

213

Ellen instructs Barra to go to the hall and get her new school bag. She's off and running instantly, singing a wee unrecognisable tune as she disappears out of the room.

'I know he wiz weird like that. Think he was paranoid that his creepy da would come back fae the grave an' get one over him.'

'This is new info. So how was the da creepy? You didnae meet him, did ye?'

Ellen is mumbling, quieting the voices, getting her story straight.

'Aye, that's right. I didnae need tae meet him tae know he was creepy. Aonghus hated him so I wiz glad when he died. Coming back here saved Aonghus's life, so it did.'

'Ellen, this place is actually totally confusing. How can ye say it saved his life when Aonghus did whit he did?'

Ellen has an image of Aonghus pulling the trigger of his firearm. She still can't understand how he had the courage to do it. She knows he had the desire though, and a mind so weighed down with his younger self that there was good reason to.

'Anita, don't. The wee one might hear ye.'

'She can't see me, Ellen, ah wiz careful about that.'

Ellen checks that Barra's still out of earshot. She is, but she lowers her outside voice all the same.

'It's Aonghus's story, Anita, but his dad was evil tae him. Aonghus wiznae a bad person, despite whit Rathlin says. It's so fucked up, aw of it. And now Breacán is...'

'Probably going tae be awright.' Ellen lets Anita close in for a hug and she settles in the embrace for a moment, wanting more than anything for the arms to be Breacán's, to hear his voice above all the shouting in her head. She lets Anita break free, knowing she's going to try and change the subject.

'And what about all this then?' Anita's flicking through

the documents and unopened envelopes on the table. 'Dae you really want me tae look at this crap or is this just a diversionary tactic tae stop ye going mental about Breacán?'

'No, obviously, that's why you're here. If Breacán comes back, we need tae sort out our future an' that means making sure the houses are under proper ownership, even when we're married. I'm no putting anything intae joint names. I've been homeless wance too many times. You know what I mean.'

'Aye, ah know whit ye mean, obviously, but married? Whit the fuck, Ellen? Are ye no getting a wee carried away here?'

Ellen is searching deep in her pocket again, feeling the comfort of the ring, the circle that's going to keep them turning. She listens to Breacán's voice and changes tact.

It's our secret, Ellen, ours until I tell Rathlin.

'For fuck sake, Anita, I'm joking. There's nae chance I'm getting married and risking losing any of this. No way. I've had enough of people walking all over me. If you cannae be bothered, forget it, I'll dae it maself.' She tries to find rage but it isn't there. There's no fight left. She can't be weak; she has to stay strong. Either way.

'Jesus take a breath. Even if Breacán does pull through he might no be right. Ah've heard about folk wae brain injuries. Ah'm just saying ye might no want this house stuff tae deal wae on top of that.'

'It's no going tae come tae that. Breacán will be fine. He's no gaunnae leave me, not now, not ever.' Ellen's ignoring her inside voice.

He's going to die. You know he's going to die.

'Well, if that's the case why no just tell his sister the now? She'll probably explode for five minutes an' then get oan wae worrying about him.'

'I'm no a monster, Anita. She doesnae need that the now.'

Anita's nodding. 'Yip. Exactly, so why not gie it a rest.

You're coming across as a bit of a lunatic. Have a bit of heart, for god sake, it'll no kill ye.'

Ellen's voices are multiplying and she bangs the table with her fist, silencing the noise in her head. Barra is staring at her, her lip trembling as if she might cry. Ellen grabs her, trying to pretend she's playing a game.

'Right, that's the big bang that says it's time to go in two minutes. Why don't you run for a pee. And no buts, quick to it, it's a big walk down tae the school.' When Barra's out of the room Ellen squares up to Anita. 'You shouldnae talk tae me like that, Anita, it's no on.'

'Aye, ah'm sorry, that was shit but this would be a lot easier if you'd just tell the bloody truth. It's all secrets, secrets, secrets wae you. It must be bloody exhausting.'

'Na, it's quite straightforward and when Breacán's better, he'll tell the truth. What does it matter if she doesnae like me. She's no the father of my child, Breacán is.'

'Aye, an' when are you going tae tell Rathlin and Breacán that wee golden nugget? Aonghus is long gone so at least there's no drama there.'

'For your information, smart arse, Aonghus knew. I could hardly pretend we were having a wean when we werenae sleeping the gether. Even I'm no that stupid.'

'This just gets better an' better.'

Ellen ignores her. None of that shit matters anymore.

Chapter Thirty-One

Rathlin

Ballynoe

The kitchen is busy with the bustle of Frances. Rathlin can feel her closing in on her. The question is coming.

'No more news I take it?'

Rathlin shakes her head. She doesn't have the energy to reply with words. Frances keeps asking. Is there any news? She cares, obviously, but the more Rathlin hears it asked, the more frustrated she gets. She doesn't want to hear *the news* she's waiting for. Rathlin is watching Frances at the cooker. The fried eggs she's flipping are making her want to vomit.

'Sit down, I'll dish up. Frank's dying for a cooked breakfast, he's starving fae helping you wae the cattle earlier. He's enjoying it though, bit different fae wheeling folk about on trollies in the hospital.'

Frank nods and starts to enthuse. It's a helpful diversion. Working in Breacán's space is keeping him close to Rathlin.

'It's no that different, love. My people-herding skills are definitely coming in handy dealing wae the cows. I have tae say I never appreciated what lovely animals they are. They've each got their own wee personality. If I wasnae seventy-two, I'd be seriously thinking about a change in career.' Frank is laughing and Rathlin dodges out of his way to circumvent the table. She's not even sat down when Frances is upon her again. This pair have negotiated a plan to maintain a consistent two-pronged attack. Frank and Frances, gargoyles by day and by night.

'You're looking a wee bit better, hen, an' you're definitely moving easier after that whack ye took tae yer chest. You'll be as right as rain in no time. In the meantime, this'll help.'

Rathlin folds her arms across her chest, the very mention of the injury causing it to throb intensely. The pain stops at her ribs and below there is numbness. Rathlin strokes her belly and then moves her hand away sharply. Guilt. And lots of it. She swallows hard and focuses on saving Breacán, not on losing something she never even had. She edges her body tentatively onto a seat, lodging herself in front of the eggs and toast Frances has placed on the table. She sighs deeply, trying to control the saliva warning her that what she puts down is sure to come back up.

'Jesus, Frances, I cannae face that. I just need a quick cup of coffee before I head tae the hospital.'

'Hen, you're no gonnae be any use to your brother if you pass out oan him. At least have a wee bit of toast before ye rush out.'

Frank is nosing in, speaking over Frances. 'I've got an appetite like a horse the now so I'll help you out if you're struggling.'

Frances bats him with an oven glove, shooing him into his seat across from Rathlin. She's letting it pass over her, thinking of Breacán lying there, unable to eat, think, talk. Unable to anything. Frances places her hand on her shoulder, kneading it gently and Rathlin, enjoying her silence, leans her head into it. It doesn't last.

'Frank, leave the wean alone, yours is coming.' She releases Rathlin and comes back from the cooker with a plate of food for her husband.

Rathlin scans the fried meat-fest and tries not to boke. She turns her attention to the mess on the worktops. Jesus,

Breacán, this chaos would freak you and your neatness completely. She feels her cheeks burn when Frances takes the hint and starts clearing up.

'Sorry, hen, we're outstaying our welcome but we're away the morra. The wean's funeral is in Glasgow the day after an' there's a few things I need tae do tae help.'

No matter how hard Rathlin tries to avoid it, she's there. In her head. Isabella. Her mind is replaying the funeral. Frank and Frances are the only people there with her. The only people who knew her sadness. Know her sadness. And there's that guilt again. She's wallowing in her own pain when Frances is dying a little bit inside too.

'I wasn't meaning anything bad wae that look, Frances. I'm so grateful tae ye both, especially when you've got so much tae deal wae yourselves.'

'I know you are, hen, but it's for the best that we're out of yer hair while Breacán's getting on the mend.'

Rathlin closes her eyes, wishing her brother was leaning across the table, nagging at her to clear up the mess. She's not daft though. She knows that when Frances and Frank have gone, the only sound she'll hear will be the kitchen clock.

'I wish ye didnae have tae go but I wish even more that your gorgeous wee great granddaughter hadnae died. It's heartbreaking but no matter whit we dae, nothing will change. They'll all still be dead.' They. She means her mum and dad. And Isabella. But now Breacán is closing in, completing the circle.

'Aye, life's shit at times, hen, but we need tae keep at it because there's nothing else for it.'

Rathlin pulls herself back from her own mourning and creates some space for Frank and Frances's grief. 'I don't know whit I'd have done without yous. You're the only grown-ups in my life tae keep me right and you're always thinking about me, even when you're both so sad.'

'Well, one grown-up. You're stretching the facts if you're calling Frank an adult.'

Frank's down on all fours on the kitchen floor, teasing Molly with a bit of sausage. Rathlin laughs, the lightness of the sound surprising her. She dips into it gladly, the image sending her back to happier times.

'I can remember ma dad messing about like that on the kitchen floor, no with a dog mind, usually wae me or Breacán and my mum would be going nuts because we were getting in her way.'

'That's a nice memory to have, and I'm sure your mum was loving it really, how could she no? Sounds like you had a lovely family. Bloody tragedy it had tae change the way it did.' Frances pauses.

No more, Frances, please no more.

She takes the hint. 'I'm glad we could come an' gie you a wee hand. It's great tae actually finally see this place.'

Rathlin is scanning the room, searching for the energy her parents left in it. 'Aye, I talked about it enough tae you, that's for sure. I wish ye were here for better reasons but...'

'It's shite, hen, but let's just hope things sort themselves out. Why don't you head up tae the hospital in Breacán's car the now an' we'll head up later wae the wee dug. She'll be missing ye after she's got fed up wae Frank's stupidity.'

Chapter Thirty-Two

Rathlin

Breacán's hospital room

Breacán's room is thick with bodies. Too many bodies. Ellen, Frank and Frances are all there and they've all crossed into Rathlin's domain. The air is stale. Her throat is constricting. She wants to run. Hard. Flight. She always chooses flight. She stands up, dragging air into her lungs. She exhales it, losing it to the other bodies. They are stealing it hungrily, their noise claiming it, spitting it back in words they think they have a right to share.

It was all fine. Ellen and her were still doing the *thing*. Being polite to one another. Friendly. It was fine. Good even. She made it turn. Rathlin did it. She waited a beat and then she tilted the room. Boom. It capsized, sucking everything down into the whirlpool with it. She made a snarky comment, the snideness sliding out of the side of her mouth like an eel.

'Lucky Barra's da is six foot under an' didnae spoil her first day at nursery.'

Why did she say it? She's spinning and she wants them all to spin with her. There. Isn't that a good enough reason? Ellen didn't seem to think so. Rathlin can't remember what she screamed back at her. It was a whirlwind noise swirling around the narrow space between her and the wall.

'For fuck sake.' Rathlin is the one screaming now. She needs it to stop. She's swinging around, wildly, spitting at everyone. 'Breacán can hear. The doctor said so just five minutes ago. Stop. You're hurting him.' In her turbulence she accidentally nudges Ellen and she's shouting back. At full pelt, the words firing at her like bullets.

'Good, cos he needs tae hear what a wee cow his sister actually is.'

Rathlin's holding her arms back, resisting the urge to grab Ellen's pointy finger and snap it clean off. 'An' by the way it wasnae me that started this. This pish is all oan you.'

Rathlin's drawing breath, lowering her voice.

Fuck, Breacán is listening.

'Christ, Ellen, why are ye even here? You're nothing tae us. Frances, can you get her out of here? I cannae breathe wae her in this room.'

It's Frank that's drawing breath to speak and Rathlin somehow knows it's going to change everything. She can hear the clock. When did they fix it? It is overpowering the room as if it's coming out of a long hibernation. Time is a winter shadow and there will be no shelter from it.

'Listen tae the lassie will ye, hen? We aw need a bit of calm the now. Our great granddaughter wiz stillborn an' we've her funeral tae get to. The only thing that's keeping us going is knowing how well Rathlin handled it when her wee lassie died so young. We don't know how she's getting through aw this on top of everything else.'

Rathlin wouldn't have believed it if she hadn't heard it for herself. The words spoken out loud. Her words. Her secret. Her child thrown into the cauldron of conversation as if she was an acceptable part of it. She can feel Ellen staring and turns to confirm it, their eyes locking as the ruckus between Frank and Frances erupts. Rathlin can see the mayhem kicking off beside her but she's refusing to listen to their hysteria. The apologies, the arguing, the noise. It's all deafening. But she can hear one question clearly. Ellen's.

'Ye had a wee daughter? I didnae know.'

Ellen's retreating. The rest are with her. They know they need to go. Frances is ushering them out of the room and Rathlin's waiting for the door to close. She knows she will collapse. She needs to be with Breacán. Her head is on the bed beside him, her scream muffled by the sheet. She raises her neck and lets out a hollow roar, empty of life, like her brother. When she sits up, she knows she needs to tell him the truth.

Chapter Thirty-Three

Rathlin and Breacán

Breacán's hospital room and Ballynoe

Rathlin is beside Breacán and she is ready. He's still in his hospital bed, still unconscious, but she knows she can reach him. And that he will listen, especially now, especially when she's ready to speak to him about her daughter. She slips into the past and wills her brother to share the same space with her. To support her through the pain. Better late than never, she whispers as she prepares to begin her story.

Breacán, it's me. Rathlin. I've got something I need tae tell ye. I've always wanted tae tell ye, but it's never seemed the right time tae break your heart again. I know Mum an' Dad dying already smashed it tae smithereens.

Rathlin is imagining Breacán's response, a slow turn of the head, the left side of his mouth drooping slightly as he tests the words behind the safety of his lips before daring to ask her what it is.

It cannae be that bad, can it?

Aye, it is. And even worse than bad. You're going tae hate me for no telling ye an' hate me for no sharing the most precious thing in my life wae ye.

Whit? More precious than me? Surely not?

She knows he'd make a joke of it because that's what he does. Laugh, avoid, run. No, hang on, she's the runner. And

224

she's still running. She's at the line though, telling him what he needs to know.

I had a daughter, Breacán. Her name is Isabella.

I always knew ye would use Granny's name. That's cool. Where is she? Can I meet her?

She knows the imagined response is a lie. He'd have been furious, then hurt, then he would have given her the support she needed but by then it would have been too late. She would have seen the pain in his eyes, seen how the loss was crippling him as much as her. She leans over, checking his eyes are still closed, his ears open. His chest is still heaving, up and down, up and down, the beeping machines now so normal she doesn't consider them to be an add-on anymore.

You can't meet her, Breacán. She's dead. She died a long time ago.

Rathlin climbs on top of the bed beside her brother and rolls on to her side. She's in a foetal position, imagining that their mum's dressing gown is pulled loosely over them both, the soft cotton resting just under their chins. She's quiet.

She imagines Breacán getting up, taking the seat beside the bed, placing the leads from the machines on the ground, the metal making brief music with the lino. He's restless. He's moving and taking Rathlin with him. She's confused at his need to shift but she's following him anyway, relaxing when she realises where Breacán is leading her.

Ballynoe.

Of course he's taking her to Ballynoe. There's nowhere else they would go. Not for this. Rathlin catches a glimpse of a shadow and she watches a blurred image stretch out in front of her, finally blending into nothing. She closes her eyes and tries to find the memory again but it has already exited. She and Breacán are still there though. Still home.

Even with her eyes closed she would know that they were home. The unmistakable scent of the past is sinking into her bones. They are back where it all started. In their parents' bedroom.

Breacán is asking her to budge up. He uses his arms to pull himself over and then up until he's resting on their mum and dad's headboard. He turns his head towards her, and she's right. He's still not ready to speak. They remain silent, the space between them magnified by the hollow ticking of the clock on the bedside table. Breacán eventually leans over, lifting the shadow from its space. Rathlin plays her part too, keeping it real.

Put it back. It's fine where it is.

Sorry, I thought you might have fallen asleep. I've been waiting that long for ye tae tell me what happened.

Rathlin laps up the sarcasm in his voice, his words, his anything. She goes further, imagining more. Her brother is alive.

I'm no sleeping as you can obviously hear.

Whoa, hold on, I'm no quite getting this. You're angry at me?

No, this isnae about you so stop building your part up. I'm angry at Frank for opening his big massive gob. I'm angry at Mum and Dad. I'm angry at Ellen, I'm angry at the whole fucking world.

Rathlin, I'm doing ma best to be calm here but I can hardly breathe. Actually, I cannae breathe for myself but you know that. One of the perils of my near-death situation. You had a wee girl, ma wee niece, a daughter you named after Mum's mum an' you didnae think that her being born an' then dying was important enough tae tell your twin brother? I don't know how tae deal wae this. It's just as well I'm in a coma or this would be unbearable.

Rathlin can't be bothered with his attempt at humour. She's like a tornado. The dog has invaded the scene and she's falling on the floor, jumping back up, regaining her protective position. Molly tries to lick her face but Rathlin pushes her away gently. Breacán needs to listen. It's her last chance to share.

Aye let's make this about you. So you're dying. Big deal. At least you get tae escape this shitty world. It's a lot more horrible for me, believe me. And why the fuck are you back on this bed anyway? It's my space now, move away will you. I cannae breathe either wae your self-righteous face glaring down at me.

Tough. I'm no moving, I've as much right tae sit on this bed as you. She was ma Mum as well.

Rathlin's looking around her, remembering he moved the scene back to their mum and dad's bedroom. She likes the shift and lets her irritation slide for a moment. It's a good space, much more appropriate for a conversation like this. Perfect for drama. She thumps her hands dramatically on the bed and swings her legs to the side. She moves over to the chair by the window, mimicking Breacán as she walks.

God will ye listen tae yourself? "She was my Mum as well you know." Fine. I'll move, will I.

Breacán's voice is charging up and down like a train turning a bend. No, listen tae yourself. You obviously think I'm some kind of monster that shouldn't meet yer daughter. At least now I know what you really think of me.

Rathlin shakes her head and pulls her knees up to her chin. She's looking out the window. Her voice is calm, quiet. Breacán strains his ears to hear her.

Breacán, stop it will ye. It's no about hurting you or hating you. Can you no hear how ridiculous that sounds? Stop being dramatic an' saying stupid things because it's no making this horrible moment any easier tae deal wae.

Which moment? Telling me about Isabella or the fact that I'm dying cos I could easily feel a wee bit left out here. Any pointers on how I'm tae deal wae this, to your satisfaction of course.

Here. Rathlin's halfway across the floor, stretching out her arm and handing Breacán her phone.

What? Do you want me tae call someone for advice?

No, here, just stop it for a minute, will ye. Take it. She's closer now, thrusting the phone directly into his hand. Have a look.

Breacán grabs the phone, keeping his eyes fixed on Rathlin until it's firmly in his hand. He's shaking. God, is this her?

Rathlin can see he's crying. Tears rolling down his cheeks and disappearing, swallowed by the stubble on his chin. Aye, that's Isabella.

Rathlin, I don't know what tae say except she's beautiful. She is. Was.

I mean it, I really don't know what tae say tae you. He's touching the image, moving his finger away sharply as if he's inflicting pain.

There's nothing you can say, well nothing that's going tae bring her back.

Breacán's examining the picture, pulling the image of Isabella closer to him. She looks a hell of a lot like Mum.

Doesn't she? Rathlin is animated as she moves closer. I thought that fae the very first moment I saw her face. And that was an introduction an' a half let me tell you. She's climbing back on to the bed, sitting alongside Breacán. The twins are gazing at the photograph. Together. It's Mum's lips. Look. She's lifting the picture of Skye from the bedside. See, they're the same shape.

They are, exactly the same. And she's got Mum's colouring. And Uncle Breacán's of course. He's ruffling his hair, but his mouth is tight. Rathlin knows he's unsure if it's okay to smile so she smiles. He's her reflection and he's smiles back. I don't know anything about wee babies but she's got loads of hair has she no?

Aye, I guess she did. It was quite thick an' all. Ye cannae

see it in this photo but it's long an' curly at the back of her neck. At least she wasnae blessed with my lifeless black hair.

She's perfect Rathlin. Well…

It's fine. Don't stress about it. Aye, she was perfect. But no that perfect or she wouldnae be dead.

I wasnae saying that, Rathlin. I wasnae being unkind. I just don't know how tae deal with this.

I wasn't picking you up, but it's the truth no matter how ye say it.

The silence is lingering, awkward and deep. Rathlin's wondering when it's going to end, when she'll have to go back to the nothingness of Breacán on the hospital bed. She's almost back when Breacán's questions keep it going.

What happened tae her? We used tae tell each other everything. Why did that change?

Life happened, Breacán. It all went to shit.

But this? He's lifting the phone, raising Isabella in front of him. I cannae believe this happened tae you. And you didnae think I would support ye. That's a tough one tae take.

It's no that. I couldnae bear tae gie you any more bad news. You had just moved into Ballynoe wae Aonghus and you seemed tae be happy.

What? We were nearly seventeen when I moved in wae Aonghus. That's ten years ago. Are you saying you've kept this fae me for a decade?

Rathlin nods her head. It feels heavy and she curls her fingers under her chin in case it drops. What does time matter? It's still the same secret whether I've kept it for a week or ten years.

No it's no. Our entire adult life has been a lie. Dae I even know you?

Ditto Breacán, if I didnae call an' text an' come tae visit I'd never hear a word fae you.

And what? I'm a guy. We don't do all that shit.

You said tae me that night, you said that you'd be there for me no matter what.

What night?

What night? That night. *The* fuckin night. When they came tae take me away to the foster home. The night of the Separation. When they Separated US. The twins who shouldn't be separated. You promised you'd come an' find me. I was fourteen-years-old an' fuckin terrified an' you said, "I'll come and get you. I promise." But you didnae. It wiz me that eventually came tae see you on our seventeenth birthday.

Aye, I said it, and I meant it. But you phoned Granddad an' told him you had a new family an' you needed tae forget us. That we werenae tae make any contact.

That's utter shit. You believed that?

I was fourteen as well, Inspector Clueso. And I was also pissed off that you couldnae just try tae stay here wae me instead of going off on a rampage every five minutes. Of course I fuckin believed him.

He's a manipulative cunt, Breacán. Why the hell could you no see that?

I did but I was busy trying to keep the peace so you an' Aonghus wouldnae be constantly getting flack fae him.

He's another prick. Don't get me started.

You've got tae give it a rest about Aonghus, I mean it. There's things you don't know.

Oh, so who's got secrets now, eh? She's shaking her head, looking at her brother with disgust.

Calm down an' I'll tell you.

I don't want tae be calm.

She's on her feet again, her phone close to her chest, her back to the window. Her weight is pressing against the glass. She can feel it behind her, wondering if it will give, imagining free-falling out of the world. Molly's at her feet, sensing it, climbing on her hind legs with her front paws resting on the pockets of Rathlin's jeans. She's barking, breaking the spell. Rathlin shifts forward on the windowsill, making eye contact with the dog.

Sit down, Rathlin. Seriously, just sit the fuck down an' listen.

What dae you think I'm doing, dancing? My arse is down and this is where I'm staying tae listen tae whatever shite you're planning on coming out wae.

Aye, okay, but be careful, please, those windows are ancient.

She makes a face, the Separation circus between them continuing. Aonghus had a hard time growing up. Granddad did really bad things tae him, for years, fae he was a wee boy.

And how dae you know all this then?

He told me, when I wiz sixteen, just before we both moved into Ballynoe. I guess I kind of knew because he wiz always asking me if I was okay, if Granddad was keeping his distance.

Jesus.

Rathlin is on her feet. Panic. The Separation fucked up her brother too.

Did he dae anything tae you?

He's shaking his head.

No, he never touched me but there was a time just before Mum and Dad died when he was being weird. I thought something horrid might happen, but nothing ever did. Aonghus made sure of that.

Fuck. Poor Aonghus. But focus, Breacán. We cannae let what happened tae him get in the way of the facts. He still destroyed us.

Rathlin, seriously, leave that shit because it's poisoning you. It was an accident. They happen. Google it. Loads of folk have tae deal with bad luck so we're no fucking unique in this.

Breacán that's completely irrelevant. If he wasnae there, it wouldn't have happened. Could Not. Have. Happened. Rathlin is tapping her foot furiously, like a bull defending its corner. Let's be clear. What he did killed our mum an' dad. I do not care a jot if it was an accident. He still killed them.

Breacán's shoulders are sinking, his chin lowering. Rathlin is wondering if he's leaving her, if he's heading back to the death scene.

Rathlin, dae you remember anything else fae that day? What Aonghus did? What any of us did?

Aye, I remember seeing Aonghus wae the gun an' then they were dead. That's all I need tae remember. Doesnae matter anyway because he admitted that the *accident* wiz his fault. Get over it. He was an arse. Abused or no.

I don't want tae argue. We don't have much time. Tell me more about yer wee daughter.

You need tae make time, Breacán. You're in control of this, no me. It's our birthday the morra. Our twenty-seventh an' ten years tae the day that Isabella was conceived.

It happened here?

She's watching him scour his brain, knowing the answer is in there.

Hang on, was it that night in the car wae Niall? I didnae even know you'd been seeing him. So has that slimy prick been keeping my niece fae me as well? Breacán's voice is louder, his fingertips whiter than the pallor of his face.

No, he doesnae know, an' I don't want him tae know. What's the point now?

I don't get it. You hadnae been here in three years. Was he coming tae see you in Glasgow then?

God, no, it was just a one time thing. Spur of the moment.

I felt crap. I'd just seen Granddad an' well Niall was the next person I saw after he…Bingo for Niall.

After he what? He's beside his sister now, peeling her arms from her face, finding her eyes under her hair. Rathlin, answer me for fuck sake. What did he dae tae ye?

She takes his forearm, circles her fingers around it.

Nothing. Well, no really nothing. He was saying heavy shit tae me, telling me I had turned intae a beautiful young woman. Seems I have a great body an' I'd make fine "company" for someone. Who even says stuff like that? He freaked me out. He always did. I didnae want the Separation because it meant losing you but I couldnae stomach living wae that creep either. I didnae feel safe. Rathlin takes her brother's other arm, running her hands down both, stopping at his hands. She clenches her fingers around his. Dae you think Mum knew what he was like?

She suspected. Aonghus told me she asked him if anything had happened but he said no. He didnae want her tae think that about him.

About him? It wasnae his fault, well that wasnae anyway.

It wasn't, no. But can we talk about Isabella now? I still don't know anything. Did you think I didnae want anything tae do with you?

Breacán, you didn't. When you found me an' Niall in the car, you called me a slut. You said you couldnae bear tae look at me.

Fucks sake, I was angry. But no really at you. Angry at him. He was going out wae someone. He didnae give two fucks about you.

Aye, and I didnae give two fucks about him. But we did create a beautiful daughter.

I'm so sorry I wasnae there for you.

I know. Rathlin is hunching down in front of her twin. Isabella was a beautiful child, but I only had such a short time wae her. It's so unfair to have someone so wonderful in your grasp and then have her ripped away. It's shite, this life I have tae live without her. And Mum and Dad. And you as well if you don't get your act together and pull yourself out of this. We've been Separated long enough.

Chapter Thirty-Four

Ellen

Ballynoe

Ellen is in Ballynoe. She has shared this kitchen sofa with Breacán many times. She's remembering how he held her on his chest, his back firm and straight against the battered leather. He'd stroke her hair and they'd talk about the day. Or she'd pull herself up and face him so she could argue with him. Who discovered penicillin? Who left the lid of the milk? Normal stuff. Sometimes they'd leave the door open to see the sunset, dreamily watching the light leave the sky, knowing there is no future if there hasn't been a past. Barra was a baby, their child asleep in the pram. Breacán loved her, even though he didn't know she was his. But they weren't ready to share their love for one another with her. And when she was older, they had to be careful of her watchful eyes, her turned-on ears. The sunsets were then shared at Kebble with Barra asleep in her own bed, her heart and eyes closed to the secret. It didn't matter then. Ellen wanted the secret. She demanded it. Aonghus had died and she was fierce about protecting his memory. He'd had enough shite in his life without people thinking she didn't care enough to mourn him.

She stands up and opens the back door. The light floods in like it's a gateway back to Breacán. It's not, it's just a diversion from the voices. Not her own, they're absent. The other voices in the room. Frances is trying to console Frank. They're annoyed with themselves. Ellen is annoyed with herself too, remembering some of the things she's said about Rathlin. *She's a wee boot, Breacán, plain and simple.*

She silences the rest, the more painful things she's said. She clears her throat, consoling herself with the fact that it wasn't her fault. She didn't know.

How did she cope?

She shivers. The bad stuff is coming back. She said a lot of nasty things. She has to be firm with her inner voice. *Stop being a fuckin cow.* She thinks about losing Barra and has to sit down before she falls down. She's lost enough. *Is* losing enough. She focuses on now, making herself concentrate on what's happening in the room and not in her head. Frances and Frank are having the same conversation over and over. First, all the way home in the car, and now back at the house. The chaos between them is as loud as the noise inside her head.

'Frank, stop beating yourself up. It wiz a slip of the tongue. It's better that it's all out in the open.' Frances is standing at the kitchen door, her weight pressing against the wood. Ellen imagines Breacán standing there, asking if she and Barra can stay. He always did that, lingered at the door when he knew she was heading back.

No, Breacán, once she knows we'll stay whenever you like. We'll tell her soon. I promise.

She shakes her head at the irony. It used to be her that wanted the secret kept. From Barra, and the judgmental villagers. Not from *Rathlin.* Breacán always said she didn't need to know. Ellen feels her anger rise again. Rathlin.

Every time Rathlin was around she was always thrust aside like a used tissue.

Enough. Be kind to Rathlin. For now.

Frank and Frances are still hammering it out.

'Poor lassie, I'm a bit long in the tooth tae be daein something as stupid as that. I just forgot that folk here didnae know.'

'Frank, sit.' Ellen's had enough of their drama. She's taking control, guiding him to the kitchen table. 'It's just one of these things.'

Frances is joining them, butting in. 'She's been keeping this tae herself for long enough, Ellen. Poor wean, what a time she has had of it.'

Ellen is listening, even though she realises the conversation isn't meant for her. They are talking it through themselves, back in the moment. Ellen wonders why everyone always has to go back. Why can't she just move forward. With Breacán. But she knows he's not moving anywhere. Frank is looking at her but talking to his wife. Ellen can feel her head bob to and fro, like she's watching a tennis match.

'Don't forget you were there for her an' I know it wasnae easy for you, no after all the babies you lost.'

'We lost, Frank. They were our children.'

Frank is rubbing his chin. Ellen is listening to the noise, the grating melodic. It's like they've forgotten she's there but it doesn't matter because she needs to know more. Especially if Breacán had been keeping it from her too.

'Ach, I know, love. Men arenae supposed tae think about it like that. It's swept under the carpet.'

'Well, you didnae dae that, Frank, you were always there for me. But what a terrible tragedy for Rathlin. I'll never forget the wee wean's face. She was so peaceful like she was sleeping. I said it at the time. Rathlin didnae let it hit her but tried tae pretend it wasnae happening.'

'I know, but we all grieve differently. Our Catherine might be the same.'

Ellen interrupts. 'Is Catherine your granddaughter, the one whose baby…'

They don't let her finish, nodding their heads, saying *died* with actions rather than words. They are kind that way and Ellen appreciates their thoughtfulness. It still astonishes her when it happens, people being kind. Ellen watches them sink into one another, their love intense and settled. She sees herself and Breacán in their place, knowing that this was the future they were supposed to have. Strong and unbreakable. Frank rubs Frances's hand with the back of his and she takes it, clasping her fingers around his.

'Ellen, you need tae be kinder tae Rathlin.'

Ellen nods at Frances. Her voices are quiet, silenced by the death of a child.

'This is between us now, but I mind she got really drunk one night. She told me what happened.' She turns tae Frank and he nods back, giving her the encouragement she needs to carry on. 'She just started talking about it so I let her speak. God knows she needed tae.' Ellen considers reaching out her hand but remembers three's a crowd. 'She could tell that something really serious was wrong when she wiz in labour but the midwife was telling her tae stop being so dramatic. Rathlin thinks she was judging her because she was so young. It's just terrible so it is.'

Ellen's about to say that she was only seventeen when she had Barra but she's not getting the chance. Frank is in there, keeping her on the outside.

'Seventeen isnae that young, love. You were no much older when you had your first...'

'Miscarriage, Frank. It's a horrible word. It sounds so cold, like we're talking about a train that went down the wrong track.' Frances is curling her own fingers then tightening her grip on Frank's hand.

'It's no easy, is it. Life.'

Frances is trying to keep eye contact with Ellen. She's back in the circle.

'No, it's no. Rathlin had this excruciating pain right down her back, but they were telling her she was exaggerating, that the pain couldnae be that bad.'

238

Ellen instinctively rubs her own back, pressing into it with her knuckles. Aonghus was with her when Barra was born. Holding her hand, saying the right things, being kind even though he was helping her deliver someone else's child.

I'm sorry, Aonghus, I didnae appreciate how hard that wiz for you. The only thing you ever did tae let me down was kill yourself but even then you did it knowing that I'd have Breacán.

Frances is still dealing with her own memories. 'And then when the wean's heid came out she was facing Rathlin. The cord was tight around her neck. She was blue. Rathlin said it was like she was watching it happen tae somebody else.'

'Jesus, that's horrendous. Was the baby dead?' Ellen has used an outside voice. She feels embarrassed, like she has piped up with a question during a minute's silence. Heat rushes through her, as if she's walking on fire. Frances doesn't seem to care.

'No, she wasnae, that's the saddest part. They got her out and cut the cord and got her breathing. Rathlin said it wiz a miracle as the same had happened tae her twin brother when he was born. He wasnae breathing right away.'

Breacán. He'd told her Rathlin saved him. It was bloody ridiculous. She was a new born baby. It pissed her off that Rathlin held that over him, so much so that he didn't want to hurt her. He owed her so much because of that. Apparently.

Hurt her? What about me for fuck's sake. This secret is hurting me.

'What happened tae Rathlin's baby then?'

'Well, they let Rathlin have a wee cuddle and they said cos she was so early...' Frances is turning her attentions to Frank. 'About six weeks early. Mind we got just such a shock when Rathlin came tae the door saying she was in labour.'

For fuck's sake, how long does it take this pair tae tell a story?

'Dae you know what, Ellen?' Frank is taking up the story and Ellen suppresses a sigh of relief.

Maybe he'll speed it up a bit.

But the voices are back, asking why she was such a dick to Aonghus, why she didn't just make it work instead of falling for Breacán.

That's obvious. I loved him when I met him. Right away. First time.

'We hardly knew Rathlin then. Whit an introduction.'

Ellen wants to roll her eyes. There was no need to break the thread with such a stupid comment but he's old, give him a break. She asks the question again. 'So what happened then?' She directs it to Frances, deciding she might be a better storyteller after all. 'Rathlin must have been terrified.'

'Well, at that point she thought it wiz going tae be okay. Loads of babies are born that wee so they said she'd be fine. Isabella went tae be cared for in an incubator and Rathlin was taken tae a ward. But the wee lassie started struggling wae an infection. I know Rathlin got tae spend the last minutes wae her but dear god, hen, how dae you deal wae seeing yer child taking its last breath.'

Ellen is horrified. That's the word she thinks. It's horrific, absolutely horrific. 'Did Breacán help her through it?'

'No, she didnae even tell him about it, swore us tae secrecy. She said she didnae want tae hurt him. That's how much she cares about her brother. But secrets are poison, hen, so you need tae tell her about you an' Breacán, whether he comes out of that coma or no. Stop hiding behind houses an' tell the lassie the bloody truth. Yous are treating her like shit, ye really are, the pair of ye.'

Ellen agrees. She stands up, knowing her legs are taking her to Rathlin. She lets them move, forwards. She's letting herself move forward.

Chapter Thirty-Five

Rathlin

The hospital cafe

Rathlin agrees to talk to Ellen but she urges her out the door quickly. They will go to the cafe. Breacán has already heard too much, even from his distant *There*. They walk quietly, Rathlin in front of Ellen. She can feel her steps in line with hers. The corridor floors are shiny, like the reflection of a torch. She wants to sit on its polished surface, cross legged, her mouth tightly shut but instead she'll talk about the moment that replaced her life.

She takes Ellen back to the day Isabella was born. The words come out like a flowering tree but the beauty isn't there. Her tone is bleak, matter of fact. Her arms are tucked tightly around her back, her hips edging forward on the plastic chair. She is hot but she keeps her jawbone moving, her tongue hypnotised by the past.

Rathlin sees Ellen searching for the courage to speak.

When she finally does, her words emerge softly. 'I'm so sorry Rathlin. You must have been terrified. And you knew something was wrong didn't you? Frances said you were telling the midwife there was a problem.' Ellen has so many questions.

Rathlin knows she's probing, but it's better than the insufferable sound of silence. Breacán knows the truth, even from wherever *there* is.

'I was, but I didnae know anything about childbirth then.

241

I've read so much since. A posterior birth is quite common and it doesnae mean there's anything wrong with the baby. It just makes labour particularly painful because of the way the baby's back is lying against yours.'

'But whit about the cord, wasn't it strangling her?'

My darling Isabella.

Rathlin can see her. Most days that moment flashes into her head, the moment she lost her identity and found a new one as a mother. Her little girl's blue face, her eyes open, staring at her from between her legs, a cord wrapped around and around her neck.

'Again, tons of babies are born wae the cord around their neck. It looks pretty terrifying but the baby's breathing through the cord not their windpipe so it's no so bad.'

'So what happened? A baby doesnae just die.'

Rathlin pauses. Ellen is pushing her, not understanding the privilege of Rathlin's willingness to respond. She remembers her mother telling her that babies share the characteristics of their parents, one from her, one from him. Breacán has Mum's colour. She used to be disappointed that she didn't have it, but her mum gave it to her anyway, in Isabella. She smiles. Mum would have loved that.

'Look, Ellen, sometimes babies do just die. She was early, her wee lungs weren't ready so she couldnae cope. It's ma fault for no keeping her safe inside me until her due date.' Rathlin can see Isabella's face, her eyes closed, her lips parting slightly but there's no sound. Not anymore.

'I don't know how you've managed tae get through this.'

Rathlin clears her throat and with it, the image. She meets Ellen's inquisitive gaze head on. 'Ach, you'd be surprised, people find ways to cope. Me and Breacán found a way to, after Mum and Dad died. I coped by hating the world and he coped by withdrawing. I wish Mum had been there after Isabella but she wiznae so I just did what I could tae survive.'

'Fuckin hell, I'm sorry. I've been such a cow but ye could at least have told Breacán. He's yer twin. He could have been there for ye.'

Fuck you, Ellen it's because he's my twin. I saved him fae the pain.

'I had Barra at seventeen an' all. We were just weans ourselves but at least I had Aonghus.'

Rathlin is feeling something new. Curiosity. She doesn't know anything about Ellen's back story, other than her being homeless when Aonghus met her. She had never wondered why.

'What about yer Mum an' Dad? Were they around when ye had Barra?'

'Na, I wish. They died. When I was five. Left me at home alone whilst they went out tae score heroin. They were teachers an' all, the pair of them, an' should have known better. But there you go, they OD'd an' left me an' the cat tae a life of shite.'

Rathlin can picture her. A version of Barra at home alone, frantic, scared, wishing it was all a bad dream.

'That's no the same cat you've got the now is it?'

'Whit, Hamish? God no, just the same name. Breacán bought him for me.'

'Lucky you. He never bought me as much as a plain loaf.' She says sorry immediately but she doesn't have to. She and Ellen are still doing the *thing*.

'It wiz a surprise. I was upset wan day missing my ma and da and he appeared wae a wee fur ball. He thought a new Hamish might be a way for me tae keep their memory alive.'

'So we're both orphan Annies. Sometimes I wonder if it wiz for the best, for me, no you. Seeing her grandchild die would have broke Mum's heart.'

Rathlin wants to rub her hands on long grass now that

the secrets are soaking her fingertips. She needs to go back to Breacán but she doesn't want to chase Ellen away in the middle of their *thing*. She rests on the windowsill and gently points out that Barra will be getting out of nursery soon.

'Aye, I'm no likely tae forget about her, Rathlin. Sorry, I'm no meaning tae be sarcastic. I'm just nervous as I need tae be honest wae you too. I'm just gaunnae spit it out real quick an' go.'

Rathlin presses her weight against the window and takes a breath. She feels as if she's going to fall, even before Ellen speaks.

'Me and Breacán, we've been seeing each other. For years, ever since I got here wae Aonghus. He didnae know until the other day but Barra is his wee lassie. She's your niece. And here, he gied me this. Mibbae ye can watch it until Breacán's better.'

Rathlin doesn't need to ask Ellen to leave. Her hair is already a shadow beyond the door frame but the room is still pulsing. She wonders where the strange energy is coming from and then she realises that it's in her chest. She's walking through the rubble of what she thought was her life.

She doesn't notice her mother's engagement ring on the table in front of her, three small diamonds perched on gold shoulders, the light of her mother's life glinting again.

Chapter Thirty-Six

Ellen

The Forest behind Ballynoe. The morning of Breacán's accident

Ellen is waiting at the east side of Ballynoe. She is keeping out of view, as requested. She's looking at the weather app on her phone for what must be the tenth time since she got here. It's already light but she hasn't missed the sun coming up.

They are meeting at sunrise but there's still a minute to go. A whole minute. She can feel the beginnings of warmth on her back so she turns around. The sun is a fire red, a proper arrival, shorn of the dance of the million veils. There's not a cloud in the sky and the sun is stretching its fingers, an orange glow circumventing everything around her. She checks the scene again just to be sure, knowing that sunshine in summer can be deceptive.

Isn't everything deceptive?

The dew is shimmering in its golden light so she turns around to face the wall. As she spins, she catches her shadow on the gable, a towering majestic presence. She checks the text message again. She wasn't going to look at it. She was angry after the fight, when he walked out of the bedroom and quietly shut the door behind him. There's something so much more dramatic about a silent exit. The impact is stronger.

There was a tingle in her stomach that scared her. Maybe

he meant it. He'd had enough. She opened the text and knew she should say yes when he asked to meet, his words all calm and orderly on the screen.

I need to see you. Come, please. We can meet at dawn. Wait for me at the sun wall. x

She's on edge, not knowing if this will be different or just more of the same. And yet there's still fire in her. She's fighting an urge to knock on the door and brazenly announce her arrival to Rathlin. She changes gear, cursing Rathlin. She always has to hide when she's around. *Wish she would just fuck off home* scrambles for attention in her head but the words fall like a stone when she sees him.

When Breacán comes into view his backdrop is a golden cloak. Ellen is mesmerised by it, so much so she forgets to watch his gait, to check if he needs any help. She often helps, leaning into his side, acting as a crutch, even though he won't ever ask for support. It's early morning and he's still finding his feet. His limbs are tight. He's using the ground to direct him, a solid base to press his joints into action. Ellen leans awkwardly in to embrace him but he pulls away, his neck turning from side to side. He's scanning, his elbows pinned to his sides.

'What's wae the drama? There's nobody about.'

He asks her to hush, whispering to remind her that Rathlin's still asleep. He tilts into her neck, his breath warm on her cheek, his hair settling for a moment on hers. She lets it encompass her like a hen brooding its nest.

'Come on, we'll go tae the woods. We need tae talk.'

He looks sad. He's had enough. He's still finished with you.

Ellen's trying to quell the riot in her head but he does it for her. He smiles. There. That's all it takes. He loves her. The words circle around her, fairy wings fluttering in the morning light. Breacán's face is puffed with emotion. His grey cheeks are tinged with pink.

It's okay, darling, I feel it too.

He takes her hand and urges her to follow him along the concrete path. Breacán's heavy boots are pitching the surface when there's a piercing cry, like a magpie alerting its young to danger. The white stone edges map the route away from the house and Breacán is eagerly following it. Ellen is taking two-step strides behind him, catching him with confidence as she reaches the old farm's boundary wall. Breacán has slowed his pace. Sheltered from prying eyes, they pause to look at the house they've left behind.

The exterior hasn't been painted in decades and yet its whiteness is swallowing the sun. The walls are pulsing the rays, bouncing the light towards the liquorice-coloured slated roof. The days are shortening. Ellen watches Breacán staring at the source of the illumination, knowing that he's thinking it won't be long before the sun begins to disappear into the night while it is still early afternoon. He's always thinking about the light and the hours of the day, charting them so he can frame them around his work.

They walk on and the path narrows, pushing Ellen behind Breacán. She welcomes his lead. His strong back is guiding her. She's watching its broadness, the way it devours the sun. She stretches the fingers of her free hand but doesn't touch, holding it in front of his back as if she were browning toast.

As soon as they curl beyond the crest of the hill, Breacán pauses to rest on a drystone wall. He pulls Ellen towards him and she pretends to pull it back, laughing as she softens and accepts him. He keeps hold of her hand but he doesn't speak. The silence again. It's awkward. Painful.

'Shall we keep going for a bit?'

She nods, flowing in his tide as he pushes on through the trees, the thick bracken underfoot like a kelp farm harvesting at sea. They walk in silence, the stillness a spider's web, poised to steal any utterances they dare to make. They are following a path created by footsteps of the past into the small forest sheltering the coastline at the end of the fields.

Ellen stops. She needs time to think. *What the fuck's going on here?* She rests her back against the rusty bark of a Scots pine. Her t-shirt snags as she slides down its girth. Breacán has stopped too and is bending his knees slowly as his body falls into the vacant space beside Ellen.

'Budge over. We could pretend we're on a wee day out tae the cinema.' He drops to the ground beside her, exhaling as his muscles relax, his joints sighing at the joy of rest. Ellen is rubbing her feet into thick black roots protruding from the soil, their glossy surface rounded like a beetle's back.

'You're such a romantic.' She's teasing, gently, taking care not to push each other back to where they've come from, to the moment when he said it was over. She leans into the moss and picks up a pinecone. She brushes the mud from it, watching as it crumbles back into the earth. 'Here, take this as a token of my undying love for ye.' She hands it to him, watching as Breacán accepts it. He lowers his eyes and she sees the angst. It's there in his cheeks, in the way the skin is sinking into the bone. She can tell he's grinding his teeth, swallowing words he doesn't want to reveal. She keeps it light. Not wanting to hear them either.

'Whit's up, dae you no like it? It kind of reminds me of us.'

Breacán shakes his head, his features giving into laughter that dashes into the blackened whin up the hill.

'Let me get this right. You think we're like a pinecone?' He's frowning at it. Ellen pushes in closer, excited to explain.

'Listen an' learn fae the master.' She lifts the cone from his fingers and raises it up so they can both see it. 'This, Breacán, is a female cone. You'll have seen tons of them before. Everyone pretty much has.'

'Okay, so you're telling me that you're common as muck?'

Sarcasm. That's cute. He's relaxed. Carry on, Ellen, he's back.

'Very funny, dick face. Patience. Will ye let me finish?'

'Yes, Miss, no, Miss, three bags full, Miss.'

'You are worse than Barra, dae you know that?' Ellen pokes him hard in the stomach and he pulls away. She ignores him, continuing with her story. 'So, Scots pine trees are monoecious.'

'They're mono-whit-ish?'

'Jeez, did Aonghus no teach you this? They're monoecious, no delicious, or superstitious, they're monoecious which means that both girl an' boy flowers grow on the same tree – different kinds of flowers mind – and then the female flowers, once the wind has done its thing with them, go green and then turn intae wee cones like this.'

'Ah got ye. This is basically a wee flower that's turned tae wood after a shag by the wind. Romantic.'

'Oh for flip sake, I'm no finished. The lassie flowers grow at the tips of new shoots and the male flowers grow at the base so it's like their love is carved intae all these wee circular bumps. Here, feel them.'

Breacán presses the cone's sharp edges. Ellen is watching, knowing he doesn't care.

He's going to be an absolute dick here. He's pulling out.

'Did ye spend a lot of time down here wae Aonghus then?'

I fuckin knew it. Ellen grabs the cone and throws it at her feet. 'I wiz married tae the guy so obviously we spent time the gether.' She crunches the cone with her foot, pushing her sole firmly into the earth to ensure its circumference is shattered. Breacán's hand is reaching out but she takes a step back.

'I've got no right tae be jealous of you an' Aonghus. Fuck sake as if I don't feel guilty enough. I'm sorry.'

Ellen accepts his kiss. She's returning it, her lips sinking into him as he lifts his hands from her shoulders to her face. She helps him as he peels off his jacket.

'Are ye too warm?'

'No, but you're cold. I seen ye shivering there.'

Her arm is loose and he takes her wrist, placing her hand into the sleeve.

'Here, put this on. That's a cold breeze now we're out of the sun.' He drags the metal zip towards her chin, tugging at its dogged edges. Ellen closes her eyes and smiles when he brushes her cheek with his finger.

'I'm no five. I can look after myself.' She is smiling, despite the heaviness in her chest. She still doesn't know if everything is all right and yet she reaches for his lips. When she finds them she kisses their coldness. She strings her arms around his neck, her foot keeping a toehold in the exposed tree roots as she uses their height to climb up to meet him. She lets Breacán prise her arms apart and pull her into his chest. She's falling willingly into whatever the day has to offer.

'Aye, true, but you're still a wee wean of twenty-one, barely old enough tae drink in some countries. And I'm sorry I've been making things so difficult recently.'

Recently? How about for the last three years.

Recently continues to sting and she peels away. She turns to face the sycamore, its branches upright in preparation for the late summer gales. Its samaras have already gathered like shorn horseshoes on the ground.

'It's fine. There are worse things in life. We can both testify tae that.'

'Aye, I guess there are.'

'So why are we here? I cannae work you out. Yesterday you said you didnae want tae see me again. I should have told you where tae go when you texted.'

'Ellen, you've no idea how glad I am that you didnae dae

that. I'm sorry about yesterday. I was a prick. I'm gaunnae tell Rathlin. Today. I just want a few hours wae her an' then I'll tell her that I love you. That I want tae spend ma life wae ye.'

Protect, protect, protect. What if he's lying. He'll no do it. He will do it. Will he?

'Did I just miss the forked lightning that zapped you on the heid? You're saying that you're gonnae tell your sister about us? After aw these years?'

'Aye, I'm fed up lying. I don't want her tae lose Mum and Dad's house. It means everything tae her. It's kinda how she keeps them alive. It's worth her hating me just tae know she's still got that.'

Alarm bells.

'So this isnae about me, it's about the fuckin house again?'

'No, it's no just about the house. Life's too short. I cannae lie anymore. I want tae tell her an' I want you tae be wae me.'

Ellen's all in. All is forgotten. Forgiven.

'We're really daein this?'

'Aye, we are.'

Ellen keeps talking, her lips hammering against Breacán's in her excitement. 'This is the most amazing thing for Barra. She's going tae be so excited that you're going tae be her daddy.'

Ding ding ding. Ding ding ding.

Ellen can feel Breacán's body weight move, his shoulders push backwards. His hips are taking him elsewhere. His arms leave her neck and there's a sharp coolness in their place, like she's fallen into a stream.

'Ellen, slow the fuck down. I cannae just be a dad overnight.'

Ellen is trying to concentrate, the voices are talking at once, all trying to grab her attention, each one thinking it's the most important. She exhales deeply, the residue of anger forming a wall of silence between them.

Just ask him outright. Why not?

'How, dae ye no want kids?'

'I never said that, I just said we need tae take it easy and no have Barra calling me Dad the morra.'

You're letting him walk all over you. He doesn't care about you, just himself and that bitch of a sister of his. You're weak. Pathetic. Play your trump card.

'Too late. You are her da. Always have been an' always will be.'

Chapter Thirty-Seven

Ellen.

The Forest behind Ballynoe.

Ellen is standing beside Breacán. He is silent. Her own voices have retreated. There is a quiet between them as if a storm has passed. She knows it is still brewing in the thickly entwined branches. She looks above her, wishing for wings. She inhales deeply, struggling to stay calm.

He's calm though and urges her to sit. She takes up the offered space, moving slowly because she doesn't want him to break the silence but he does anyway.

'How did I no realise? She's always been Aonghus's daughter tae me. I've never looked at Barra and saw my reflection.'

'We've always been so complicated. It wiz one less thing for ye to worry about.'

'That's patronising bullshit. Was I just some kind of joke tae you, a daft prick who didnae even recognise his own daughter?'

'Of course ye weren't. I love you. Aonghus loved you, for fuck sake, that's why we did it.' She leans forward and tries to separate Breacán's clutched hands but he tightens them.

'Whit, he knew an' all? Jesus, I'm supposed tae believe that yous lied tae me about my own daughter cos you loved me. Okay then, explain. Let's have a laugh at least.'

Ellen clears her throat. *Fuck, this is not how this was supposed tae happen. Well, you've done it now. Speak or run*. She chooses fight. 'It's complicated. Aonghus needed me. If I left he'd have done something stupid, I know he would of. It worked the way it was. He had me an' I had you.'

'Ellen, you refuse tae tell me the truth even now. We both know what he did. Fuck, I cannae believe he knew I wiz stabbing him in the back. Is it our fault he killed himself?'

Ellen looks up beyond the trees. She can see nothing but sky. 'No, it wasnae. Aonghus was depressed because of what he went through but he found a way tae save me an' I owed him. He needed me. And he loved you too. He wanted you tae be happy. And by the way, how ye feel now has no bearing on what ye would have felt then so don't be all self-righteous. You'd have told me you didnae want a wean.'

Ellen knows she isn't misrepresenting him. They were both consumed by grief when they met. They needed to be bound, body and spirit, but there was never any talk of a baby. He's blindsided now but then he would have left her.

'Who knows, Ellen, because I've had that chance tae choose taken away. Why wait until the now tae tell me? She's my wee lassie. Dae you no think I'd like tae have known that? She's four-years-old, for fuck's sake.'

'Is that supposed tae be a serious question? Fuck sake you're telling me it's over half the time because ye care more about yer sister. Why would I want Barra tae be caught up in yer self-indulgent whining about no wanting tae hurt Rathlin? She's always been the most important thing tae ye. Me and Barra cannae compete. But listen, it's no aw bad. At least you have a good relationship wae Barra. Is that no something ye can build on now ye know the truth?'

She's watching his features change, softer she thinks, but she's holding her breath anyway.

'Of course it is, I love her like she's ma own already but it doesnae make what you did tae me right. Ma head's about

254

tae explode wae this. I don't think I can dae this, Ellen. We're just poisoning each other. We always have been.'

Ellen can't wait. She needs to hold him. She needs to bring him back to her. She pulls Breacán's head towards her. Her fingers clasp his jawline, her heart skipping a beat when she feels its tightness. The sun is slipping through elm leaves, forming little overlapping circles on the fissured bark.

'Stop. Please. Ten minutes ago you were gonnae tell Rathlin that ye love me and want tae be with me. And what about your wee lassie? I even named her after ye. Mind how ye told me Barra was supposed tae be yer name before ye were born? That's why she's Barra, she's your daughter. How can ye walk away fae her now?'

He stands up, his shadow drowning the circles with darkness. 'Don't blackmail me, I've had as much of that as I can take.'

Ellen lifts her chin. 'You don't have tae. I'm sorry. The house is yours an' Rathlin's, of course it is. Let's just go back tae where we were.' She's on her feet too, her fingers searching for the warmth of his neck.

'Ellen we can't undo the fact that all of a sudden I've got a wee lassie wae ye. I'm gonnae have tae tell Rathlin about us, and then about Barra. This is going tae hurt her.'

Well that makes a change, hurting her. It's usually me that takes the hit.

The voices are intense. He's hurting too. Good. He should be hurting. Breacán is walking. He needs to think. You do, my love. You've had a shock with this but this is also a good day. We're going to be a family. A family. Ellen is inhaling short sharp breaths. She hasn't had a family since she was five-years-old.

They are still walking, their feet echoing in the hard earth. The sea is close and Ellen is imagining its familiar beach, the waves sieving the sand. Time is different there on the shore. She's thinking about the ease with which Breacán swims against the incoming tide, and how he dries his wet back sitting next to his shoeless daughter, a bucket and spade in her hands. Absorbed by his tales of water wraiths, Ellen would not be able to coax her away. She hears a gull crack its call overhead, breaking her comfort. She is back with Breacán and his disappointment in her.

There's always something.

Breacán slows his pace and they grind to a halt. His shoulders slump as he steps on a small embankment where the beach will come into view. Her heart is racing. He'll hear the sea, its rush swirling hard and fast in his ears.

'Shit, I'm sorry Ellen, I didnae even think when I started walking this way. Are ye okay? C'mon we'll turn back.'

She hadn't even noticed the incline is stretching in front of her. Her voices want her to stop but her legs keep walking. She's ready to face it.

'It's fine, c'mon.' She opens her arms, stretching them wide as though she had wings. She faces the tree. The bark is discoloured where the bullet hit, its shell burrowed deeply into the trunk. The blood, albeit blackened, is still visible. The gradient has drawn it to the softened earth below. She had found him there, at the foot of the tree, hours after the stricken search. 'I could never work out why he did it here. It doesnae make any sense tae me.'

'Maybe it's because of ma mum an' dad. It's no the same place they died but it's no that far. He could have been confused in the pitch dark.'

It was Ellen who found the note from Aonghus but it could just as easily have been Breacán. He often visited when Aonghus was out and Barra was taking her nap. The note didn't say a lot. It didn't need to. Ellen knew it all already. Enough was enough. Ellen takes her hands from the tree and thrusts them deep into her pockets. She turns to face

Breacán. She needs to connect through the searing loss children feel when parents die. Ellen and Breacán share that as well as a daughter.

'I expected him tae do it at Kebble. That's where the biggest part of him had already died, back when he was just a wee boy. I should have been there for him more, but I wasnae.'

She's looking at Breacán, unsure why he's not agreeing, why his head is shaking back and forward.

'I'm sorry you and Barra couldnae save him. He was a good man, he really was. He loved my da, and you too, in the way he needed to. An' I love you, Ellen.' Ellen can hear branches rustle as Breacán drops to his knees. She looks at his head, imagining a bullet. 'I had planned tae do this today, even before I knew about Barra.' Ellen is swallowing mouthfuls of her own hair, unable to see what's in front of her except the fear that something awful has happened to him. When she finally hears his words, her voices are silenced by shock.

'I want ye tae have this. It's my ma's ring, her engagement ring.'

Ellen folds Breacán's fingers, hiding his palm from magpies. 'But what about Rathlin?'

'She's my sister Ellen. I cannae be with her in that way.'

Ellen's laughter tumbles over them and she wonders what the ring will look like in the afternoon sun.

'But seriously, Rathlin has always said she'd be too sad tae wear it. She said I should give it to the woman I want tae marry. And that's you. Will ye take it and be ma wife Ellen?'

Ellen has no words, no voices. Finally she finds a response which comes directly from her. 'Yes.'

That was enough. Ellen lets him slips the ring on her finger. She nods when he tells her to keep it safe, their secret, until he tells Rathlin later that day.

Chapter Thirty-Eight

Rathlin

The field between Ballynoe and Kebble

Rathlin can feel Breacán's absence. She's thinking about before, when a darkness was falling in the living room. They were laughing a little, easing back into some semblance of a relationship. He was curled up on the sofa, falling asleep, his body still on top of the throw, her own carving a hollow in the seat beside him.

There's no change, but there will be a scan later in the day and then they'll know. But she already knows. She's getting ready to say goodbye. She kisses his forehead, her fingers caressing his hand and his ears. She hopes he's listening when she tells him she'll be back.

She drives home to Ballynoe, the memory of getting there gone, as if the journey never existed. When she gets out of the car, everything has a different form because life is different now. Again.

She needs to see Ellen, know more, fill the gaps on the empty ruled lines that tell the story. The sky is fluffy white, bending gently towards the earth's jagged edges, like snow on a hilltop, but the wintery scene is an illusion as she walks to Kebble. She marches under its illusion, her boots holding her ankles taut as she pushes through the bracken. She imagines Breacán's reaction to Isabella, his isolation, loneliness, his pain because of her pain, her face crumbling when she says the words. My daughter died, Breacán, my beautiful baby girl.

She changes tack. A detour. She goes to the graveyard first. Mist hangs low on the water's edge, the soft haze lingering ghostlike above her parents, and Aonghus. She kneels beside them, her knees pushing into the soil, bone searching for bone, ashes to ashes, dust to dust. She caresses the dedication to Skye and Joseph, but her head spins when she reads the line below.

In Loving Memory of Aonghus Doherty, 1981-2016

'In Loving Memory' is a lie. She hates every fragment of the dedication. She pushes her anger into the cold stone wanting to topple it out of place. The emotion that beats against her back is like a winter wave. It's always there, a tightening of her throat when she remembers what she can of the day her mum and dad died. Aonghus. The gun. The blood. The silence. And a menace that hangs in the air. It gnaws at her but she settles back into the truth she trusts.

The word forgiveness isn't in her vocabulary, despite what others might think. She climbs to her feet, retreating, discarding the pregnancy test she bought at the hospital pharmacy into the wee bin on the lamppost at the end of the cemetery path. She ignites a bit of paper and tosses it in beside it. She watches it burn, knowing that the fire won't change a single thing.

Rathlin begins the climb back up the hill in front of her, the path eventually forking in two directions, one to Kebble and one to Ballynoe. She heads for Kebble.

Rathlin braces herself. Someone is coming towards her, crossing into her domain. She is uncertain about meeting Ellen in the open where the surroundings could be claimed by either one of them. She opens the collar of her jacket, lets in the cool air from the summit above. She wishes Breacán were here, everywhere. She tunes in for news on him and finds nothing. He's still alive, or whatever he is while attached to those machines.

She forges forward, clenching her fists, her fingers gradually uncurling when Anita lowers her hood. It isn't Ellen.

'Hey, I was wondering when I'd see you again. You okay? Sorry tae hear about yer brother.'

Rathlin smiles back, her lips forming the shape of thanks.

'No prizes for guessing that ah'm *that* pal of Ellen's.' Rathlin is confused and flashes her eyes, undoubtedly with suspicion. Anita explains. 'Ah'm the wan helping her wae the legals for the hoose. Ah'm no a lawyer, but ah studied law at uni. That's enough for Ellen. Listen ah'm sorry about everything.'

Rathlin shakes her head. She hadn't made the connection, hadn't had the time to think about any of that. She presents her hand. Anita shakes it and the two of them laugh at the formality of their second meeting.

'I should have worked it out but Frances didnae say your name when she said she met Ellen wae her lawyer pal.'

'Aye, we bumped into her when she was out wae the dog. We thought mibbae she had an update on your brother. How's he doing by the way? An' where is the wee dog?' Anita looks past Rathlin, searching for Molly in the field beyond her.

'She's in the house wae Frances. I came straight fae the hospital.'

'Ellen's no long back an' all. She said there wiznae any change?'

Rathlin knows the bike is close by but she's resisting the urge to look. She doesn't have to because she knows exactly what a mangled mess it is. 'I thought I'd lost him in that moment.' Her eyes lift to find Anita's. 'I suppose I shouldnae kid myself. I have. He's in a coma.' Rathlin can hear her voice tail off with the weight of the words. 'There's no much hope.' Rathlin follows Anita's gaze to where she didn't want to go. To the crash site.

'Ah don't know how you're managing tae be so strong. Ellen's the closest ah have tae family an' ah would freak out if anything happened tae her.'

Rathlin knows she's waiting for a response, but she's no energy left so when it comes it's weak. 'Guess you don't need tae be blood related tae have a bond.'

Rathlin lets the silence between them settle, then turns away to the calm of the sea. 'So, what you up tae then? You heading down tae the village?'

'Just getting some air while Ellen's getting the wean fae school. Might keep clear for a while, house is like a bomb's hit it and she'll flip that ah didnae tidy it. One wee lassie can dae a lot of damage ye know.'

Rathlin's mind is back with Isabella. When she returns, Anita is watching. Rathlin knows she knows. About Ellen and Breacán and the ring. She's hoping there is nothing more.

'Ah don't suppose ye fancy coming a wee wander with me, show me the sights?'

On the other side of the conversation Rathlin is looking at Anita, trying to decide if she should even answer. Sightseeing is not on her to-do list. She responds, trying to find an energy to match Anita's pace.

'See when you got off the bus an' walked along the street, the one before you turned up the road to get tae Kebble?'

'Ah dae an' it'll stay long in the memory.'

'Well, that's the sights. You've seen it all.' Rathlin is trying to be witty but she can hear the flatness of her voice.

Anita pushes her way into Rathlin's red zone. 'Sorry, ah shouldnae be joking about stuff. Ellen texted me an tellt me that she told ye about her and yer brother. Ah'm guessing that's aw ye need on top of everything else.'

Rathlin shrugs, a person she wasn't a moment before. She ignores the comment. 'So Ellen's definitely no in?'

'No, like I just said, she went tae get Barra.'

Rathlin looks at her phone, no news, no calls, no nothing. 'I need tae talk tae her.' She's looking into the distance, in the direction of the school.

'Come up tae the house an' wait. Ah guess you'll want tae see Barra an' all now you know yer her aunt. Auntie Rathlin's got a no bad ring tae it.'

'I'm no sure I'm ready tae have a laugh about it all, Anita.'

'Sorry, that wiz shitty. Barra must be a major shock on top of everything, but it's better out in the open.' She takes a cigarette from a packet, offering one to Rathlin. She turns to shelter from the breeze.

Rathlin follows her lead and lifts a cigarette to her lips. She leans into Anita, her fingers flicking the lighter until it ignites.

'This is a first fir me.'

Rathlin watches Anita lips open and close around a cigarette, her head sheltering in the inside of her jacket.

'What's a first?' Rathlin follows the smoke from Anita's cigarette as it bellows off into the distance.

'It's the first time ah've considered asking a lassie out in the middle of the darkest of traumas. No the most romantic oav moments.'

Rathlin draws her jacket closer to her chest. 'Timing is everything.'

It definitely is because Rathlin can see Barra and Ellen coming towards them. Barra's running ahead, excited, she thinks, to see her. But maybe it's Anita. She must know Anita better. Rathlin's staring. This is Breacán's daughter. On the day she tells her brother her baby girl is dead she learns he has one of his own. She can see her properly. She has his gait, not his arthritic limping but his bullish way of sending his torso forward first, his legs catching up. Her hair is the same colour as Breacán. God, it's identical and her eyes, her cheeks, the shape, like his, and their mother's. She has his skin colour too. Rathlin shakes her head. She can feel her heart stretching inside her chest like a rubber band that's about to snap. Her own little girl should be running across the field to meet her. Her beautiful little Isabella. She looks at Barra and sees Isabella. They would have looked so alike, the Doherty genes strong in both. Almost twins. And with that word, she knows what she must ask.

'When's her birthday?'

Ellen is out of breath so her words are laboured when she responds. 'March. How?'

Rathlin is bending down, moving closer to Barra. Still looking, still seeing her own little girl in Barra. She needs the confirmation. She needs to know.

'What date in March?'

'Rathlin, there's no debate about who her dad is.' Rathlin watches her turn her head, making sure Barra can't hear. 'Like I said tae you, I just wish I'd told him sooner.'

'Sooner?'

'Aye. Sooner than the morning of the accident, when he gave me the ring. But he was gaunnae do that anyway. He had it aw planned. I told ye aw this at the hospital he'd only just found out. What's going on Rathlin?'

'I don't think that really sunk in earlier. That's good.'

'Good? I'm no sure that anything is good about this. I'm sorry we lied tae ye, but there were reasons, there's always reasons, I guess, and I know fae experience that that doesnae make anything right. He wiz gonnae tae tell ye. Everything.'

'It is good. Good that he knew. That morning outside Kebble. Before the accident. He knew that Barra wiz his wee lassie and when he wiz hugging her, he wiz hugging his own flesh and blood. I'm happy he got the chance tae dae that. I did too, wae ma wee lassie.'

Ellen is quiet.

'Ye still havenae answered my first question. Whit date in March wiz Barra born?'

Ellen touches Rathlin's arm, leaving a ghostly imprint. 'It's the twenty-fifth.'

'It's the same day. Isabella and Barra were born on exactly the same day. No the same year obviously but they share a birthday, just like me and Breacán. Ellen, that means something.'

Chapter Thirty-Nine

Breacán

The Forest behind Ballynoe, August 12th, 2005

Breacán's not awake but he's aware. He's not travelling in a dream like Rathlin but he is going willingly in the direction the road is taking him, searching for answers, craving his mother's voice, his father's firm hand that almost always ends in a warm hug.

It is their twelfth birthday. He is visiting *Then*. This is the day the end began. He knows that what is happening to him now, in his hospital bed, can be traced back to that day.

Breacán is watching his sister riding her new bike. He is happy because she's happy because it's white, a boy's bike, nothing pink to taint her sense of self. He's remembering the moment. He was smiling *Then* and he is now, but he did not know *Then* that his happiness would soon be stolen.

He's still back there, on their twelfth birthday with the presents they have bought for one another. The gifts are the same, a meeting of minds, a moment of impenetrable closeness.

His friend, Annie, is with him and his mum is being kind, getting her a drink, making sure she has food. Dad is winking, giving the thumbs up behind her back, having a father-son moment with Breacán. Even though he's smiling and making the right gestures Breacán's not interested but he doesn't want to hurt her feelings by telling her to go away. He knows she's changing, that they are both changing. Annie's carving out time for the two of them, shutting out Rathlin, edging onto another path where he will never catch up. He didn't know *Then* that time was something you inherited, something that was passed on to someone else. He is passing his on now, but not yet, he needs to taste the cold sweetness of the past before the clock stops.

Breacán is watching Rathlin place her bike against the wall. She cannot see him and he's not really there, not *Then*. But he's there now, watching her walk down the path, going in her own direction.

Breacán lets go of his adult self and returns fully. He is twelve. It is his birthday. He needs to be with his sister, to watch out for her in the final moments of the lives they used to live.

His mum and Annie answer his question before he asks it. Rathlin's just away for a wee wander. She'll be back in time for the picnic.

Breacán watches Rathlin walk away from Ballynoe and though he's only twelve, he feels its significance. He's sad that they are not wandering together, stealing hours alone before the birthday picnic. They are in a different class now. Mum and Dad explained, it wasn't good for them to spend so much time together. They'd looked at one another and asked why. He's remembering Rathlin's temper, her outrage at the suggestion that they separate on school days, find new friends, do less with each other and more with others. He remembers trying to express his anger too, but it only came out as silence, a sullen huff, an inability to fight his corner. He remembers the feeling of retreating into himself and doing nothing.

He's walking down the hill with Annie now. Mum and Dad are at the door. Mum is shouting but the words are lost in the wind. He's shrugging, moving on beyond the gate, listening as Annie explains that Mum is probably reminding

266

him not to be late. She's taking his hand and he's letting her.

Breacán is ready to go back and get ready for the picnic when he sees his uncle Aonghus in the hay field. He is staggering. Breacán lowers his eyes. Aonghus is drunk. He's always drunk these days. His granddad is walking alongside Aonghus, annoyance falling from his lips, his head bobbing, his shoulders uneven. Granddad is angry. He's always angry these days.

Aonghus is cutting across his father, trying to block him. That's when Breacán feels fear. He drops Annie's hand. She's not happy. She stamps her feet and asks what's wrong with him.

Don't you like me anymore?

Breacán doesn't reply. He has forgotten that Annie is there. He's watching his granddad, noting the flames that crackle in his every movement. He tries to avoid eye contact. But when his granddad looks at him, in that glance he sees all the future pain.

Aonghus still has a way to go to fully cross the field. He's holding Breacán's attention as he staggers nearer, raising his arms, shouting *Happy Birthday*. Through his fear Breacán smiles. He loves Uncle Aonghus. He doesn't love his granddad. He's never told anyone that. He never will. How can he?

Despite the warnings, loud now, Breacán hears himself say, yes, I'm coming, when his granddad shouts at him to come to the woods. He follows. What else can he do? His granddad has issued instructions.

Aonghus is calling out. Telling him to stop. To turn back.

Don't you go into those woods, Breacán Doherty, it's not safe. Get home now to Ballynoe.

Breacán hears Aonghus but he can't defy his granddad or persuade his legs to change direction. There is no going back. His grandfather demands his attention. He demands that he follow him into the forest.

Breacán obeys, following his grandfather into the woods even though he knows what's going to happen to him once he gets there.

He's back *Now*, knowing that it's over, that he's going to die and that Rathlin will be at his side watching.

Chapter Forty

Rathlin

Breacán's hospital room

The scan results are back. The doctor's words pierce Rathlin. No. Brain. Activity.

She presses her temples with her fingernails, trying to contain the pain. If it escapes, she'll tumble to the floor. Part of her wants to believe they've got it wrong. Completely and utterly. Watching her brother, she knows he's travelling, that he's thinking and feeling despite what they are saying. He's on a journey. She can feel his movement even though she can't see it.

Where to though?

It's not a question he can answer. He looks busy. Rathlin tells the doctor. My brother, he's thinking about something. Is he begging them to stop?

Don't turn off that machine. Don't kill me.

They explain again with calmness and authority. This time the nurse doesn't take Rathlin's hand but sweeps her fingers across her face, mopping up tears. Then they stand back. The voice becomes firmer, the language clearer.

I'm sorry. He's already dead.

Rathlin is holding her hand inside his. His warm hand. There is blood running through his veins. Hot blood. Blood that is pumping to her fingers, pulsing from his heart to hers.

His heart is beating because of the machine.

They explain as if saying it for the first time. Because she isn't taking it in.

Once we turn off the machine, Breacán will be still. Forever quiet. Does she want anyone to be with her?

No, definitely not. We came into this life the two of us. It should just be me. I'm his other half.

And then she panics. Rathlin searches her brother for an answer. She runs her finger along his cheekbone and then under his chin. She rests her hand alongside his neck. She stays still for a moment, feeling the life that's left in him and then moves her hand down and places it on his chest. She reaches over him, replacing her hand with her face, her ear tuning into the rhythm of the beat. The machine's or his? It doesn't matter. She hears his message.

No. I don't want to be alone, she says. He would want his girlfriend here. His fiancée. She nods when the nurse asks if she should make the call for her. Rathlin shouts her back.

Wait. Tell her she can bring their daughter too. If she thinks it's right.

The nurse closes the blinds. The room isn't dark and it's not light. Rathlin sees the digital numbers on Breacán's machines as through a rain-soaked window. The doctor has turned off the sound and the quiet is louder than the beeping. They're leaving her alone now, they say, until Ellen gets here. Rathlin hopes she'll hurry. Then she hopes she'll stall and it won't happen and her life won't be changed forever.

A life without Breacán isn't imaginable. She decides not to try. She'll go back to Glasgow and think of him in Ballynoe. She will spend quiet moments imagining him on the farm, working, his confidence in himself building with the passing years. His skin will give in to the sun and tan a deep golden brown and his birthmark will blossom, its redness intensifying so the moment he came back to her will always be tattooed on him. She will always be a part of him in the way that he is her.

Ellen hasn't brought Barra. Rathlin is relieved but doesn't pass a remark. She accepts Ellen's embrace when she arrives, crashing through the door as if she's been running for the train and only just manages to snake through the doors as they shut.

Ellen apologises. Rathlin can't respond. She must keep her words to herself because there are so few left. Instead, she smiles, kind of, pulling her lips across her face. She knows Ellen can feel the kindness of the gesture. The *thing* between them is all they have. She nods when Ellen asks if she can take his hand and Rathlin watches her walk around the bed, her knee clattering noisily off the frame when she bends down towards his face. She looks to Rathlin for approval before she kisses him gently on the lips. Rathlin knows he's still warm so is not surprised to hear Ellen says it out loud, the hopelessness of hope making her voice sing a little.

'Dae ye think they've made a mistake? He feels fine?'

Rathlin shakes her head. She's further along the journey, feeling her own heart beating slower, pushing its weight deeper into her chest.

'No, he's leaving us. I'm sorry ye cannae have that life together that ye both wanted.'

Rathlin is watching Ellen cry but she's thinking about the path to Ballynoe and how sometimes when it rains, it is lost in mist. It didn't matter to her and Breacán. They'd always find home. The navigation was rooted in their feet, the terrain embedded at birth in the tips of their toes. Even in the dimmest moonlight they'd find their way. Rathlin nods to Breacán realising that they were the way, the map. The twins, their parents, they were the human part of Ballynoe. Yes, she sighs to the non-believers, even though the conversation is with herself. Houses do have a heart and a soul.

Ellen is crying but her sobs are muffled by Breacán's hand so it sounds like the rain when it used to beat off that same path. She holds his hand against her face, his elbow still lodged on the bed. Rathlin can see that his limbs aren't loose or normal. She wants to share the thought that pops into her head but she doesn't. It seems odd, disrespectful even. He looks like the Action Man she had as a kid and she's resisting the urge to reset him, to bend his knee joint back and forth just because she can. She shakes her head, pulling herself back from the grief.

'What happens now, Rathlin?'

'We wait. We love him until he's no longer him. Until he's a shadow that we sometimes catch a glimpse of on summer days.'

Chapter Forty-One

Rathlin

Ballynoe and the Forest behind Ballynoe

Rathlin places Breacán's unopened birthday present on the kitchen table at Ballynoe and carefully straightens the creases on the wrapping paper. She rewrites the label, mouthing the words as the pen moves from left to right.

To Barra, love Aunt Rathlin.

She touches her lips with her free hand knowing that there are so many words unsaid. She puts a small ring box beside the parcel and places a note in front of it. She writes the message calmly.

Ellen, give this to Barra when the time is right.

Molly is beside her, walking expectantly in tight circles, wanting to go out. Rathlin sits on the floor and the dog follows her lead, snuggling against her legs. She can feel Molly's pulse against hers, her hunger for their story to continue.

You've heard this a million times, Molly, but seeing as you're being so sweet... Once upon a time, when ma soul was tormented by its constant need tae hold Isabella in ma arms, a wind blew and with it came a sudden warmth. That warmth was you.

Rathlin is talking to the dog's nose, her hands caressing the velvet softness of her ears.

You lightened the darkest of shadows an' put a gentle sound into a space where there was silence. God, you were so teeny tiny. So cute. Your little bendy arms an' legs. Yer red hair, just like wee Isabella's. I held ye like a wee baby, like I would have held her. I saw Frank and Frances look at each other, thinking I wiz heading for a fall. And they were right, but no in the way they thought. I wiz falling, for you. I didnae have my angel but I had you and you've been the most perfect friend since. And dae ye know what, right now Ellen an' Barra need a friend just like you. I need ye tae look after them, just like you looked after me.

Rathlin climbs back to her feet now and asks Molly to sit. Stay. Ellen and Barra will walk you when they wake. And they will keep walking you. She bends down and steals another hug, lingering into the warmth until she has to stop. Go.

She opens the front door and stops on the threshold. The pain is slowing her down but she also wants to see the hope the space used to yield. Before what's left of it turns to dust. She looks at her surroundings, remembering a time when she and Breacán thought it would be endless, a time when they were untroubled by death. She stretches her arm behind her and closes the door without turning towards it. She won't look back at the house. It won't let her go if she does.

There's a dunnock on the path, it's tininess admirable, it's appearance distinctive. Has it shuffled from the hawthorn behind the wall and the flowerbed underneath? It flicks its tail and turns, losing interest. It reminds her of the wood pigeons that breed in August and she walks to the linden looking for signs of life. She eventually finds them, the squabs only visible when her eyes give up on finding the nest. There are two, pruned and nourished, ready to expand into their lives.

Rathlin carries on, resisting the pull of Ballynoe. She's walking to the woods, to the spot where her parents died. The trees are bending in on her, their branches bowing, as she passes through. They are solemn and melancholy, in mourning for Breacán too, their leaves rustling. They create a path for her, twisting in and out, learning the magnitude of her grief. They deliver her calmly to the place. Morning is disappearing. Rathlin is leaving it behind. Already it feels too invasive and she wants it shorn like the pine needles underfoot. She finds the courage to turn, knowing Ballynoe is somewhere deep behind the trees, wobbling on unsure legs. She spies a deer asleep in the long grass in the hollow. Its black hooves are like basalt soaking the sun, a little sign of the igneous fairies of Rathlin's childhood.

She's here. Where it happened. She lies down on the hearth of heather, rolling on to her front, wriggling her hips until she has sunk into its blanket. She hauls her rucksack towards her and pulls the build-a-bear from its clenched mouth. It falls into her hand and she uses her teeth to unstitch the thread on its back. The knots are taut and singing, its tune circling overhead. A magpie is watching, waiting for a steal. Rathlin holds its gaze, her glare saying everything has already gone.

Rathlin removes the bear's stuffing, her fingers penetrating with the precision of familiarity. She pulls a silver box from the empty torso, clasping it tightly in her fist. She folds her arms across her chest, pushing her hand firmly on to her heart. Her elbows are supporting her weight but little else. She's falling and this time she won't stop. She digs her toes into the ground and clamps her knees together so she can push her body into the soil beneath the heather. When her words come, they will slip with ease into its sweet guise, the tiny flowers swallowing the sadness.

I've never come back. Not once since ye left me. Here.

Her eyes are stinging, like she might cry, but they stay dry. She carries on, her words dropping softly, like petals being peeled from a daisy.

I didnae need tae come. Every single day I have flashbacks

of you lying here, the way you were. It's horrendous. But now there's more. Hurt. Pain. I wanted tae show yous a fragment of what should have been.

Rathlin places the silver box on the heather and still it surprises her. She takes a second glance as if she's not responsible for its arrival.

I had a daughter. Isabella. She died. I bought a bear tae put in her coffin but I couldnae part with it. She'd have loved it so I keep her name band and her wee hand and foot prints inside it. I've got a wee lock of her hair too. Red hair, just like yours, Mum.

She opens the box and curls the tiny band around her fingers. She's saddened by the smallness of it each and every time she allows herself to look at it.

I don't know how tae tell you this but Breacán died. It was an accident. It was all my fault. We had a fight and I stormed off. He came racing after me and...

She's thinking about him now, seeing her and her twin on separate sides of thick glass.

He was in love. So much in love he wasnae thinking straight but he was sorting it. He was going tae get married. To Ellen. You don't know her. Long story. My heart's too broken the now tae talk much.

Her voice is breaking. A lark swoops in, assessing the intrusion before flying off into the distance.

I cannae bare tae see my brother going into the ground. Or live a life without him in it.

She's crying now, hard. She rolls over and gathers Isabella's things, holding them against her chest. She tightens her fingers around them, like trying to pull heat from a stone.

I want tae die. I've been thinking about it since Breacán...

I decided that I was gonnae shoot myself, right here, on this spot so they could all say, oh the irony, fifteen years tae the day.

Small problem. I don't have a gun. What a mastermind plan that was. Not to worry though. I've got another solution. But first I just need tae lie here and hold you both. And then, well, that will be it. I don't want this anymore, no without you, or Isabella, or Breacán. It's like I'm rattling off a shopping list aw the shit in ma life. It would be funny if it wasn't so fuckin tragic.

There I said it. We're a tragedy us Dohertys. The witches o'Ballynoe.

I was thinking that maybe I should stay. For Breacán's wee lassie. He and Ellen had a daughter. Her name's Barra. She's cute, but everything else is just cruel.

Rathlin is wondering what would what happen if she had the courage to climb the tree beside her and look back. Ballynoe would be palely lit but strong against the skyline. It wouldn't need to call to her twice, she knows that. She's anchored in it and it would drag her, puncturing her with memories like a rush of drugs. Just the good stuff, until she's inside and then it will all still be there. The Pain. The Separation. Forever this time. It's the shove she needs. She unplugs the thought and sinks with it. She won't be climbing trees today or any other day.

Barra looks like Breacán. A wee miniature wae red hair. Just like Isabella. They were born on the same day. Breacán's daughter an' my daughter. Isn't that so weird? Twins who arenae twins. Maybe there's a name for that. If there isn't there should be. Sibling twins. They would have had such a strong connection.

Rathlin can smell blood. It's heavy in her throat. She tries to clear it and it rattles like a magpie. She's going back. There. To *Then*.

Chapter Forty-Two

Rathlin

The Forest behind Ballynoe, August 12th, 2005

She's walking backwards, to the edge of the wood and everything is happening in reverse. She's hearing her mum's voice. She's remembering seeing her bike, upturned, the wheels spinning, she's rubbing her knees, seeing the blood trickle, she's fallen off but she's not too badly hurt so she carries on running. She's heading into the trees, turning sharply, her hips moving at angles, she knows where she's going, she's been here before. She's heading for them but she can't remember who she's searching for.

It's Granddad, his shirt soaked with sweat, in front of the tree, there's something in between him and the bark. She's running towards it, still not sure what it is, who it is, if it's even anything but she knows it must be something because she's crying, shouting out a word, a name, she's running through the word, snaring it only when she reaches the other side of it.

Her ears are hearing it as Breacán.

Breacán, why am I shouting Breacán? She doesn't know why. He's probably in the house with Annie, stealing their birthday time with her. She's pulling her binoculars to her eyes, snatching a peak when Granddad moves to the side, his arm on the small of his back. Whose back? She's asking, trying to see, she's running diagonally, seeing his other hand, Granddad's other hand at the base of his neck. He, him, whoever it is, has his back to her, the name she's calling, the person isn't turning around, he's not listening to her, he's listening to him.

She's running faster, tripping over, clambering back up, seeing him. Not him, another him, Aonghus is running too, his gun cocked, he's running to Breacán. He's going to shoot Breacán. She's chasing him, in line now, shouting, shouting his name as loud as she can, she's hearing her mum now, and her dad, they're shouting for her, and Breacán, their voices loud, but she's still running, getting there before Aonghus, pushing Granddad out of the way, tearing his hands from Breacán, kicking him, screaming, standing in front of her brother, seeing the shotgun is still coming, Aonghus aiming it in their direction.

Rathlin is watching everything unravel. She can see that is twelve. It is her birthday then and now. She has run to the woods. No, she didn't run. She was dragged there. She and her brother had been stolen, like the children seized by the water wraiths. They are in the forest, not the one with the gingerbread house, their forest. She's replaying the scene for the first time since Then. She's trying to save Breacán. From Granddad. He's the monster. But what about Aonghus? She wants to shout to her younger self and ask but there is nothing but phlegm in her throat.

This time she doesn't heave herself out like she normally does at the crack of dawn. This time she keeps her fingers connected to the earth. She knows she's heading here, to the monstrous scene. The place where her parents' shapes remain. She runs her hands along their imagined sculptures and glances at her hands. They are heavy. She pits them against her ears and curls up tight, making space for her brother. The ground is thrumming and there is nothing in her field of view but the past.

Twelve-year-old Rathlin is ready when the gun comes

close. She's cocked too, exactly like the butt of it. There's a sharp pain in her chest but she didn't notice then, the way the metal clattered against her chest. She's ignoring the impact, reaching for the weapon, knowing in that moment that she is going to kill him. Granddad.

She's twisting and pushing Breacán down, saving him, spinning Aonghus around the gun so she can do it. It has to be her. She must avenge her twin. Granddad's clothes will hang unused in the wardrobe and he'll rot in the ground and her brother will be safe. She's grabbing its barrel. She's only ever held it once. On birthday number eleven when Aonghus let her and Breacán shoot congealed vegetables that had grown in the weeds. Her hair was longer then, childlike, and she had tied it in a band at the base of her neck. She was older than Breacán so he had to wait. She shot first, catching nothing but her shoulder when it forced her back. They recalibrated and Breacán crossed the boundary, his shooting clearer, harder. Now she has to be the hard one.

Rathlin can see it. What's about to happen. She can see her mum and dad just out of reach. She could have stopped them coming closer *Then*, if she'd tried. She would have saved them from herself. They would have lived and Breacán would never have died. She's biting into her lip, tasting the blood she knows will come. She tries to shout but memory is not the same as reality and she's screaming aimlessly into an empty life.

Open your eyes.

Can't you feel their shadow on your face?

You're going to shoot Mum and Dad.

It's exploding. The gun. Once. Then once again.

Now Rathlin is watching in slow motion. She is chasing the bullets, trying to catch them with her own body, throwing her stomach hard in its direction but it's in the past and she can't alter their course even though she's screaming, finding her voice in the present, begging them to bend, to fall, to be somewhere else.

Then Rathlin's eyes are closed and she can't see what she is doing. Has done. She doesn't see Aonghus taking the gun. And the blame.

Her mum and dad are falling to the floor. The bullets have ripped through them. They're on the grass, Skye tumbling onto Joe, their hips soldered. They are dead, together. Forever.

. . .

When Rathlin comes back, Breacán is there but not there. Not there because he's dead, but there because she can see him. He's lying beside her, trying to suppress her distress, holding her body until it stops fighting and her skin begins to cool.

It was me. I killed Mum an' Dad.

You didn't mean tae. You were saving me.

I thought Aonghus was going tae shoot you but it wiz Granddad he was after. I wanted it tae be me that shot him but I shot Mum. And Dad. I killed them. I bet you're glad you're dead. You wouldnae want tae see me now ye know whit I did.

I've always known. I was there, remember. We all did. It was an accident. They happen.

But Aonghus. He said it wiz him. I thought it wiz. He told the police. Everyone.

Of course he did. He loved you. He didnae want ye tae blame yourself. It was an accident.

No, it wiznae. I killed them. Just as well I've decided tae kill myself.

Rathlin. Stop. We cannae both leave Barra. Take your

twenty minutes an' twenty seconds and use them for as long as you need tae keep her safe.

Rathlin's thinking about the photograph of her mum and dad she kept beside her bed. She's looking at it from a different perspective now, from somewhere between the living and the dead.

There's always something on our birthday. By the way, that's some present I got you this year, telling ye I killed our mum and dad. Match that.

No, you havenae, you got me the exact same thing I got you.

That's impossible.

She's sitting up, her wrist slack as she gathers Isabella's things and places them gently into her silver box.

There's no way you even know it exists – the thing I got you.

Aye I do. I got you Hannah Frank's *Woman and Trees*. And you got it fir me. It reminds me of Mum, and you a bit too. I knew you'd need it, Rathlin. We both dae.

Rathlin's lips are taut, silenced. She has shared enough. She knows she has given enough. She is resisting him, determined not to sink into the *us* that was Ballynoe. She will not exist as one half of a whole.

She knows what she has to do.

Chapter Forty-Three

Rathlin

Rathlin Island, August 12th, 2020

Rathlin Island's sky is beguiling. Its grey clouds are the fate its namesake is holding in her hands. Their intensity has diminished on the journey from the north but they are still advancing across the sky with purpose, ready to scour a cliff face in a horizontal lashing. For now the rain is soft, the kind that settles gently and glistens on a wild rabbit's back.

Hardy to its surroundings, a gannet is preparing to swoop into a sea of broken glass, its prey somehow resplendent and exposed beneath the low hanging mist. Rathlin is waiting for its pounce but she is distracted by an artic skua scanning the coastline, soaring spectacularly beyond the jagged cliff edge. When it disappears into a distant field she takes command, shifting her focus back to where she's come from, gathering in a glance the strength she needs to continue. She repeats her mantra, just to be sure, but her soul knows she doesn't need to. She will not exist as one half of a whole.

Across the water in Kintyre, wind generators on Machrahanish are tightening the distance between the two headlands, their pas de deux graceful in the smoky curtain call light. Rathlin nods to that part of her life and continues on her journey. She is going to her mother's island home. She dances a path across the colourful landscape, her feet leaping in and out of an underlay of wildflowers. Bog pimpernels, brooklimes and knapweed are flowering in abundance and inching up the hillside, collapsing into a crescendo she can't see. Harebells and fairy flax are forming tiny shadows, figments of imagination that will manifest as folktales, intense narratives to provide company on lonely, candlelit nights.

She knows she will see Maoil na nDreas soon. The whiteness of its walls will appear behind the twists and turns of the road and it will be as if she is standing at her mum's glass etching on the hall window at Ballynoe.

As the chimney comes into view the wind is suddenly strong and vocal, its intensity tossing the sea into a sky thirsting for connection. She keeps her eyes high. Turf is burning from the direction of the house, its heavy hue racing to greet her.

Rathlin quickens her pace, navigating the nooks and crannies of the lane. Its footholds are carved out of basalt stone that has shaped wet hearths and memories. When she is close enough to see but remain unseen she stops. She doesn't want to venture further, she does not need to add new memories to her day, not when she is reconnecting with the past.

A final hurrah.

It's been how many years? She's counting on her fingers, her eyes glued to the ditch that's courted as many cattle hooves as people. Twenty-two, twenty-three years? Yes, twenty-three. She was four the last time they came. The final time. Mum didn't want to visit after that. The window gave her the memories she craved without any of their pain. Rathlin's memories of the visit are loose, a tiny fleck of bog cotton. Even at that, she's unsure if they are real or imagined. She closes her eyes and tries to remember the sights and smells but all she can feel is her mother, talking to her and Breacán by her window at Ballynoe. They would slide down onto the floor beside her and listen to the story of the little girl dressed in white who roams the island looking for the mother she lost.

Rathlin searches for her along the cliffs, not yet aware that she is craving her own reflection. The sea is licking its coves and caves but the only white she sees is that of glaucous gulls circling overhead, and her shoes, her own footprints are shaping the story, adding a final chapter. The little girl who finds her mother.

She knows she has to stop stalling now. She has to begin the end.

She takes a breath. She has made a mistake. The house, when she finally turns to examine it, is a mirror of home. Its walls are white, its windows and porch a confident green. She can hear the voices of its past congregating in the garden before stretching out to sea. She knows she has to hitch a ride with them, quickly escaping the pull of Ballynoe. She joins their noisy trail to the east.

They take her to the place swiftly, the wind whistling around her ankles. The Coire Bhreacan whirlpool at McDonnell's Race is below her, swallowing the ocean into its hungry cauldron. She stands on the cliff edge watching the waves pitch and roll like a nest of snakes furling and unfurling. She is tiny in what is now an enormous beast of a day. Even from a distance she can taste the sea in her mouth, its saltiness thick with the smoky turf cut from earth that is rising and falling, giving in to the twisting wind.

It is time. The speckled seals are clambering from the rocks making their way out to sea. She knows she needs to join them.

She scours her surroundings for a route to the water's edge. To Breacán's cave. She finds a battered wooden gate and knows she has stood here before. With her mum and dad. With Breacán. With her family. A chaffinch pierces the moment with its incessant call and she opens it so she can go to them. She continues down the coastline, threadbare heather illuminating the path to her final descent.

She stands on the shingle and she sways as it crunches underfoot, chanting a tune she recognises. She watches the swell, its tide uncoiling. She waits.

Finally she can see the werewolves shifting, striding towards the shoreline, their curves echoing familiar shapes.

Rathlin steps into the waves. For a moment she stays still, letting the water lash around her ankles. Then she squats and plunges her hands into the squalling froth. When she stands again, she straightens her back and runs over sand and stones, laughing, as she heads for her own transformation. She does not look back.

THE END

Acknowledgements

This book is dedicated to Art (Arthur) McIvor but there are many people to thank in its creation. Jessica Bates and Beccy Swain read early versions of *Almost Then* and were supportive and kind in their feedback. Thank you both. Lynn Michell at Linen Press has been wonderful and if it wasn't for her faith in me and my story, *Almost Then* wouldn't be in the hands of readers. Thank you also to Lynn for her insightful editing and endurance as the manuscript sailed back and forth between us on its voyage to publication. I owe thanks also to Hannah McAuliffe at Linen Press who edited with precision, an' wasnae wance perturbed by the Glaswegian dialogue.

I owe a debt to my beautiful children, Daniel and Siobhán, who make me proud every day and ensure I feel the love that is embedded in my writing. Thank you, both, for blessing me with grandchildren who give me more joy than I could ever have imagined.

A word for my parents, Margaret and Michael, who ensured my roots were fortified in Rathlin Island. My home on the island, at Maoil na nDreas, is very much at the heart of this story.

Last, but certainly not least, I thank my twin, John, for ensuring that the bond I write about in this story is authentic.

As twins, we are a family within a family.

Lightning Source UK Ltd.
Milton Keynes UK
UKHW020739210621
385893UK00015B/1721